Books by Eric Smith
available from Inkyard Press

Don't Read the Comments
You Can Go Your Own Way
With or Without You

WITH OR WITHOUT YOU

ERIC SMITH

Recycling programs
for this product may
not exist in your area.

ISBN-13: 978-1-335-45807-0

With or Without You

For questions and comments about the quality of this book, please contact us at CustomerService@Harlequin.com.

Inkyard Press
22 Adelaide St. West, 41st Floor
Toronto, Ontario M5H 4E3, Canada
www.InkyardPress.com

Printed in U.S.A.

For Preeti Chhibber, Swapna Krishna, and Lauren Gibaldi,
who always show up. I couldn't do it wit'out you.

And for Saray Fitzhenry, who taught me how to cook that first year in Philly.
Thank you for making sure my diet wasn't only hummus.
I'll fire up the grill.

chapter one:
jordan

Thursday, Ten Days until Truck Off!

"Wow, Cindy already has a line down the block."

I look up from the onions I'm slicing to see that Steve has arrived. Instead of hopping right in and getting to work, he's leaning out of the truck, gripping one of the metal handles on the inside so he can look around without stepping outside. He's like a sailor in a war movie, tilting himself over the bow to get a better view of something, only the conflict we're fighting isn't all that serious and a food truck is far from a battleship. Though considering how my family behaves, you'd think this food truck was the *Battleship New Jersey* docked over in Camden across the river.

I pull open the window shutter in front of me just a little bit, and squint through the crack.

He's not lying about that crowd.

Ortiz Steaks has a line sprawling from their food truck

across the square, and it looks like it spills out around the corner, but I can't tell how far. I nudge the shutter closed again, and Steve swings in, settling next to me.

"Sorry I'm late," he says. "Toad in the Pothole has a new sandwich special, had to try it. You know they're using white cheddar?"

"God that…" I look up at the ceiling and close my eyes, exhausted by the play on words. "That *cannot* be the name of their food truck."

"They can't be all as groundbreaking as 'Plazas Steaks,' bro." Steve laughs and starts shaking out some mushrooms from a small container. He stares at them for a beat before his eyes flit up to mine.

"Do you think we should—"

"No," I scoff, tossing the freshly cut square chunks of onion into a metal container along the grill. I grab another whole onion and start cutting. The trick is to slice it in half lengthwise, and then make several long cuts along those halves, so when you chop right along the side, boom. Small cubes of onion, ready to be sprinkled on the hot grill.

"It's just yesterday—"

"Steve, I *know*." I stop and roll my eyes at him, and he backs off, a grin on his face, hands up in a faux surrender. I get back to slicing. "Dirt on mushrooms is normal, it's *natural*. If we wash them hours before cooking, they're gonna get all slimy."

"Yeah, but that lady who asked for raw mushrooms made such a fuss over the, like, *globs* of *actual dirt* in her sandwich last week."

"First of all, that's what you get for asking for raw mushrooms on a cheesesteak. It's justice. Secondly, did she die?"

"Not that we know of." He nudges me with his elbow. "You gotta stop being such a...cheesesteak purist." He pauses for a moment and exhales. "Have you figured out the sandwich for Truck Off yet? Or you know, your magic ingredient?"

"No." I exhale, chopping down a little too hard on the onion I'm cutting. But a little flash of anxiety rushes through me. Truck Off is in two weeks—ten days, really—and I still don't know what we're going to serve at the competition. I've experimented with a few different ideas, from mini-cheesesteaks that are basically just the same thing we make right now but made...well, mini, to attempting cheesesteak egg rolls in the never-used truck fryer my family mostly stores condiments in.

Neither were a hit.

The prize money is huge, and it's all I've been able to think about since the spring. My grades even slipped a little, leading up to graduation. Winning it could change everything, and yet I'm still stuck.

Steve nudges closer and joins me in preparing the one topping we allow in the truck. He makes quick work of the whole white-capped mushrooms, cutting them up into thick slices, before putting them into the container next to the onions... which do *not* count as toppings. Onions are a key part of the cheesesteak, as much as the cheese, steak, and bread. Mushrooms are the unwelcome interlopers, but Mom and Dad were asked about them so many times, they finally caved.

Though with mushrooms, come consequences.

"Look, I know you're stressed and there's a lot riding on

the competition," Steve presses, slicing away. "But we...you... *have* to think of something."

"I know, I know..." I grumble.

Steve's been here with me nearly every weekend these last two years, in my family's cheesesteak truck, splitting tips while saving for his own dreams. And now it's the summer, and we're spending as many days as we can slinging lunches and spectacularly late-night meals for folks in South Philly. I couldn't ask for a better sous-chef, and I couldn't ask for a better friend. But he knows how my whole family feels about change. After my parents lost their diner years ago, they try to play things as safe as possible. Give people what they want, and that's it.

New ingredients? New sandwiches? You start messing with the menu, and bam, that's when your deli gets turned into an H&M, Dad likes to say, swapping out small eateries for big retail chains each time. Coffee shop into a Sephora. Bakery into a CVS. Greasy spoon into a RadioShack.

No one says greasy spoon anymore and RadioShack hasn't existed for a really long time, but what can I do.

Mom and Dad aren't thrilled about me entering this competition in the first place, especially since they know what I want to do with the money. I've had to sneak new ingredients into the truck to experiment with, which hasn't been easy. But it'll be worth it, if in a few months I can hit the open road.

Even though I'm trying hard to make sure everything changes, I can't help but want to savor it all *before* everything changes. I don't know if that makes sense, but I've come to realize it is possible to foster those two emotions at once inside yourself. The need for change that I feel, and the want for things to stay the same that my parents cling to.

I swipe at my eyes, some of the onion vapors starting to sting a bit.

Yeah. Yeah, that's it.

"You really need to start wearing those protective glasses." Steve says, nodding at the goggles hanging above the grill. The clear plastic has a film on the lenses from days, weeks, and months of grease splashing on them. I've never put them on, and I don't think Mom or Dad have ever used them on their own shifts in here.

"I can power through." I sniff, blinking through the pain. "Great work comes from suffering."

"Yeah, okay, Daniel Day-Lewis," Steve scoffs, and I laugh. God. I'm going to miss this, being here, with him. The chop busting, the hustle. The sound of the gathering crowd rings out over the hiss of the grill, and I glance back at the shutter just as it rattles open from the outside.

"Hey, nerds," a voice chimes in through the metal slats. I don't have to turn around to know who is there.

"Hey, Laura," I say, wiping my onion knife on my jeans. Steve gives me a nudge with his elbow and nods at my pants.

"Come on man, be sanitary," Steve complains.

"Jeans are self-cleaning, it's okay." I move to slice an onion when he grabs my arm, giving me a look. "*Fine.*"

"I loathe to think what food prep looks like in this truck when I'm not in here," Steve says, shaking his head. "Or when you finally head off on your road trip."

"I bet he tastes every single cheesesteak before handing it off to people," Laura instigates, and the truck rocks around a little bit as she takes a seat on the edge, where the side door opens inside. "Just licks the bread and wraps it up."

"Don't," Steve says, holding up a finger. He's always had a thing with germs and things not being quite-so-clean, which makes his work in a food truck with a grease-coated floor slightly ironic, so I give Laura a look to not push any further.

"So, what are you guys doing today?" Laura asks, the strum of a guitar chord echoing through the truck. I see she's brought her acoustic with her, which shouldn't surprise me. Since the start of the summer, she's been out here just as often as Steve, fiddling over new songs, sometimes busking and playing covers in the square. She's wearing a dark blue jean jacket littered with enamel pins that's way too warm for the weather right now, but I know Laura. That's the look. Best not to question it.

"Just the usual." I sigh.

"Hmm," Laura grumbles, tuning her guitar. "Not gonna win with the usual."

"That's what I keep telling him!" Steve shouts.

"Okay, you two!" I exclaim, laughing, grabbing another onion. "I know. I'm gonna figure it out. What time is it?"

"Uh..." Steve fumbles around awkwardly for his phone. He is—even though he will never admit this—a little too tall for this truck. I fit in here fine, but he's a little over six feet tall and spends a lot of his time stretching outside or leaning through the shutter window. Meanwhile Laura's nearly a foot shorter than me, a small, angst-filled emo powerhouse in jean jacket armor. "Almost eleven."

"Alright, it's time. Let's toss some onions on the grill." They're not actually for cooking anything, not yet. But once the food truck starts smelling delicious, people know that we're open. If the winds are right, the smell of onions sizzling will lift the right person off the ground like an old cartoon character catching a whiff of cooling apple pie.

"Oh, and open that up and ready the counter, would you?" I nod at the shutter. Steve looks eager for some air anyway.

He moves to jump out of the truck and Laura shifts out of the way. She spins her guitar around by the neck and peers back inside.

"I'm gonna go snag a bench," she says, glancing over at the Ortiz truck with a smirk. "Any requests?"

I smile.

"Surprise me."

I grip a squeeze bottle full of canola oil and spray it over the grill, steam rising from the blackened silver surface. I add some of the white onions, a loud sizzle immediately filling the truck. That sound, that smell, reminds me of my family—of being a kid in Mom and Dad's old diner, or back at home, the aroma of spices and onions clinging to their clothes. It's inescapable, and that's fine with me.

The heat from the grill warms my skin, and as I flip the onions around, I can already feel beads of sweat starting to form on my forehead. I've only just gotten started, but that's a Philadelphia summer mashed together with the steamy interior of a food truck for you. Sweltering mornings and late afternoons when you can see the heat rising off the cobblestones, brick, and concrete. The hope that a break from it all is waiting in the chilly evening.

There's a reason why my favorite bands, like The Ataris and The Wonder Years and Yellowcard, sing about summer so often. Maybe I can get Laura to play "The Boys of Summer" or "Dismantling Summer" or "Always Summer." Something with *summer* in the name. My favorite bands are not subtle.

The shutter rattles open, making a *chunk-chunk-chunk* sound as the metal slats and rivets disappear into the ceiling of the truck. The summer air brings some immediate relief from the heating up grill, far more effective than the cheap, poorly mounted fans tucked in the corners of the truck, and for a moment I close my eyes, feeling the late morning breeze on my face.

God. I love it here. And if I win Truck Off, it'll be so much easier to get my own. The dream.

Steve unfolds the small steel countertop on the front of the truck, puts out the napkin holder, and then reaches into the truck for the mason jar under the window.

"Can't forget this." He grins, wiggling the jar in the air.

It's empty right now, but last week we wrangled up nearly five hundred dollars in tips. It was rough saving the measly tips from only working weekends during the school year, but now that we've graduated and summer is here, there's just this wild flood of extra money from working full weeks.

I'm not sure if it'll be enough to buy my own truck with though—at least, not the ideal one. Maybe something will pop up, but food trucks really don't get listed all that often. People keep them running until they fall apart, and the ones that are still in good condition go for tens of thousands of dollars.

Tens of thousands, I do not have. A few thousand that I've spent every week working toward these last two years? Sure. But the Truck Off winnings would put me in a great spot to make this dream a reality.

It doesn't have to be perfect. An old junker that needs some love would do just fine, as long as it moves and is fixable with a few YouTube tutorials. Meanwhile Steve's got his eyes set on ICA here in Philly, the Philadelphia Institute of Culinary Arts, and constantly rattles on about molecular gastronomy, to the point that Dad won't let him come over anymore. If it isn't salt and pepper, Dad doesn't want to hear it.

Me either, really, but he's one of my best friends. Mom likes to joke that I was born with my arms around Steve, Laura, and a spatula.

I scrape a terribly charred section of the grill down a little, but not much. This slab of metal has *seen things* and so many flavors. Better to leave it a little oily, a little burnt, and very seasoned. With the shutter open, the bustling of Bardhan Square in South Philadelphia breaks the constant sizzling, the scratch of the metal. The cars trying to navigate the nearby roundabout, people out with their dogs, Laura plucking her guitar strings. If I close my eyes, I can almost hear the water from the fountain a block away.

Instead, though, I look at the Ortiz truck.

Parked on the opposite side of the roundabout, across the small grassy area with tiny city trees, shrubs, and benches, sits the Ortiz family cheesesteak truck. Well, if you can call it that. I'd argue it's more of a hoagie truck, as their "cheesesteaks" come with lettuce, peppers, and ugh, Jesus, *tomatoes*. Fruit doesn't belong on cheesesteaks. Lately they've introduced cheesesteak wraps, where they sometimes substitute the steak for chicken, and I'm sorry, at that point you are just a deli.

But the people turn up for it, I'll give them that.

And if I hope to win Truck Off, I'm going to have to do

some more innovating than me or my family have been comfortable with. Our menu is simple. Cheesesteaks. Three options for cheese: American, provolone, whiz. Onions. And for the brave, foolish few…mushrooms. Our menu is a sentence, and the Ortizes's truck's menu is a novella. And as much as I love it, staying true to what my parents wanted, I know I'm going to have to come up with something different, something a little more…novella-ish, if I want to win the competition.

Steve hefts himself back into the truck and joins me in leaning out the window. He squints at the crowd and nudges me with his elbow again.

"It begins," he says as Cindy Ortiz gets out from the back of the truck somewhere and hurries around the front. She hoists up the entire metal flap that slides on top of the window, and pulls out large poles, creating a cozy canopy.

A few of the people in line rush to get under it as she walks back around the truck, looking relieved for the shade. Some more are off to the side, eyeing up the menu that's revealed itself since she raised the shutter. It's written in colorful chalk, like something you would see outside of a fancy café.

Their whole truck sparkles and shines and looks brand-new. While ours…doesn't. It makes me think about my own future truck, and what I'll do with it—

"Hey!"

Cindy is in the window of her truck, and she's glaring right at me, gesturing with a narrow metal spatula. I don't know why she bothers straightening her jet-black hair when it will inevitably be a curly disaster by the end of the day. Especially since we both spend most of our time in hot food trucks smack in the middle of the concrete prairie that is the South Philadelphia business district.

"Nice line you got there, Jordan," she snaps, smiling, waving in my direction with the spatula. Even from here, I can see her dazzlingly white teeth. She tilts her head down a little, peering at me from behind her thick oversize glasses. Two of the people that were reading her chalkboard menu start making their way towards our truck. I cross my arms and give her the smuggest look I can muster.

"Losing customers already, Cindy?" I shout back. When I turn to the pair as they reach the counter, they look at each other, small, amused smiles on their faces. "What will it be?"

"Just two cheesesteaks with provolone please." One of them says, expression turning anxious as he looks at his friend. They're both grown, probably have kids my age, but seem utterly terrified now that they are ordering. It cracks a smirk out of me. Ah, such power. Such wild, useless power.

"Wit' or wit'out?" I ask.

"Oh, oh. Uh...wit'!" one guy exclaims.

"Wit'out for me," says the other.

"We'll have that right up." I smile and the two of them appear relieved. I turn to the grill, tossing the shaved rib eye we source from Dad's friends at Rossi's in the Italian Market onto the grill. The meat sizzles and snaps, and Steve busies himself cashing the guests out. I take a hefty portion of salt and pepper and dash it over the rib eye and snag two seeded cheesesteak rolls from Amoroso's. There are cheesesteak joints all over the country who import those rolls in their attempts to make authentic sandwiches in their respective states, something I can't help but laugh at. It's nice that they want to try.

Though Steve has asked me how I can judge them so harshly when I've never even been out of Pennsylvania. Unless you count that time I took the SEPTA to Trenton, New Jersey, by accident, or my plan to enter Truck Off in Camden. Which he does not.

I've got plans to change that, though, and to go way farther than just across the Delaware River by mistake. Two more months. I'll win Truck Off, have enough for my dream truck, and then I'm in the wind. A whole year on the open road, or at least, however long I can make it work. I'm prepared to sleep in the truck if I have to. Amber Fitzpatrick, a girl who graduated last year, is off doing that "van life" thing, sleeping in a tricked-out passenger van, traveling all over the country and taking sunset naps and photos at the Grand Canyon. Sure, her parents are wealthy startup people, but if she can do that, I can snuggle up in my food truck in, like, Connecticut.

And goodness, if I win that prize money, maybe I wouldn't *have* to sleep in the truck. I wouldn't *have* to get a junker. I could get something that really shines.

As the meat sizzles, I toss three thick slices of provolone on top, mixing it in with the steak. I press the rolls facedown on the grill to give them just a tiny bit of extra crispness, char, and warmth, as rolls from Amoroso's are already perfectly crusty, and ease the meat and cheese on it. I take a heaping portion of the onions that have been slowly simmering on the edge of the grill and slide them onto the one sandwich. The one that was ordered "wit'."

Wit' means "with onions."

I slide the two cheesesteaks over to Steve, who promptly wraps them up in shimmering sandwich paper.

"One wit', one wit'out," he says, reaching over to the window and placing the sandwiches on the counter. "Ketchup is right there if you need it."

"Is...is that allowed?" one of the guys asks, eyeing me like I'm going to reach out through the window and snatch the sandwich out of his trembling hands.

"Yes," I mutter from inside the truck, and as I scrape some of the melted cheese away from the surface, I hear the *pbbbbbttt* of the ketchup bottle outside. I'm not against ketchup on cheesesteaks, but tourists in Philadelphia have this fear of ordering cheesesteaks wrong at our truck, ever since Dad introduced the bell.

I wonder how many times we'll have to ring it today.

"Thanks, guys!" Steve exclaims. I turn around and join him at the window, leaning out, feeling the warm summer air on my face. I glance off to the side, but there's no line. No one is out here for us. Not yet anyway. And what looks like three wrinkly dollars sit inside the mason tip jar.

"Wow!" shouts Cindy, again, from across the way. Her line hasn't really slowed down, and she's handing something to someone. She ducks back in her truck and reappears in the window with another sandwich for the next customer. "That was quite the lunch rush. You two okay? Need a break? When I wrap up here, I could maybe help fill in?"

I just scowl at her.

"Any chance Michelle Branch here is going to play something decent?" Cindy asks, staring daggers at Laura.

Laura takes a break from strumming her guitar to give Cindy the finger without looking at her, and then gets right back to it.

"Whatever," she continues, rolling her eyes. "It'll probably be an hour or so before anyone else even stops by your truck—"

"Hey screw you, Cindy!" Steve shouts, lunging forward a little against the counter. The force shakes the truck a bit.

"Hey, man." I reach out and grab his arm, pulling him back in from the window, talking through my teeth. "Come on, cool it down."

"Oh, sorry," he says, wincing. "Was that a little too much or—"

"No, screw YOU, Steve!" Cindy shouts back. I groan and shake my head, and by the time I look back to her, she's already out of her truck and storming toward us, spatula in hand.

Here we go.

A few of her customers are laughing, taking out their phones, ready to record the action.

"You two have something you want to say to me?!" she hollers.

Ugh, Steve. *Why.*

I walk out of the truck and tear my apron off, tossing it over the countertop. There's still no line for us, so it doesn't matter.

"Go back to your truck!" I yell, pointing across the street.

"Make me!" Cindy yells back.

A bit of panic surges through me. What am I even supposed to do here? By now, most of the crowd has their phones pointed at me, and Cindy's fists are balled up and shaking.

I step toward her, and in a quick motion, Cindy hurries closer and whips out the spatula, holding the thin metal edge to my chin. Like some kind of warrior in a fantasy novel.

The corners of her lips inch up in a half smile. Laura strums a dramatic chord on her guitar, and I turn to glare at her. She shrugs.

I raise my hands and back away from Cindy.

"Figures," she scoffs. "All talk, both of you." She sheathes her spatula, literally, into this holster-looking thing around her waist. If there's one thing I've learned in all these years of our trucks being at odds with one another, it's that for her and her family, it's over-the-top or nothing.

"Good luck with your cheap ingredients and horse meat. You hear that, everyone? Word on the street is the Plazas family uses horse meat in their steaks."

Jesus. Speaking of over-the-top.

"Oh, come on, that's…" I look at all the customers with their phones out. "That's not true and you know it isn't. Go back to your truck with your…your…vegetables…"

"Oof!" Cindy says, putting a hand up to her chest, like she's just been shot. "The comeback skills, my God. Your insults are as weak as the seasoning you use on your steaks."

"Salt and pepper are all you need!" I bellow, my father's words coming out of my mouth, and turn around, hustling back to my truck. Heat billows up behind my ears, and I feel like I'm sweating again. I hear people laughing as I make my way inside, and Steve has his phone out, videoing the whole thing.

"Really?!" I snap at him, pushing his hand down. I steal a quick glance through the window, and Cindy is already back in her truck, the people around her applauding. She takes a few little bows and everything.

"What?!" He laughs, putting his phone away. "That was

pretty funny. The spatula? Laura's busy with her guitar, and
she would have wanted me to get that on video."

"Ugh, I hate this," I grumble, turning back to the grill.
I do love it when Laura is armed and ready with her phone,
because at least she makes sure I look good. Not too sure
about the video Steve's got, or the throngs of people across
the street with their phones. Great. Can't wait to see how the
truck gets tagged on Instagram.

I scrape the grill's surface a bit, silence in the air between us.

"Hey, you okay, man?" Steve asks.

"I don't know..." I huff. "Everything with her and her
family, all while trying to figure out what to serve at Truck
Off, it's just...getting to be a bit much. It's the summer. If I
don't figure out what to serve, if it's not perfect..."

I exhale and look up at him, his face awash in worry.

"Steve, I'm not sure how much longer I can keep this up—"

"Excuse me?"

I whirl toward the window, where a woman is standing
and squinting at me. She doesn't look that much older than
I am, maybe right out of college, with a blazer and jeans on.
Probably in town for a conference, which is how we get a
good chunk of our tourist business, but I don't see a convention center badge.

"Oh, sorry," I mutter. "Did you want to order something?"

"Definitely. I heard you guys make a really good cheesesteak..." she pauses, looking back and forth between us "...
with mushrooms?"

Steve sputters out a laugh.

I grin and cross my arms.

"If you're gonna order one with mushrooms, you *do* know

you'll have to face the shame bell." I reach under the window and pull out a large bell, handing it to Steve. It's an old, large, brass thing that looks like it would be better suited hanging up in a fire station or an ocean-side lighthouse, ready to warn beachgoers of high tides. I often wonder where Dad got it.

"It is the consequence of such a topping," I continue. "Our only topping."

"The shame bell," she says, deadpan.

"Yes."

"It's a bell."

"It is."

"For shaming."

"Correct."

"For people who order your food, who pay you to make it, and ask for mushrooms."

"I'm afraid so."

She stares at me for a beat, her eyes flitting to the bell and to Steve and to the truck. She looks across the intersection to Cindy's truck, the line still long and not really moving that much. For all her smack talk, Cindy really needs to start asking for help more often. Like, why not have her parents working in the truck once and a while? But... I don't see that happening. I've never met more of a Taurus in my life.

"Alright," the woman says, turning back to me, a little smirk on her face. "A cheesesteak with provolone...and mushrooms."

"SHAME!" Steve shouts, a little too loud considering he's right next to me. He walks out of the truck, ringing the bell. The woman takes out her phone and starts to capture it on video. No surprise there. It felt like she might have known what we were up to here. Some people come for the whole experience.

"Shame, shame, shame!"

People across the street at Cindy's truck are staring at us, as are a number of neighborhood folks just making their way through the area. A man walking a small French bulldog tries desperately to calm the pup down, as it barks madly at the noise. Laura's set down her guitar in the middle of the square, and is taking a video of Steve, a huge smile on her face.

I'd be embarrassed if it wasn't tradition passed down from my parents. But at the same time, I'm painfully aware that this tradition needs to change if I'm going to win Truck Off in the coming days. I have to do something different, come up with something different, and maybe not shame people for wanting a change.

I start making the woman's sandwich, while the bell and Steve's shouting echo through Bardhan Square. I try to focus on the meat, the cheese, on the mushrooms that Steve sliced up earlier, but I keep seeing Cindy in my head. All that fierceness, staring me down, the narrow spatula in her hand like a sword.

It pulls a little smile out of me, a bit of warmth creeping up my neck.

And it's not just the heat from the grill.

"Jordan!"

I startle and drop the spatula in my hand, sending it clattering to the floor of the truck. I bend down to scoop it up, and then turn around to face my dad.

"Hey!" He's standing outside the truck, his thick hairy arms crossed, a bundle of papers flapping in one hand. He's wearing his favorite Eagles shirt that just says Go Birds on it, which is meant to be a slogan rooting for the Philadelphia Eagles, as though other teams with like, blue jays or penguins simply do not exist.

But that's Philly, I suppose. We're gonna have an attitude about everything, including denying the sheer existence of other feathered animals.

I try not to stare at the papers in his hand. I know what they are, and I'm not here for it.

I move toward the grill, desperate to avoid this conversation.

"Best wash that before you use it again, kiddo."

I look at the spatula in my hand as if waking from a dream, then down at the floor, the patterned metal interlaced with rivers of grease and grit. There's salt and pepper dotting the trapped liquid, like sand in a rain puddle.

Yeah, I was gonna wash it. Before you startled me.

I toss it into one of the trays full of cleaning solution under the countertop and grab a fresh one from a box next to it, avoiding his gaze.

"Hi, Mr. Plazas," Steve says, peering over the counter, doing his best to be some kind of buffer, as always. He clangs the bell up on the countertop right next to him, and the woman waiting for her cheesesteak stands a few feet back, fiddling on her phone. "We're just getting started over here."

"Hi, Steve…hey, tell me…" There's a long pause, the sizzling of the grill keeping things from being totally silent. Dad's eyes flit down to the papers and back to me. It's like a standoff in one of those old Clint Eastwood movies he likes so much. He was supposed to take over the truck tonight so

I could go out, but that's *tonight*. It isn't even noon yet, and I know a guilt trip is coming. "Did *you* get your application in for ICA?"

I knew it. Here we go.

"Oh, um..." Steve says, hesitating. He glances over at me for a moment, worrying at his lip, then turns back to my father. "I did. I... I got in."

"What?" I ask, nearly dropping another spatula.

He mouths an *I'm sorry* to me with a wince.

"Oh, your parents must be so proud!" Dad exclaims. "And your grandfather. Just imagine, an ICA trained chef. Think of what you could do at his deli even. It'll be like that...what's that show we watched, Jordan? The young man who's a chef and goes back to a sandwich shop?"

I groan, shaking my head.

"*The Bear*," I mutter.

"Yes, *The Bear*!" Dad says, laughing. "That's so wonderful."

"Well, Mr. Plazas, I mean, I want to study gastronomy to do things a little more complicated than that." Steve shrugs. "Fine dining and—"

"That character in *The Bear* wanted to do that too, and what happened?" He slaps the countertop. This is what he does when he's excited. Lots of slapping tables and legs and arms. "Sandwich shop."

"Let's not crush Steve's dreams before he gets a chance to try, okay?" I grumble. I'm talking about Steve, but goodness, I know I'm talking about myself too.

"Backup plans are important," Dad presses, leaning against the counter, and I suppose it's his turn to do that to me. "Laura, she knows she can't make a living playing guitar on the street like that." He gestures to Laura, who happens to catch him and waves. "Look at her. Looking like some kind of urchin."

"Dad this isn't a Charles Dickens novel." I laugh.

"She's going to Arcadia! To major in business! You should do the same," Dad says, his voice getting louder and louder. Sure, she's going for business, so she can work in the music industry and play music on her downtime. And that's fine. But I don't want to run a food truck on my downtime, I want to run one on my all-the-time. And I don't need a college degree to do it. "If me or your mother had that kind of opportunity, we could have done something else with our lives after what happened with the diner."

"Dad, you *like* working with food," I say, treading carefully. His and Mom's shuttered diner, The Stateside, is a sore spot with our family, and with good cause. "And you both work at restaurants. What else would you have done?"

"They aren't *our* restaurants, and that's not the point." He huffs, pressing the bundle of papers at me. "The point is having options. I want you to take these."

"Dad I'm *working*," I huff back.

"It's not too late to apply for rolling admission at these schools!" he says. "While you're off tonight, I want you to fill a few of these out."

"Dad!" I shout. "Come on, we've been over this. I'm not going to college. And I have plans!"

"That's fine. For this year." He rolls the papers up and sticks them right into the tip jar. "I'll show up an extra hour early so you have time to work on these. Maybe if it's not busy, Steve can help."

I flash Steve a *don't you dare* look.

"What time do you boys need me back here?" Dad asks. "Six good? Seven?"

"I don't need to wrap things up until around eight—" I start, and immediately regret it.

"Okay! I'll be here at seven." He pats the applications. "I'm going to head over to the Italian Market, see if I can't do a little haggling." He cracks his knuckles like he's going to physically arm wrestle someone into giving him a better deal on rolls.

And with that, he's off, already power walking toward the Italian Market and Christian Street about a half mile away. He moves like he's on a mission, his big arms aggressively moving back and forth. Dad's a little bit shorter than me—I definitely get my height from Mom, who is a good six inches taller than him—but he carries himself like he's the biggest person in the room, on the block, on the street. He's like a Latinx version of Jack Black, beard and all.

The woman is still waiting patiently for her sandwich, tapping at her phone, so Steve and I whip up her order and she finally gets on her way. Since no one else is at our counter just yet, I grab the applications out of the tip jar. There are a whole bundle of rolling admission papers in here for schools in the city, like Drexel and Penn, and a few right out the outskirts, like Arcadia, where Laura is going, and Rosemont. None of these places have degrees in running a food truck though. I just do not see the point, but Dad, and Mom for that matter, insist I should go for business or something.

"Have a backup plan." Dad loves to press.

I know why he does that. I might have been a little kid

when they lost the diner, but I still remember... I don't know, the *energy* in the house. At home. The way it felt like we were all on this tightrope and I was too young to really understand why. But I do now, after all these arguments about college and the food truck. I know how serious it was, that our family fell on hard times and almost lost the house.

But I don't need a backup plan. This time I *do* understand.

"Hey," Steve says, an apologetic grimace on his face. "Sorry I didn't tell you about...you know, ICA and all that."

"Oh." I try to snap back to here and now, away from the college applications and Dad's expectations. "It's fine, but... yeah why didn't you say anything? That feels like kind of a big deal."

"Well, all *that* for one." He swats at the papers in my hand, and I tuck them under the countertop. He grabs the bell off the counter and walks back around to come inside the truck. "I just found out yesterday and, well, I know how hard your family is on you about that stuff and I didn't want to give them any more ammunition, you know?"

"Yeah, I got you." I nod because today's revelation has absolutely done just that. "Thanks."

I reach out and clean up the countertop, putting the tip jar back, moving the napkin dispenser and condiments into place from Dad shuffling them around when he leaned over and nudged them all.

"So...*do* you want help filling those out?" Steve asks.

I just glare at him.

"Okay, okay." He laughs, getting back to prepping some onions and mushrooms so we're ready for our next customer.

Laura starts strumming on her guitar, playing what I think

might be a Taylor Swift song, but I'm not really sure. My phone buzzes, and I slide it out of my pocket.

Cindy: Hey, I saw all that with your dad. You okay?

Cindy: Also, please tell me Steve got our spat in the middle of the park on video. I've been practicing the whole spatula-sword move

Cindy: I hope you're alright. See you tonight? <3

I peer over to the Ortiz truck and see Cindy looking right at me, her phone in her hand.

I smile at her, and I swear, I can see her eyes glittering from here.

She turns away, tucking her phone into her pocket, and I get back to the grill.

chapter two:
cindy

Thursday, Ten Days until Truck Off

The streetlamps that line the sidewalk, as well as the hanging white twinkle lights in Bardhan Square, are all glimmering brightly. It's not quite evening, but it's just about 7 p.m., which means its quitting time. My phone buzzes, and I can't help but smile. I know what time it is, they know what time is, and it can only be about one thing.

Eesha: You on your way home yet?!

Ariana: You absolutely cannot miss the episode tonight. The previews have been wild

Ariana: I need to watch this live so we can post about it together before recording tomorrow morning

Eesha: Hello?!

Oh yeah. Just as expected.

Me: I told you guys, I've got plans tonight. I'll watch it later or in the morning before we record.

Eesha: UGH. It's not the same!

Ariana: Is your mom at least going to watch it live? Maybe we should add her to the group chat

Eesha: Oh wow, that's a good idea. At least she seems dedicated

Me: Oh my God, shut up you two

Eesha: You love it

I laugh and shove my phone in my pocket. I don't love missing *The Secret Lives of Beacon Hill Wives*, a reality TV show set back home in Boston that we're all wildly obsessed with. Posting our live reactions is a great way to interact with other fans while drawing attention to our podcast that's dedicated to the series, and a lot of our live reacts end up working as notes for our recordings. A few weeks ago, one of Eesha's snarky tweets made it onto *Beacon Hill Wives'* live evening wrap-up.

Eesha likes to call it accidental multitasking. How posting about the show leads to chatting with viewers, which ropes in new listeners, but for me, it's just fun. And ever since I moved away from Boston, the podcast has been the best way to keep doing something with my best friends. Saving up tips from working in the food truck has definitely upped my game when it comes to my podcast equipment, that's for sure. The latest Yeti microphone each year, a new MacBook back in the spring, some soundproofing gear for the closet where I record…it doesn't feel like I'm just investing in our project, but also our future and our friendship.

I'm aware we've created a show that just recaps another show, but if Eesha's nerdy boyfriend can listen to podcasts that unpack every Marvel movie, we can do this.

But… I've got plans tonight. The sort of plans I don't get to make all that often.

After I shut down and clean off the grill, gathering the left-over veggies that won't be good in the morning, I head outside, stretching and wiping at some of the grease that clings to my cheeks. I take a deep breath of the South Philadelphia air, but all I can smell are my truck, the sharp scent of organic olive oil, and garden grown onions…

And Plazas Cheesesteaks across the street.

While my line tends to quiet down as the evening approaches, Jordan and his family's truck just gets busier and busier the later it is. And I know why. All the drunks that party through South Philly, up and down Passyunk and along the bars on Bardhan Square…they want a basic cheesesteak at the end of the night. Meat. Cheese. Onions. Salt-pepper-ketchup. They're not interested in the locally grown and sourced steak sandwiches and sundried tomato wraps we've got.

Which, fine.

Some people just have no literal taste.

I fold down the awning that expands over my truck's window, and something collides with my shoulder just as I finish.

"Oh, hey, sorry," someone slurs, the smell of beer following them in their wake. I watch as the person stumbles their way across Bardhan Square toward Jordan's truck and can't help but roll my eyes. At least the punk rock princess and her guitar are gone.

Jordan and his pal Steve lean out of his truck to hand a sandwich to someone. A bit of it falls out of the paper wrap the second the person bites into it, splattering on the sidewalk, and the people around him laugh.

"Hey! Get a handle on your customers, Plazas!" I shout across the square. If I have to close up shop while boozy tourists and locals swarm around him, the least he could do is keep his guests in line.

His eyes flit up to me, and I have to stop myself from biting my lip. His hair is a tussled mess, and he's wearing a tight white T-shirt that shows off his toned, permanently tanned arms. I swear, even from all the way over here, I can see his hazel eyes flash a little as he breaks eye contact with me and turns to another customer.

Whew. Right now, he's the enemy. *Hold it together, Ortiz.*

A few customers in his line give me the finger and shout a bunch of unintelligible nonsense, and I just shake my head. It's not terribly late, but it's summer, so that's early enough for the partygoers to already be out and about. Jordan and his truck will be out here for hours, but it's definitely a wrap for me, so I take out my phone to text Dad.

Me: I think we're finished for the day. Our truck's line is dead. Plazas is taking over.

Dad responds with an animated GIF of someone flipping over a table.

Me: Why can't you just use normal emojis like everyone else?

Dad: Because I am 45 years old and GIFs are the way of my millennial people.

Dad: Why can't you learn to drive?

Me: Hah hah

I can run a food truck. But I definitely can't park one.

Maybe I'll get the whole "learning how to drive" thing under control eventually, but this is Philadelphia. A city with tons of cars, absolutely no parking, and zero reason to drive, especially if that reason is "Cindy can you drive the truck to the car wash." I can walk just about everywhere or grab the Frankford or Broad Street Lines to make it around the city. It was the same way back home, when we lived in Boston. Wandering through the neighborhoods with Eesha and Ariana, like the city was ours, grabbing ice cream or Italian ice (sorry, Philly, I will never call it water ice) at J.P. Licks or Emack & Bolio's.

I wish Philadelphia felt that way. I like it here, but without the people who make a place a home, it's just that. A place.

But I'm hoping I can make it back to Boston eventually. After my gap year road trip, I'll kick things off at the Community College of Philadelphia to save some money, and then maybe I can get myself home. That city has been calling to me, asking me to return someday like an Augustana song.

I did have a…moment, in the spring, when I wasn't totally sure about this whole yearlong break, and neither were my parents. I sent in a late application to Northeastern to humor them—and maybe myself if I'm being honest—and got wait-listed. But I know the odds are slim, miniscule, nonexistent even. It's not even a real option.

Right now, I'm focusing on what I can control. My podcast. My summer job. A year off. And these plans with a beautiful boy I've got across town.

So I huff it over to the Broad Street Line.

I take a seat on a bench in the Fishtown Rose Garden, a small, triangular open space near a large condo lined with dedicated bricks and blooming shrubs. One of my favorite plant boutiques, Krumm's, just opened a second shop in this neighborhood, and I keep meaning to swing by. The assistant manager at the Old City location, Whitney, frequently hits up the truck, always trying to get me to hang plant baskets from our tiny awning. I admire the hustle.

Fishtown. Why did Jordan want to meet in Fishtown—

"Hey," a voice says from behind me, startling me. I turn around and see two people holding hands, waiting to cross the street. The woman, who looks just a little older than me, smiles apologetically. "Sorry to scare you, but well… Team Ortiz."

I chuckle and wave. "Thanks."

The rivalry with the Plazas family and their cheesesteak

truck has been going on since I was in junior high. Me and my family moved to Philadelphia when my parents' urban farm outside of Boston lost its nonprofit funding, and they took jobs at another urban farm here. They had a food truck in Boston as a way to fund some of their bigger projects. Back then, they served up lettuce wraps and buffalo cauliflower and small salads in mason jars—fresh from a farm smack in the middle of a brick-and-concrete paradise.

They just mixed things up a little, when we moved here.

By getting a new truck and adding cheesesteaks.

The old one had to stay behind with the farm, sold off to nip away at the debt that followed my parents here. Spending my summer days in the Philly truck, and my weekends during the school year, helped with making my own way. Paying for my podcast gear, saving so I have financial breathing room in college. Anything to take that off Mom and Dad's plate.

It's what I can control, just like the audience who revels in the dueling truck hijinks.

The thought of Jordan Plazas bumbling over his words in the middle of Bardhan Square while I was yelling at him sends a fit of laughter through me, washing away some of the worry. The spatula sword move was too good. He was absolutely frazzled, and I loved it.

I exhale, leaning back, until a familiar-looking flyer catches my eye on the community bulletin board in the tiny park. I get up, stretching a little, my muscles still a bit stiff from being cooped up in the truck all day, and walk over.

TRUCK OFF, PHILADELPHIA!

Join food trucks from all around the Philadelphia region as they compete for prizes and serve delicious dishes all afternoon! It's all going down at the Camden waterfront. Participating trucks include:

Romaine Calm (West Philly salads + veggie wraps!)
War & Peas (Philadelphia's only falafel truck with a Little Free Library attached!)
Me, Myself & Thai (Thai food from Manayunk's favorite truck!)
Love at First Bite (Visiting from New York!)
Not Yolking Around (Artisan breakfast wraps!)
Schmear Today, Gone Tomorrow (Bagels from New Jersey!)
Good Korma (Indian food and lassi drinks from Drexel Hill!)
Hot Noods! (Ramen from South Philadelphia)
Plazas Steaks (The best cheesesteaks in all of Philadelphia!)

And many others! Want to sign up? Visit our official website for details.

I scowl at the listing for Jordan's family's truck. Best cheesesteaks in all of Philly? That's all pretty debatable. His is also the only truck without a fun name. Sometimes I wonder if we should give our truck a snazzier title. I feel like having our family name attached to it makes the rivalry with the Plazas truck more powerful though. Like a historical blood feud in a Chloe Gong novel or something.

I look around the rest of the board. There's an ad for a band's concert here, an art gallery opening there. A local acoustic night at Cousin Charles, a popular café mixed with a small music venue.

I try not to glare at the name "Laura Lim" on the roster. Jordan's friend with the guitar, playing songs she knows I can't stand in the park near our trucks. Sometimes she shoots videos of our spats, but I swear, she only tags me in the clips that are particularly embarrassing.

Are you a cinematographer or a musician? Pick a lane, Laura.

"You know, there's still time for you to enter," a voice whispers in my ear, and I scramble forward, nearly colliding with the bulletin board. I turn around quick, the flyers and business cards and postcards scratching my neck.

And there's Jordan Plazas.

He's smiling, his floppy, curly hair a disaster. He grins down at me, his hazel eyes piercing, a sweet smile on his face, his neck speckled with a few cooking oil burn scars.

"Nah." I shrug, looking back at the flyer. The prize money is outrageous, but events like that aren't really made for what my family does. "Everyone entering has some wild, greasy, madly unhealthy thing. That's what wins. Not the healthy stuff. It's not special enough."

"Hey." Jordan's hand gently touches my shoulder, spinning me to look back at him. "Don't kid yourself, you're special to me."

He leans forward, and I press my hands against his chest.

"Wait…" I whisper, looking around.

"What is it?" he asks, following my gaze.

"Nothing, I just…there was a couple that recognized me earlier. But they're gone." I run my hands up to his shoulders and pull him in for a kiss. He reaches up and holds my face in his hands as his lips brush mine, and with all the heat swirling around me, it's like I'm back in front of the grill again. I tighten my arms around him, pulling us closer, before exhaling a sigh and moving away.

"We can't do *that* in South Philly." I say, feeling flustered. Warmth flutters in my chest, tickling up my neck. "Is this why you wanted to come to Fishtown?"

"Maybe." He grins wickedly, reaching out and sliding a thumb over my cheek. "You know that spatula move back there was kinda hot."

"Oh yeah?"

"Definitely." He reaches for my hand, and I hesitate. We're like five miles from the trucks and our neighborhood, so really, I shouldn't worry, but I can't help it. Jordan absolutely notices.

"Cindy," he says with an exhale, his voice like honey. "No one really knows who we are away from the trucks, you know." I intertwine our fingers, but he wriggles free. "It's okay, you don't have to."

I can tell it isn't okay.

"Soon, we won't have to worry about *anyone* in Philadelphia," he continues, the light back in his eyes. "It'll be you and me, on the road. An entire year, going where we want, seeing what we want. We won't have to hide." He looks up, away from the park, and down Frankford, before his eyes flit back to mine. "Come on, I've got a surprise."

He starts walking, and I regret not holding his hand.

Even though I'm looking forward to my year of freedom with Jordan, I do love our little splash of reality television-esque drama. Our fights between the trucks, the way the videos go wild online. How customers come back just for the spectacle. It's like we've got our own version of the shows I love so much.

But more importantly, I see the attention it brings the trucks, which helps with customers and money. Which I know both my family and Jordan's rely on in a big way. Mom and Dad are still chipping away at the debt they fell into back in Boston, when the farm went under, the subject of a lot of late-night fights when they thought I was asleep.

Hell, they're still paying off the actual truck I work in.

Without the rivalry, we're just two cheesesteak trucks taking up the same space, eating one another's market. With it, we're a whole show that provides for our families and our passions. I can't let that fall apart because of my carelessness. Philly is a small town—it would just take one rumor to burn down the entire operation we've built here.

And then I can see it. Mom and Dad fighting again. Me at the top of the stairs, wondering when it'll be over. Wondering how I can fix it.

"So have you really not given it any more thought?" Jordan asks as we make our way out of the garden, walking along a large condo with a bunch of cute shops on the bottom floor. A brightly painted ice cream shop stares back at me, Eleanor & Margot's, the smell of caramelized sugar and vanilla weighing heavily in the air like a fog.

"Given what more thought?" I ask, still distracted by waffle cones and weird flavors and thoughts of my family. Goat cheese ice cream. Who does that? Definitely something Jordan's best friend Steve would be into.

"Truck Off!" he exclaims. "I know your family isn't really into, you know, the local scene and all, and yes, junk food usually wins those food truck fairs, but it could be fun. The two of us, shouting at one another at a festival, with all those people? I know you'd love the drama."

"Oh, I don't know." I shrug. "You know how competitive my dad can get. And besides, the way you've been stressed over it, I wouldn't want to add to it. I'm surprised you haven't lost all your hair."

"Wow, don't even joke," he says, running a hand through his hair like he needs to make sure it's still there. I reach out and tuck a strand behind his ear. He's got the kind of unruly curls that I swear he doesn't even style or brush, yet they look perfect every day, a little too long in the front, like a rock star from a bygone era.

"I'll figure it out eventually," he says after a pause. "If I can't come up with something soon, I don't know, maybe I won't even do it."

"Yeah right," I scoff, trying not to roll my eyes. "You're gonna come up with something. That festival has been your entire personality for months."

"It has not!" he laughs, smiling at me.

"It has." I shrug, and he slows down his pace, stopping in the middle of the sidewalk. I turn to check out what he's so zeroed in on, and it's Goldfarb's, a cooking supply shop right on Frankford. An enormous glass window peers into a beautiful setup that reminds me a lot of the huge Williams Sonoma on Broad Street, bright stainless-steel appliances and copper pots and pans, a line of cookbooks along the windowsill, a mix of celebrity names and local icons. A Jose Garces cookbook sits comfortably next to Marisa McClellan.

Anytime we've walked by a shop like this, he stares at things inside like he's a toddler looking at a puppy in a pet shop window.

"I mean, that kind of money would definitely fund my truck," he continues, looking through the shop window, but his actual gaze seems so far away. "I just want to get something really nice, so I can make sure it's as comfortable as possible." He turns to me and smiles softly. "For you."

As sweet as the sentiment is, I really wish he'd dream bigger outside of that thing. The truck. There are like a million colleges in Philadelphia. So many choices. Why that, why a truck? Don't get me wrong, I like food. Working in my family's food truck is fun, most of the time, and saving money for college and upgrading my podcast gear has been great. But ever since I ran my old junior high's YouTube channel and helped with the morning video announcements in high school, I wanted to do something in television. Launching the podcast with the girls has been a great way to stay connected, sure, but it's also been another step in that direction. Toward my career goals.

I feel like the only reason I really do the family food truck anymore is to help my parents and plan for a future that's away from here, shooting these videos of our spats. Our faux rivalry. My own little slice of reality television, with the boy I can't get enough of. Well, as long as no one knows about that part.

"Just you wait until you and I are inside that truck every single day," he carries on, unable to keep the excitement from his voice. "Every day, we can go wherever we want. Every day we can…wake up together."

He almost whispers that last part, his eyes shying away from mine. I can practically feel him blushing at the same time as me. That's um…*definitely* a conversation I've left out with my parents when it comes to this adventure he's been planning.

"And I'll let you choose the playlist." He nudges against my shoulder, breaking the tension. "I think you've spent enough time listening to Laura's choices in the park."

And that blush flushes off my face like someone just threw turpentine on some paint.

Laura.

He must notice my expression sour because he says, "This again?" He runs a hand through his hair. "She's one of my best friends, Cindy. My *neighbor.* We literally grew up together. You see her all the time, there's nothing there."

"Yeah, I see the way she's been looking at you lately." I stop, crossing my arms. "I see her playing music she knows I hate."

"Come on, that's all part of the rivalry," he huffs. "She… likes you?"

He laughs a little, his tone unsure. I give him a look, and he continues, "She and Steve are my closest friends. They're the only ones at school who even knew about us. Please just trust me."

"So, are you going?"

"To what?"

"Her show at Cousin Charles, that music café."

"She didn't even tell me about it. I saw her today, you saw her today, and she didn't bring it up." He exhales. "You really need to let this go. There's nothing for you to worry about."

We walk in silence for a beat.

"Are you gonna be at the truck tomorrow?" I ask, circling to something familiar. Comfortable. That's where we're the best. I mean, cheesesteaks *are* comfort food.

"For a bit." He nods, like we didn't just step through a minefield. "I'm still trying to come up with the right thing for the competition, so I might field test an idea or two this weekend."

"Oh?" I smile. "Like those egg rolls?"

He groans loudly and hides his face in his hands.

"I'm never gonna figure this out." I tug at his arms until he raises his head and we keep walking.

"Sure you will." I lean against him for a moment then pull my phone out of my pocket. It's been buzzing nonstop since we've been walking. There are a flurry of absolutely unhinged updates on the show from Eesha and Ariana.

Eesha: Kelly De La Jensen just flipped a table at brunch!

Ariana: James Scarpella is threatening to leave the show!

Eesha: It won't be the same without him OH MY GOD CHRISTY SNYDER THREW HER SANDWICH AT KELLY

Cindy: YOU GUYS, SPOILERS

"Want me to pick up any ingredients for you?" I ask, sliding my phone back into my pocket. "I'm gonna hit Reading Terminal tomorrow for the family picnic on Monday."

"Reading Terminal on a Friday at the height of tourist season?" He scoffs. "You'd have so much more free time on the weekend if you weren't like…trying to find the most organically grown, ethically harvested lettuce."

"That's not true!"

"It is! You and your family need to make sure your tomatoes were free range and lived an entire life before you can use them." He turns to me, dramatically. "This tomato… *had a name.*"

"Yeah okay." I playfully shove him away. "And you're the one serving nothing but bread, meat, and cheese."

"Hey, hey." He slows down and turns to face me. His eyes are straight up shining with adoration, and I swear, when he does this, which is often, I can see his pupils dilate. A little grease burn cuts a tiny line above his lip, and I just want to kiss it. He takes my hands. "Let's save all those jabs for the trucks tomorrow."

I smile, and he smirks back.

I make sure no one is looking before I lean over, giving him a quick kiss on the cheek. I linger, whispering in his ear, "I can't wait."

He leans back and then grabs my hands in his, squeezing them. The sleeves on his T-shirt shirk up a little bit more, revealing a slightly longer cooking scar on his bicep, like a scythe. I remember when he got that, when he first started working in the truck and leaned against the hood above the grill.

He lets go and looks down at me, a mischievous smile on his face.

"We're here," he says and nods off to the side as we turn a corner off the main strip.

Head and the Hand, a small bookstore up off Frankford,

is all lit up despite it being after closing time. It sits wedged between two other small shops, with apartments and condos above them all.

Living above a bookshop. Talk about a dream.

"Wait, what?" I ask, looking through the window. There's no event going on, but it's brightly lit, and the middle of the tiny bookstore is cleared out like they're going to set up chairs and a space for someone to speak. Twinkle lights are shimmering around the store, twisting and turning around bookshelves and up and over the windowpanes. It's really gorgeous.

"Come on," Jordan says, taking my hand and opening the door to the shop. A little bell chimes as we duck inside, and I'm awash in the smell of well-loved used books. That unmistakable sweet papery smell that makes me think of autumn, and I immediately have the urge to brush my fingertips across the uneven book spines.

"I think they're closed or something," I say, glancing over at a row of romance paperbacks, spotting some familiar romcoms that my mom has reread several times. Emily Henry, Jasmine Guillory, Ashley Herring Blake...

"Well come on in, you two!" a voice exclaims.

I look up, and there's the owner of the shop, Shannon... something. I've come in here a few times, but I'm not like Jordan. I don't know every single person in every single shop and café around the city, the way he and his family do. But I know she's close to my mom's age and dresses infinitely cooler, with tight, deep blue jeans and oxblood-red boots that come up to her knees. She flicks her hair back, big curls like mine that she's just let take over her head, and points toward the back of the shop.

"I'm almost ready, just pulling out the chairs—"

And that's when it hits me.

I'm here with Jordan.

She's seeing us here.

Together.

"What are *you* doing here?!" I shout, reeling around to Jordan. I push at him, my finger out, pressing against his chest. He looks wildly confused and then laughs, grabbing my hand. "You let go of me—"

"Babe, it's okay…she knows," Jordan says gently as I wrestle against him.

I stop and feel my eyes go wide.

"She what?!" I snap.

"It's okay, it's okay." Jordan has his hands up, in a sort of surrender. He glances over at Shannon, who is wincing, her eyes darting back and forth between the two of us. "Me and Shannon talked, and she's agreed to keep it a little secret in exchange for some free cheesesteaks at the truck."

"With a Mountain Dew," she adds. "Whenever I want."

"Well, yeah, as long as I'm there." Jordan smiles back at her, tilting his head. "It's not forever."

"I know, I know." Shannon laughs. "You two *lovebirds* sit tight, I'll be right back."

God the way she said lovebirds. It was like she took real joy in knowing our truth.

"Jordan, what is going on—"

I can't even finish the sentence. Shannon has emerged already, two folding chairs slung over her shoulder, a small table wedged under her arm. She puts them in the middle of the bookstore, unfolding everything, and then walks over to the shop's register, where she pulls out a small tablecloth and a picnic basket from behind the counter.

She places the cloth over the little foldout table and plops an electric candle in the middle of it all.

"Can't have a flame in here. You know, store full of paper and all." She places the picnic basket on the table. "Enjoy and remember to pick out a book for yourselves on the way out. I'll be in the back listening to a podcast, so if you need anything just walk in."

And with that, she vanishes into the back of the store.

"Jordan!" I snap. "What is this?!"

He shrugs sheepishly. "It's date night," he says, walking toward the table in the middle of the bookshop. He holds a hand out and I take it, letting him lead me to the charming setup. He pulls out my chair for me and I sit. Despite how uneasy I am about being out in the open, I'm feeling...cozy. Snug.

"Listen I know...we've been losing places this summer. *Our* places," he presses, reaching out the table to rub the top of my hands with his thumbs. His face is gently illuminated by the electric candle, his eyes twinkling under the golden lights strung around the store. "But you know, we have to make new ones. Spaces for each other, until we get out of here."

I sigh. He's not wrong. With so many of our classmates graduating and sticking around Philadelphia for college, or also taking some time off like we are, it feels like every day another coffee shop or pizza place in neighborhoods away from South Philly, including all the way out in Manayunk, have random acquaintances running the register or slinging cups of tea. People we were barely friends with in high school who could easily post something online about seeing the two of us together, clearly not being rivals.

We've been losing places where it's safe to just be...us.

I glance at the picnic basket.

"Go ahead," Jordan says, settling back in his chair.

I peek inside, and oh my God, the laugh that erupts from my mouth manages to scare me a little.

I reach in and pull out a Choco Taco.

"How?" I ask, looking at the ice cream, wrapped in a shiny silver packet. "They stopped making these!" The photo on the wrapping paper shows a taco shell made of wafer, the sort you see on waffle cones, packed with vanilla ice cream and chocolate drizzle. It's freezing cold, and I flip open the rest of the basket, and there are even more in there, sitting comfortably in what looks like some kind of insulated fabric.

It's my favorite ice cream. I haven't had it in... I don't even know. A few Philly restaurants have tried making them as a dessert, but it's just not the same.

"Well..." Jordan shrugs. "A few days ago, Steve's grandfather was cleaning out the freezer in the back of the deli and found a whole box just sitting at the bottom of it."

"Oh..." I stammer out and look at the expiration date on the ice cream. I exhale with relief. It's got another two months left.

"Don't worry," Jordan says as he plucks his own out of the basket. "They might have been in that freezer for like two years, but there's still time." He looks at the wrapper on his and frowns, promptly putting it back and pulling another one out. "There was...not any time left on that other one but this one is good."

I laugh, contentment washing over me. This is so wildly sweet and romantic. I suppose this is safe, so far away from our stomping grounds in South Philly. I try to push away the anxiousness in my chest and settle down into the moment here. We have to make our own space. I like that.

"Let me get the drinks," Jordan says, winking. "It's, you know, not wine. Not anything wild."

"How did you even come up with this?" I ask, stopping him from getting up.

"I didn't. This place offers date nights in the shop. They book up pretty fast, though, and Shannon managed to squeeze us in. A free cheesesteak bribe will do that."

"*Cheesesteaks*," I hear Shannon shout from the back room, stressing the plural.

Jordan rolls his eyes and walks toward the back room. I take a moment to check my buzzing phone.

Eesha: Fine, fine, no spoilers, but you're gonna have so much to catch up on

Eesha: We should be reading the live Reddit reality show threads together by now

Ariana: We should record right away in the morning, like... spectacularly early. Since we can't record right after the show and all. Please picture me glaring at SOMEONE right now

Eesha: Maybe like, eight?

Ariana: Earlier would be better

I look at the time. It's nearly 9 p.m. I'm surprised I haven't gotten a bundle of texts from Mom yet about the show. Though to be fair, I think she knows better than to spoil it for me.

Me: I'll catch up on the show tonight, my mom is recording it

Me: I'll be ready to record tomorrow I promise!

Jordan returns from the back room, two cartons of Arctic Splash iced tea in his hands, the most ridiculously sugary sweet iced tea in existence that feels like it belongs to Philadelphia, when it's made in, like, Texas or something.

He smiles, beaming as he walks toward me. He hands me a carton and holds it up in a toast.

"To making space." He beams.

I tap my carton against his, and even though my phone keeps buzzing against the table, I ignore it.

Reality can wait.

Pilot: Confessional Shot Transcript (Jordan)

Jordan: Ah yeah, Cindy. We've known each other since her family moved here in junior high. Later in junior high, at the end of it all, like eighth grade. That's around the time our parents started their trucks.

According to my dad, our families didn't always dislike one another. Her family had posted something in our neighborhood's Facebook group when they were moving to the area, and my mom rushed to welcome them to town. Even showed them how to go about getting a permit for their truck. That's just the sort of person she is.

If it wasn't for my parents, I don't know if they would have gotten started as fast as they did.

But then something happened. Her parents wanted the same corner as mine for their truck, the spot my dad had called dibs on. They fought over the spots a lot. I remember all that, all the way up until the city permits came in and they had locked in their locations across the square.

Her family got the "good" spot, according to my dad. He's still salty about it.

But the whole public rivalry thing really only took off when we both started working weekends in the trucks during the school year with our parents. I walked over and asked her if we could borrow some ketchup and she made it into this whole thing, "How DARE you ask ME for ketchup?" Someone caught it on video, and suddenly that was it. People started coming by, kids started sending that video and others around school, and everyone just seemed to hope to catch us fighting. It's been a battle ever since.

Do I wish we were friends?

laughs

Yeah right. Have you met her yet? No way.

Pilot: Confessional Shot Transcript (Cindy)

Cindy: Jordan?! Don't get me started. He's as basic as the ingredients he uses.

I feel like... *sighs* I don't know, maybe in another life we'd be friends, right? We both love food, we both love cooking. Our families have similar stories about why we're here. We lost our urban farm, his family lost their diner. Why not, you know?

But between the drama over the parking spots and how we've just been shouting at one another through the entirety of high school, that just doesn't seem like it's in the cards.

It's not exactly a Romeo and Juliet situation, our families don't want to kill each other. They don't like each other, fine, but I'm sure all of that would ease over if they just got to swap parking spots once and a while.

It's not... Montagues. More like Manchegues. Like the cheese. Manchego...get it...

long pause

Can we edit that out?

chapter three:
jordan

Friday, Nine Days until Truck Off

"Okay, okay," Steve says, sitting me down in his parents' kitchen. I'm not sure exactly what he's been working on all morning, but the small space is covered in a wide array of pots and pans, the smell of burnt sugar and cooked milk permeating the air. There's not much of a kitchen table in here, not really, just a small cast-iron thing with two barstool-esque chairs, pressed up against the wall farthest from the fridge.

The mess here is...very un-Steve-like. But I suppose it can't be helped.

It's a pretty typical small kitchen you see in most Philadelphia trinity homes, where the staircases are as twisty and narrow as a gnarled tree branch, and the rooms are small and skinny. How Steve, the over-six-foot giant he is, navigates it is beyond me, and I watch as he ducks and swerves around

the microscopic kitchen with the same grace he does in the
food truck...

He slams an elbow against a kitchen cabinet, and I wince.

"Argh," he groans, gritting his teeth. He closes his eyes and
exhales, and then focuses back on the countertop near the
sink, which is absolutely overflowing with dishes and utensils.

After a few minutes, he spins around and, with a flourish,
places a plate in front of me.

I blink at it.

It's some...some kind of hardened, arched spiderweb? Or,
maybe, one of those white fabric doily things my grandpar-
ents used to have in their living room, underneath ancient
bowls of strawberry candies or, ugh, Werther's Originals. I
reach out and poke at it, and it doesn't move, just stays there
retaining its shape.

"What do you think?" he asks, and while his face is absolutely beaming, I can practically see him vibrating with
anxiousness.

"Steve, I..." I clear my throat. "I'm not sure what I'm looking at. Is this...food?"

"Ugh." He reaches around me, breaking off a piece of the
delicate web. The arch tilts over on the plate, but still mostly
stays together despite the brittle pieces scattered about the ce-
ramic. He holds it out to me. "Try it."

"So...it *is* a food," I say, taking the spindly bit of... I don't
even know.

"This is what I made to get into ICA!" he shouts. "Well,
one of the things from my portfolio. It's crystalized egg
whites, created using coconut oil infusions. Parmesan cheese
helps to make it crisp like this."

I pause for a beat, looking at the edible spiderweb.

"Steve, are you telling me this...this is a *frittata*?!"

"Exactly!"

"But why?!" I ask, barely able to hold back my laughter. "What's the point of it looking like this? Why would you do this? Who is this for?"

He rolls his eyes at me and breaks another piece of spiderweb—I'm sorry, crystalized and infused frittata. He pops it in his mouth, and the thing crunches loudly, like he's eating rock candy crystals we used to make in third grade.

"I'll have you know this is delicious," Steve insists, and then crosses his arms. "And if you're going to win Truck Off, you're going to need to think outside of the box too."

"Yeah, dude, I don't know about *that* outside the box." I laugh. "You could stand to be, like...just a little closer to it. This is, like, outside the box and across the state line."

"You're sounding like your dad right now, you know," he says.

I glare at him for a beat.

He lifts an eyebrow, a challenge.

Fine.

I take a bite of the crystals in my hand, and... I feel my expression change from amused and doubtful to pleasantly surprised. It does taste like a frittata, maybe with just a little too much coconut oil, but I'm not about to shatter the joy on Steve's face right now.

"See?" he says, smugly.

"Yeah okay," I admit. "It's good. Weird, but good. But that's not what we need in the truck, you know that, right?

I mean look at all this!" I point at all the dishes and pans piled up.

"Of course," Steve scoffs and grabs one of the tall barstool chairs at the tiny kitchen table. I sit down at the other. "But look, man, you need to figure out what that thing is. I thought this might...stir up something. Trying something new can get you out of your comfort zone. It can inspire!"

"God you really *are* gonna be like one of those fancy chefs in television shows." I laugh, thinking about Dad yesterday.

"Har har," Steve says. "You finish those applications?"

"I'm just gonna tell him I filled some out online." I wave Steve off, remembering that I left those papers back at the bookshop last night.

"You know he's going to ask for the email receipts or something. Just fill them out and humor the man, so we can enjoy the summer...and focus on what's important." He holds up the spiderweb egg creation, and I break off another spindle.

The sound of a door opening makes Steve shoot up from his seat.

"Oh no," he says. "They're home early." You'd think he just got caught with a girl over or something, but it's far worse than that.

It's a kitchen that looks like a war zone.

"Steve?" I hear his mom from the other end of the house. "Are you home? What's that smell? Have you been—"

It's a trinity home, so it's small. And before she can even finish that sentence, she's already in the doorway leading into the kitchen.

"Oh. My. God," Steve's mom says, her eyes wide, surveying the wreckage of the kitchen. "What did you even make this time?!"

"Hi, Mrs. Giles." I wave.

"Yeah, hi, Jordan," she says quickly, still staring at Steve. "Well?"

Wincing, Steve holds up the plate with the broken leftovers of the crystalized frittata spiderweb.

"You have got to be kidding me." Mrs. Giles exhales, pointing at the plate. "You're both going to clean this disaster, right now, before you even think of heading toward the truck."

"Oh, well, Mom, we were going to—" Steve starts.

She glares at him, and Steve stops talking. Her eyes flit over to me and then to the basin of dishes.

"I'll make you two a deal." She crosses her arms, nodding at the disaster behind Steve. "Make me a breakfast sandwich, and I'll take care of the dishes."

"Breakfast?" I scoff, and Steve gives me a pleading look. He might be something of a neat freak, but he does not want to clean these dishes. "Uh, okay. Sure, Mrs. Giles."

She walks out of the kitchen and into the living room, flopping down on a couch. I look over to Steve and then the fridge.

"Breakfast, then." I nod and move to see what they've got available. I don't even have to ask, Steve starts cleaning off one of the cast-iron pans he used to make his weird spiderweb frittata thing. I find two eggs left—and briefly wonder if it took the rest of the carton to make that thing of Steve's—some vibrant orange American cheese, a hardened kaiser roll, and some bacon.

"That cheese looks like it has seen better days." Steve laughs, peeking over as I get situated on the small kitchen table. I give it a little flick with my finger, and it is…not entirely soft the way cheese should be. The more neon American cheese gets, the more ancient it has become. No one really gets hyped for "aged" American cheese on a menu, since it's mostly made of chemicals.

If your cheese has to be called "cheese product" that's usually a bad sign.

But whatever. It's delicious.

And it'll melt just fine.

I splash some olive oil on the cast-iron pan and heat it up on high, tossing a few strips of bacon in. Steve busies himself with cleaning up a little bit here and there because let's be real, even though his mother said she'd take care of all this, the guilt is just going to be way too much for either of us. I dry a few dishes as the bacon starts to sizzle, and then crack two eggs into the skillet, and watch as they fry up.

Bacon, I can let sit unwatched for a spell. Eggs, definitely not.

You want everything around the yolk to fry up nice, and if you get the egg whites just thin enough, you can even make them crispy. The trick is making sure the yolk doesn't break, and if possible, even stays a little bit cool. Just warm enough that, you know, you're not gonna get sick. But if you overdo it, the yolk will gel, or eventually just get solid, which kills all the flavor.

Some people like the yolk gelled. It's delicious in ramen, whew. But on a breakfast sandwich? It's just not the same.

That yolk should run like someone seeing Gritty for the first time.

"Salt, pepper," I say, sticking out my hand.

Two grinders appear there from Steve, and I put a heavy sprinkle of each into the whites and the bit of yellow that is just visible underneath it.

"That smells outrageously good," Steve says, and I glance over to see him looking down at his artisan frittata creation with a little regret on his face. I slice open the slightly stale kaiser roll, put the neon slice of brittle cheese on one side, and the bacon and egg on the other. The yolk jiggles inside its protective sheath of fried egg white.

Perfect.

I give the other side of the roll a few seconds on the hot cast iron, letting the bread warm up while melting that chemical cheese, and then put it all together in one fantastic smelling sandwich.

Steve's mom peeks her head back into the kitchen.

"How's it going, boys?" she asks, and then her eyes settle on the sandwich in my hand. "That is what I'm talking about."

She walks over and takes it from me, and when she bites into it, a bit of the yellow yolk explodes from the bread, dribbling down her hands. She exhales loudly and smiles.

"Perfect."

It's nearly 11 a.m., and I pop open an energy drink as we wait to cross Broad Street, the can hissing loudly as though the liquid is literally full of energy. It tastes like battery acid, but it keeps me going.

"Jesus." Steve shakes his head. "You're weirded out by culinary excellence, yet you drink those things."

"It's natural?" I say, but my voice lilts up a little because I'm actually not sure. Steve yanks the can out of my hand, some of the liquid dribbling onto the sidewalk. "Hey!"

"Caffeine. Ginseng. Guarana. Ginkgo biloba…"

"Mmm-hmm, so far so good," I say, trying to swipe the can.

"CYANOCOBALAMIN," Steve shouts, lifting it out of my reach.

"Fine, fine, you win!" I grumble, and he hands me the can back.

"You could just drink *coffee*, you know. There are plenty of great cafés right near the truck."

He starts to cross the street, but I stop him.

"Let's uh…go this way," I say, moving back down the sidewalk.

"What why…oh." He mutters, realization washing over him. "You're just torturing yourself, and therefore, torturing me. Is this because of my frittata? Or making fun of your energy drink? Or because you had to help do some of the dishes at my house? Alright maybe I do deserve this."

I smile—even Steve's grumbling can't keep me from slowing down, as if I'm being pulled forward by a magnet.

Are there faster ways to get to where our truck is parked? Of course. Do those paths skirt along the used car lot that borders the nearby performing arts academy, all the way on the other side of Broad Street? They absolutely do not. As buses and trucks zoom down the busy street, tall fencing comes into view.

"There we go." I walk along the edge of the metal fence, Steve muttering something under his breath next to me. And then finally, I see them. At the end of the large, sprawling used car lot. I lace my fingers through the chain link, the rusty edges nipping at my skin as I take them in.

The food trucks.

It's not like they have a huge selection or anything. It's a used car lot in South Philadelphia, after all. Most of the stuff here is what you'd expect to see at a dealership like this— your average sedans for commuters, minivans and SUVs for families, a couple of Range Rovers for people with low self-esteem.

But there *they* are.

There are four in the lot right now. One was added in just a few months back, but I have a strong suspicion the other three have been sitting here forever. An old dessert truck with its own name misspelled (Just Deserts), a fresh salad truck that served their meals in mason jars (something that Cindy's family apparently used to do back in Boston), and a pizza truck complete with a stone oven inside called Quarter Slice Crisis, a spin-off truck from a pizza place in Jersey that tried to expand down here.

They're all a bit faded and sad looking, from years of just, well, being there. And it is kind of depressing. I get why Steve doesn't love me walking by, my heart full of yearning for one of them.

But there's no denying how beautiful Big Red is.

She's painted the color of a fire truck. Bright red with dark maroon panels, bright yellow text along the side. Jalapeno Your Business. Horrible name. Just horrible. According to Mr. Quirino, the dealership owner, it used to be a taco truck, and I should "stop lurking outside" until "I can actually buy something."

"Just think—" I start.

"About it," Steve finishes for me, leaning against the chainlink fence, sending it rattling. He does his best impression of me and keeps going. "A fresh coat of paint over the name, new kitchen gear inside, maybe some new wheels because who knows how long it's been sitting—"

"Okay, okay." Laughing, I reach over to shove him. I look ahead at the truck for a beat before turning to Steve. "What did our tips end up at last night, after I left?"

"Eh, not much." He shrugs. "Hundred each."

"Hmm." I think back to the week. "We're definitely coming in under the five hundred dollars we split last week..." I glance back at Big Red and sigh. "I feel like I've been saving for a truck for years, and I'm nowhere near being able to get something like *that*."

"You don't need something like *that*, though, right?" Steve asks. "Haven't you always said you'd be happy with a heap?"

"Sure, but..." I huff. "I mean just *look* at that truck."

"I see it. It sure is a truck."

"Shut up," I laugh. "I just... I feel like we're going to need to do something extra nice. Cindy won't be comfortable in a truck that's rusting and falling apart, no matter how much I'm working to fix it. I want her to be happy while we're out there on our road trip."

"Yeah, man, I guess," Steve says, rubbing the back of his head.

"What is it?" I ask.

He shrugs. "I'm just gonna miss this, you know?" He smiles faintly and looks at me. "Sure, food trucks aren't where I want to be, but it's been so much fun just hanging out every week-end over the years, and this summer has been awesome..."

He exhales and leans his shoulder against the fence.

"Growing up sucks a little, sometimes."

"Yeah, I hear you." I join him in leaning, the metal squeak-ing beneath me. And I do hear him. But I've been daydream-ing about this trip since the day Cindy first kissed me, the same way kids at school talked about prom or homecoming freshman year, even when it was years away. Some kids dream about the perfect promposal, I dreamed about the perfect road trip with the perfect girl.

And now, everything is nearly within my grasp. And if working for myself and setting out on my own is growing up, I'm not sure I hate it that much.

Steve starts to say something to me, and then hesitates.

"Steve, come on."

"It's..." He huffs, pushing himself off the fence, nodding at Big Red in the lot. "Look, we're not gonna magically make a lot more money by doing what we've done every single day this summer, bro." I must give him a look because he gives me one right back. "You *know* I'm right. Those locals and tour-ists aren't going to abruptly tip more because they've heard you have a crush on a truck."

"I don't—"

"You gotta change. You gotta adjust. Or Big Red is gonna stay right here forever." He keeps going before I can protest. "I know you and your family are stubborn as hell, but...and hear me out, I think we should try out *breakfast* cheesesteaks this week."

"Whoa, whoa, whoa." I laugh, shaking my head. "Are you kidding? Really?"

"Dude my mom practically left my father for that sandwich you whipped up today. And you made that with a stale roll and American cheese that should have been thrown away."

"Yeah, it was starting to look closer to red then orange, and it wasn't even supposed to be orange."

"I'm telling you, that's it," Steve says, urgently. "It has to be it."

"Who is going to want breakfast that late at night?" I ask.

"People eat breakfast at all times of day, especially late at night." He pauses. "But… I think we should actually work some morning hours too."

"Oh, I dunno…" Something twists in my chest a little, some nerves, I think. "The morning and early afternoon, that's kinda Cindy's family's whole territory."

"Psh." Steve rolls his eyes. "Her customers aren't going to abandon whatever healthy thing she's whipping up. Besides, aren't you two rivals?" He winks.

"Shut up."

He nods at Big Red. "Listen, if you want that truck, if you want that road trip…" He reaches out and grabs my shoulder. "I need you to trust me."

"Of course I do, it's just…" I sigh. "I swear, if I didn't know any better, I'd think you were trying to get rid of me."

"I am." He smiles. "That's what best friends do. I want you on the road chasing down that dream of yours." He claps his hands, rubbing them together. "Okay. Okay, okay. I'll go hit up my grandpa's deli before things get hectic at the truck, and tomorrow, we try something new."

"Steve—" I start, as he turns to head down the block.

"You bring the energy drinks! I'm not gonna let you do this on your own!"

I look back at Big Red in the parking lot. The city buzzes with promise. I know Dad won't love the idea of me making something that wildly different at the truck, but if it's going to get me a few steps closer to what I actually want, it's worth a shot.

For now, I've got to head to the truck for the lunch rush.

Tomorrow.

Tomorrow, I'll try something new.

chapter four:
cindy

***

Friday, Nine Days until Truck Off

"Oh my God, Cindy, you have to stop yawning," Eesha grumbles at me through Zoom. I blink and shake my head, patting my cheeks a few times, and take a deep breath. The air smells like wool sweaters, which isn't all that surprising considering I'm wedged in the downstairs closet, also known as my podcast recording studio.

Thick wool sweaters make for excellent sound proofing, you know. That, combined with the actual sound proofing I've put up on the inside walls, makes it the perfect nook... albeit a little less roomy when it comes to fitting jackets, umbrellas, and an actual human.

It's eight in the morning on a Friday. It's the summer. I was up until two after my date with Jordan, catching up on the episode of *The Secret Lives of Beacon Hill Wives* and reading all the Reddit recaps and behind-the-scenes leaks so I could be ready for recording this episode with the girls.

I suppose I did this to myself.

But that bookstore date. The discontinued Choco Tacos. Afterward, it turned out that the date included two books which I could pick out from the shelves, since Jordan had prepaid for them. I eventually passed out in my bed with a copy of the newest Laura Taylor Namey title on my face.

"Cindy!" Ariana shouts. "Focus!"

"I am! I'm here." I shake my head again and grab the latte Mom had ready to go for me this morning, tightly secured in a metal mug with a lid. I can steal sips while Eesha or Ariana are talking. Their setups, which I can see through our Zoom session, are a little bit sunnier than mine. Literally. Eesha is in her kitchen, the warm morning light shining in through a gorgeous bay door, giving her a little halo, while Ariana is in her bedroom, seafoam-green walls dotted with some of our favorite Boston bands, like American Authors and this group The Receiving End of Sirens her dad got us listening to.

And here I am, crammed in the closet, with a little television tray on my lap holding my computer, my microphone, and my coffee.

My bedroom is way too loud, and I don't have a closet in there. The only other solid hideaway nook is the closet in my parents' room, but I don't need to see Mom and Dad's underwear all around me.

I clear my throat and take a sip of the latte.

"Okay, okay." I exhale, focusing. I'm awake. I'm here. I'm in control. "Let's go."

"Three...two....one..." Eesha counts down, and then claps,

so when she edits the podcast, it's easy to find the point that all our recordings kick off. "Welcome to *Beacon Street*. I'm Eesha."

"I'm Ariana."

"And I'm…"

The yawn that escapes me, I swear, it practically rattles the closet. Ariana and Eesha both nearly fall out of their seats on video, and shout at me at the same time.

This…is gonna take a while.

Reading Terminal Market roars with the sound of busy customers. Dad walks ahead of me, purposeful in all the chaos, and my senses are immediately awash with the smells of the open air around me. Sharp cheeses, roasting meats, sweet chocolate…it's an intense barrage on my nose, and so powerful that I can taste everything in the back of my throat.

God, this place. This city market is starting to wake me up better than the two shots of espresso I had. Maybe we should have recorded later in the day.

Smack in the middle of downtown, the over-a-century-old indoor farmers market spans the width and length of an entire city block, with almost a hundred vendors smattered throughout. Fresh fruits and veggies carted in from farms around Pennsylvania, desserts made right there in kitchens set up inside of stalls, hulking masses of roasting ribs shaved off into sandwiches, bread so fresh and fluffy it's like a freaking cloud…everything is here. Even live crabs that twitch from where they're on display, sprawled out on their backs on top of countertops, ready to be lunch.

We had spots like this back in Boston, like the Mission

Hill markets. And of course, all the places where Dad and Mom drove their urban farm's produce around. South Boston. Dewey Square. Beacon Hill, where they film the show, or at least parts of it. Ashmount. But nothing quite like this.

Jordan would live it up in a place like this. If only his family didn't stick to the Italian Market in South Philly for their basics. Last time I tried to convince him to come with me and my dad to shop for the trucks, he said, "My cheesesteaks don't need pomegranates."

Which...okay fine, but...he's missing out. Especially right now, struggling to figure out what his fancy sandwich is going to be for the Truck Off. I make a mental note to look for things for him, even if he doesn't particularly want me to. There's just gotta be *something* here. Out of everywhere in Philadelphia, this would be the place that has it. Whatever *it* is.

I yawn and wipe at my eyes, nearly colliding with a stack of wicker baskets outside a stand. When I collected myself, Dad is staring right at me, a smirk on his face.

"Don't say it," I grumble.

"Sweetheart," he starts, his accent putting a "hah" in the middle of *heart*, "I'm just saying—"

"Dad."

"You and the girls should really just watch those shows of yours on Hulu or something!" Dad teases, walking ahead, weaving between folks. "Staying up so late, it's bad enough with you and your mom doing that too. It's a lot! And then recording like that in the morning. It's not a job, darling."

"It *could* be a job someday." I yawn again, then clear my throat.

"Fine, fine," Dad concedes, slowing down. "I know there

are some things I just have to accept I'll never quite get. Your reality shows, TikTok, and why cars can park on the sidewalk in this godforsaken city."

He stretches and peers around.

"Okay. Dollar bags first?" He smiles at me. His darkened features skipped me, leaving me looking more like my mother though I've definitely got his way-too-thick Peruvian eyebrows. I join him skirting by some people in suits waiting for freshly ground coffee. Just the aroma feels like I'm waking up a tiny bit more.

It's not just food industry people here early on the weekend, or during the week, for that matter. If you work in Center City, there's a good chance Reading Terminal is a favorite place to grab breakfast, lunch, dinner, you name it on the go.

A little girl runs by me, and someone chases after her, with the tone of a frantic and stressed-out parent.

Right now, it's packed with a little bit of everyone.

Me and Dad make our way over to one of our favorite stands, Sparowanya Farms, run by a wildly hip young farmer from New Jersey. I can spot her dark red hair that's buzzed along the side long before we get to the stand.

"Christine," Dad says, nodding at her. She glances up, smiling at him, before she notices me.

"Hey, Cindy." She tosses a cotton tote that I just barely manage to catch. There are some beets on the front, wearing bathing suits. I squint, trying to figure it out.

"Hot beats," she says, winking. I roll my eyes. Why does every single person who works with food insist on punny names? She grins. "You two have fun."

The veggies that line the farm stand's bins and shelves are

bright and wet and colorful, beads of water glimmering on leaves and skins like gems. I run my fingers over some lettuce, making my way to the back to the dollar section, where small paper bags line a hard, wooden countertop, the contents hastily scrawled on the surface in poor handwriting. But I can read it easily because we've been coming here since I was in junior high, ever since the truck opened.

Tomatoes.

Misc. Stone Fruit.

Assorted Root Veggies.

Gala Apples.

I scour each bag, peering inside and dropping a few solid finds inside the tote. A lot of the dollar bags are fruits and veggies that'll likely go bad in another day or two but are otherwise okay. Maybe some heavy bruising on the sides, some wilted leaves. It all looks and tastes just fine when you slice it up in a sandwich, and anything that we can't use goes right into compost for the farm or to the local Philadelphia ASPCA. They've got a lot of bunnies who are more than happy to get fresh but wilting produce.

"Anything good?" Dad asks, appearing next to me. He's got a few bags of tomatoes under his arm.

"Some tomatoes in here too." I pat the tote and peer into a few more grab bags. "Do we need onions? Or..." I squint, trying to make out what's inside. "Sprouts? Asparagus?"

My dad chuckles. "Not unless you've got some wild new sandwich idea." He peeks into a couple of bags, and sucks at his teeth. "Slim pickings today, but that's okay, I've got plenty from the farm back home. Don't fuss too much over anything.

We're gonna use a lot of this at the family picnic, so it can be a little soft or squishy."

He starts loading up some potatoes into a plastic grocery basket, eyeing up the green beans before tossing a couple bunches in.

"Figure we can roast these in some Cajun spices, have a little remoulade on the side to dip them in." This cracks a grin out of me. There's a gastropub across town, Grace Tavern, that he and Mom go to weekly that serves these fried green beans, and he's always trying to figure out the recipe, even if he won't admit it.

"How were things at the truck yesterday? You haven't said anything." He lifts his basket, testing the weight. "I think I've got a few more stops in me."

"It was fine." I shrug. "We could stand to figure out a way to keep the truck open later, you know."

"Nah." Dad shakes his head and grabs a bag of oranges. "We're good at what we do, Cindy. No need to give in to gimmicks or anything like that. Let the Plazas family deal with the drunks who want something greasy. That's not our jam."

"Yeah, but we could be making so much more!" I exclaim. "We wouldn't need grab bag veggies."

The words spill out of my mouth too quickly for me to realize what I've said.

Dad winces and I immediately feel terrible.

"There's nothing wrong with grab bag veggies, kiddo." Dad smiles gently, recovering. "Sure, sometimes we get a carrot that looks like a person's hand, but it saves money, and it's also a good way to contribute to less food waste. All a part of the mission, sweetheart."

The mission, not contributing to waste, sure. He says all this, but I saw that pained expression on his face. We're still pinching pennies because of his mistakes back in Boston, leaving him and Mom in a credit hole when the farm shuddered. It's the weight they're both carrying that we just don't talk about.

Debt. The word we don't say.

"You know, sometimes I worry those reality shows you and your mom watch are getting in your head a little," Dad says, squinting at me. "You know stuff doesn't have to be all... I don't know, glitz and glamour to be worthwhile. Right?"

"I know, I know," I huff, grateful for the levity. "I'm not *that* shallow, Dad."

"Alright, I'm just saying. But hey, think of it this way— cheaper, but still *good*, produce just means more money in your college fund." Dad grins. "Have you heard anything back from Northeastern? The wait list and all that?"

"No." I sigh, a little surprised at the feeling of disappointment in my chest. I want the road trip with Jordan. But still...

"That's okay," he says, shrugging, the bags jostling in his arms. "County when you get back from your little trip is gonna be fine. You're gonna be fine, but I..." He grunts from the weight of everything in his hands. "I am not. So, on second thought, I think this is a wrap. Need anything else? I could drop all this at the car, and we could come back."

"No, no, it's okay." I look around in the stall and feel a twinge of jealousy at someone grabbing a little plastic basket of truffles that has got to be at least a hundred dollars. I bet I could cook up something wild with those. Some truffle aioli? Shaved truffle in a cheesesteak? A few weeks ago, there was an episode of *Beacon Hill* where some of the women were out to dinner, and a waiter brought around a truffle board, and it was like fifty bucks each time he shaved one sliver on their chicken or whatever they were eating.

One of them just kept it going for the cameras, smiling at her friends. Because she *could*.

I sigh, feeling the weight of my own life expectations and, vicariously, the weight of those bags my dad is carrying. "Let's go."

"Alright, we'll pick up some rolls for the truck and the picnic, and then I'll drop you off."

The picnic, that's right.

We make our way toward the exit, passing by a massive stall full of seafood, with fish that seem impossibly huge to be, like, in Philadelphia, fresh and under ice. Boston, it made sense. But here? You don't exactly see fishing boats in the Schuylkill or Delaware. There's red snapper and swordfish steaks, oysters galore, and piles of crawfish. A soupery stand, with heaving caldrons like something out of a fantasy novel, smells astonishingly good as we walk by. I snap a photo of the to-go containers of clam chowder, one Manhattan, the other New England, and text it to the girls.

Me: Not sure I know which one is better anymore, to be honest

Eesha: Oh my God

Ariana: You absolute traitor

Eesha: Blocked and reported

Eesha: I'm almost done editing the show, by the way. I managed to snip out all your yawns

Eesha: I don't know how we're going to record when you're off in a food truck for an entire year

I feel the smile on my face fall off. I hate the idea of our episodes being delayed or missing a recording while we're on the road. *Beacon Street* is important to me. I've talked to Jordan about it, and he doesn't see it as much of a problem. "You can watch the show on your iPhone!" But I don't know.

If that wait list came through, I could be there as early as August. With my girls. No being too tired to work on our show, no timing our viewings together, no worrying about trying to respond to listeners while next to a sizzling grill. I could be recording in Eesha's kitchen, or sprawled out on Ariana's bed, the way we used to as kids having sleepovers, only this time with podcasting gear.

I yearn for it something terrible, and I feel so guilty thinking like that. All this planning Jordan is doing, the way his eyes light up when he talks about the places we'll go and the freedom we'll have. But college in Boston, with Eesha, with Ariana…

I know. I *know* every warning that every guidance counselor gives about not going to college for somebody else. Usually someone you're dating, or a friend you've had the last year or so. But I've known Ariana and Eesha since we could crawl. It's different. They're family, the same way Steve is to Jordan.

As we keep making our way out of the market, we pass a bakery with gigantic cookies and then, a rare sight.

An empty stall.

Dad slows his brisk walk, eyeing up the space. It looks recently cleared out, and he stares into the stall, searching.

"Do you remember what was here, Cindy?" he asks, putting one of the bags down. He runs his free hand over a glass case, gingerly, before looking to me.

I shake my head.

"Yeah, me neither." He looks back up, and something in his gaze feels far away. "Sorry." He shakes his head. "I just wonder sometimes, you know. About back in Boston, at the markets. If people noticed that we were gone. If anyone would notice if that happened here."

"Dad?" I ask. Maybe what I said earlier, about the dollar bags, cut a little deeper than I thought.

Or...are we in trouble again? I haven't heard him or Mom fighting over finances since we moved. I thought we left all of that behind.

He gives the stall a little pat and lifts the tote bag full of groceries.

"Come on." He clears his throat. "Let's go get things ready."

I follow along, my mind spinning.

Pilot: Confessional Shot Transcript (Cindy)

Cindy: Well, Philadelphia is kind of a small city.

Like, okay, I know it's not. It's a huge city. But it has that... I don't know, feeling, you know? So sure, we bump into the Plazas family now and again, sometimes they're out getting ingredients at the same time as us. Like in the Italian Market. And I went to school with Jordan and his circle of friends. So he's kind of unavoidable.

But no, our families don't really talk. What would we even say to each other? Fight over the parking spaces again?

The people closest to me, they're back in Boston. Minus my family, of course. Eesha and Ariana. They actually both really love reality television and will likely lose it hearing their names on here.

Hey, girls. I miss you.

Being here in Philadelphia, it's been hard. I feel like a lot of the other kids I've met, starting in junior high all the way through high school...so many of them had been through school together since first grade. I met these cliques that had been tight for a decade, even though we were all thirteen at the time.

laughs

pauses

I dunno. When you see a lot of people with those kinds of close relationships, it's hard to wedge yourself in. To ask people to make space for you. I know some people are good at that sort of thing, but not me.

I've never been good at asking people to make space for me.

I just kinda...wait for them to do it.

Pilot: Confessional Shot Transcript (Jordan)

Jordan: Look, change is...difficult, for my family. My dad was always a big believer in the fact that once you've nailed a recipe, once you've perfected something, there's no need to meddle with it. We've been doing the same cheesesteak at the truck since I can remember.

I don't really see us changing.

Why try to fix something that isn't broken? When it works, it works.

chapter five:
jordan

———

Saturday, Eight Days until Truck Off

I rub the sleep from my eyes as I make my way down Broad Street.

It's still dark out, not even 6 a.m. I can't believe Steve talked me into this. My whole body feels like it's dragging, and I wonder how many energy drinks it's going to take to make it through the morning.

I'd say I wonder what other kids from school are up to on a Saturday morning, in the summer after graduation, but I know. They're all asleep. Or hey, what are my old classmates doing at 11 p.m. on a Friday night, when Steve and I—and sometimes just me—are serving up cheesesteaks to drunken tourists or grad students? Surprise, also sleeping. Maybe with each other.

I can't help the sigh that escapes my chest. Good for them. I'm not saying I want a different life. I love the truck.

There's a road trip coming with my and Cindy's names written all over it at the end of the summer. I think about how in the cold months, we could maybe work our way down to New Orleans, or maybe just go all-in with the cold and head to Maine, meet some of the food truck community serving up lobster rolls. Or just leave the coast entirely and head toward California, serve up traditional Philadelphia cheesesteaks on the boardwalk by the Pacific.

I suppose there's the question of how to get the right bread to last a journey that far but…whatever. That's a problem for future me. First thing is first. The truck.

I'd be gone already, but I promised my parents that I'd stick around this summer and give some serious thought to college and the culinary institute, which was a mistake. I know that now, considering the way Dad jammed those applications in my tip jar. But the heart wants what the heart wants. And in the case of mine, it wants the smell of grease and the searing of onions, for as long as I can take it.

And Cindy.

Oh goodness, does my heart want Cindy, and I really don't see any reason why I can't hold on to both. The two of us on the open road together, traveling state to state, untethered. Where we won't have to worry about hiding in order to maintain the illusion of the feud. As long as I have enough in my savings after buying the truck, we can absolutely make it. I've heard about some of our classmates backpacking through Europe for their gap year.

Neat. Their families have money so they can do the *Eat Pray Love* thing. Not mine.

I'm excited to see the mountains in the West, the lakes along Michigan, the smoky mountains in the South...

All with her.

The old row homes and tucked-away ancient mansions that dot Broad Street down here, south of Center, sit quietly in the dawning morning. A few people shuffle up and down the sidewalks, maybe walking toward Temple or up to city hall, but it's quiet this time of day. The rumble of a SEPTA bus interrupts the hush, the dim lights silhouetting the handful of riders inside.

The city changes noticeably the farther you walk up Broad, the closer to city hall you get. Old homes start to get replaced by newer builds made of steel and plastic, wedged between landmarks of brick and stone. A Starbucks right next to a hundred-year-old school. All things that Dad likes to grumble about while glaring at his phone in the kitchen at home, complaining about neighborhood changes with other local dads on Facebook.

And then there's the shuttered diner.

The Stateside.

The old building comes into view just a few minutes into my stroll to the square from home. It's unavoidable. I could, I suppose, walk through our neighborhood, taking small side streets on narrow sidewalks, but I eventually have to cross Broad. And unless I want to go an entire two or three city blocks around it, the quick route past the diner is the only real option.

And I don't know, part of me needs the motivation, I think. It's a reminder.

To avoid staying in one place, where other people can make decisions for you.

The diner has started to look more and more out of place as the years have gone by since it closed. It's just a small building, its glittering silver exterior now faded, on the corner of a city block that has a towering condo next to it, and several new homes on the other side of the block. The old parking lot is cracked, full of weeds growing up through the craters. A bit of life in a place that's sadly dead.

Thick wooden boards are up against the windows and the front door, graffiti over the surface, the same old scene I've been seeing since junior high. I remember looking out those windows to the bustling city beyond while Mom hustled around the dining floor, handing out orders and talking to everyone. Dad over the grill in the back. A legion of cousins and coworkers and friends everywhere.

But rising property taxes aren't friendly to small-town diners in the middle of a city, no matter how many years or families they've been attached to.

I kick a piece of dislodged concrete on the broken sidewalk, sending it flying into the parking lot and clattering against some trash…when something catches my eye.

A sign. On one of the boards.

That…is something new.

I walk across the small parking lot, and notice another sign wedged in the front door.

Coming Soon: A New Project from AmeriBank
Twenty-four brand-new units, perfect for growing families,
complete with planned retail spaces that are available for leasing!

Fully Furnished Units Starting at Only $600k! Estimated Project Completion—

I tear the sign off the door.

Only $600,000.

The sheer nerve of that word, *only.*

The computer-generated model of the condo building looks like a giant stack of LEGOs, like some of the new buildings that have been springing up, taking the place of old homes and faded businesses. The sort of structures that infuriate Dad, all metal and steel, looking more like spaceships than houses.

I make my way over to the boarded-up windows, everything in me shaking. I already know what the pasted sign says. I've seen signs like that, on decaying row homes and closed businesses through South Philadelphia and other neighborhoods. When time or money or both have just run out for the people inside.

Community Notice: Building Marked for Demolition

And it's the date underneath that sends my heart reeling.

Mom and Dad's diner.

It's coming down in just a few days.

I try to grab the paper off the wooden board, but it's glued there. Wheat paste. I claw at it like an animal in a cage, trying to grab a corner, my nails scraping against the particle board, like that will in any way prevent the inevitable—

"Hey!"

I spin around.

And exhale with relief.

It's Steve and, much more to my surprise, Laura. It is *way* too early for her.

"So, uh..." Steve starts, walking toward me. Laura follows, unexpectedly guitarless, still clad in her jean jacket full of pins though. A little fabric messenger bag is slung around her shoulder, a Paramore patch carefully stitched onto it, and I'm guessing it's full of notebooks. A lyrics day, then.

There are two huge totes in Steve's hands. "I got a bunch of eggs and bacon from my grandpa's deli for the new sandwich. He was a little pissed at me taking so many supplies this early in the morning, but he'll get over it."

"Maybe we take some quick videos of the process," Laura chimes in, pulling out her phone. There's some weird thing sticking up from it, coiling up on a little wire. She presses something, and a bright ring light illuminates from the wire, making me blink to regain my vision.

"Sorry," she laughs, turning it off, but there's something sad about the way she's looking at me.

Steve nods at the diner. "What's—"

"Nothing," I mutter, walking toward them. "Laura, I'm surprised you're up this early."

"Well, you know, gotta support my boys." Her eyes flit back and forth to me and Steve. "Besides, I gotta work on my song..."

I move to keep walking, but Steve slides in front of me.

He holds out an arm, tote bag dangling. Laura takes a few steps toward us.

"Come on, bro, bring it in." He puts the bags down on the sidewalk. He grabs my shoulder, and lowers his head, his forehead touching mine. "Hey. Talk to me. Us. Your bros are here."

"Uh, excuse me?" Laura scoffs.

"Get in here, you're one of the bros," Steve says, reaching an arm out. Laura grumbles something but comes closer.

I can't look at either of them.

"So," Steve says. "Is it happening?"

"I don't know how..." I stammer the words out. "How I'm going to break the news to my parents. Do they know? Do you think they—"

"Come on," he says and pulls me into another hug, Laura quickly joining in. He smells of sandalwood and food truck grease, and Laura's long black hair is awash in the orange Creamsicle shampoo she's been using since we were in second grade.

"Let's go," Steve says, letting me go after patting my back. "We'll take the long way, maybe walk by Big Red."

"I'm gonna wrap back around and grab my guitar," Laura says, giving my shoulder a squeeze. "Maybe I'll play a little Ed Sheeran in the park today, really get Cindy mad. For you."

I smile a little.

"There we go," Steve laughs. He turns on his heel and starts walking, carrying all the supplies, bags slung over his long arms. Laura hustles after him, and I follow, but stop for a moment to take another look at the diner.

This is it. This is why I want my own truck.

Because no one will be able to take it away from me.

Pilot: Confessional Shot Transcript (Jordan)

Jordan: There's not much to say, really. I basically grew up in the family diner. It was just...there, you know? The way a neighborhood friend is. You just always assume they'll be around, until one day they tell you they're moving, and just like that, they're gone.

Mom used to make these pancakes there with... M&M's in them?

I know, I know, it sounds gross but hear me out.

They'd melt a little into the pancake batter and you'd see the food coloring bleeding through, and I'm telling you, the chocolate mixed with syrup mixed with slightly-too-sugary pancake batter is just *chef's kiss* a thing of beauty.

She doesn't make them anymore.

I think...maybe it reminds her of the place. The diner?

That's the thing about food that some people don't really get. It can transport you. And what happens when something you used to love reminds you of a place you can't go back to?

long pause

I'm sorry. I don't really want to talk about it anymore. Can we talk about something else?

When my parents had the diner taken away from them, I promised myself I wouldn't be in that position. My dad talks about how we rallied, how he and Mom got new jobs, but it's not like that happened overnight. Jobs don't just...appear, for people like us. That's not a thing.

I remember my parents making every penny stretch. The struggle.

I don't want that. I want to chart my own course.

And I don't see the problem with starting now.

chapter six: cindy

It is...weird, hearing my own voice in the car, coming out of the speakers, but Mom is smiling and laughing, her eyes darting back and forth from the road to me as the podcast plays.

"Sweetheart, this is maybe my favorite episode," she says, reaching out and grabbing my leg. "You and the girls get funnier and funnier each one, I swear."

"Thanks, Mom," I yawn out, wiping at my eyes. She slows down at a traffic light, and glances over at me.

"God, we shouldn't have stayed up to catch *Watch What Happens Happens Live*," she says, shaking her head. "Are you sure you don't want some help at the truck today? It's the summer, you really should be relaxing."

Relaxing. Like she or Dad know the meaning of that word. She's got on a pair of permanently dirty jeans, a short-sleeve flannel shirt, and I can see the grit under her fingernails as she grips the steering wheel. The two of them really throw everything they've got into that farm, just like it was their own back in Boston. And the more work I put in at the truck, the more I can save for...well, everything. The road trip, college, my podcasting gear, all without having to make them worry about anything.

For a moment, I think about Dad back at Reading Terminal, the way he looked at that farm stand, all broken up. Like it was something that didn't just happen back in Boston, but was something actively happening right now. And I wonder if I should talk to Mom about it.

But I remember those fights back in Boston, over money. If something's wrong, maybe Dad is already fixing it. Maybe it'll be worse if I say something.

No. Better to focus on what I can control.

"I've got this," I press, wrestling with the groceries between my legs from Reading Terminal. She parks around the corner, and we both lug those and the other bags from the back of her hatchback toward the square.

"Huh," Mom says, as we reach the truck. "That's...different."

It *is* different.

There's a *massive* line outside Jordan's truck today, something that never happens in the early morning. A twinge of... I don't know what, jealousy, maybe, prickles in my chest as I unlock the truck—its sides shiny and glimmering in the morning light thanks to Dad getting it cleaned this weekend—and start unloading all the veggies and meats from Reading Terminal. I hurry around to the front, Mom making her way to put some more groceries inside, and open up the truck's little canopy and faux patio.

I stand outside, trying to figure out what's going on over there. The air smells like the usual except…there's something else, lingering in the scent of onions and cheese.

"Is that bacon?" Mom asks.

Bacon.

I wrangle my phone out of my jacket and tap over to the Plaza's truck Instagram page. There are a bundle of new photos there, in the stories and on the profile, of some kind of new sandwich. There it is on the grill in one shot, some ingredients spread out in another, and then sitting in Steve's massive hands. I glance up at the truck, just in time to catch Steve hand a sandwich off to someone, who takes their own photos of it before chomping in.

Ugh. Laura's there too, phone out, shooting some video, it looks like. I spot her guitar leaning against the side of the truck. I swear, I feel like when she plays in the square, she picks songs specifically to annoy me. If I have to hear her strum out another Daughtry song on that thing, I'm going to scream.

But the photo of the sandwich.

It's such a good idea.

It's a long-seeded cheesesteak roll with eggs that are so runny they don't even look cooked, yellow yolk soaking the surrounding bread. There's bacon and I think cheddar in there, I can't tell what kind of cheese, really. Could be white cheddar or white American. Definitely a bit of shaved rib eye. While our Instagram lists every individual ingredient, Jordan's family's truck just says stuff like "bread, steak, cheese" and expects people to be fine with that.

I mean, they are. But still.

They're calling them "cheesebreaks" like *breakfast* and *cheesesteak* combined, and I wonder when Jordan became a father in his fifties making dad jokes.

"Wow," Mom says, her voice in my ear. I shirk back to discover she's looking over my shoulder at my phone. "I wonder if I can sneak over and buy one without anyone seeing."

"Whatever," I grumble. "It's just more greasy food. People like our healthy options better."

"If I didn't know better, I'd think you were actually jealous," Mom says, and I can hear the smile in her voice. "Maybe I'll just DoorHub a sandwich from them, wouldn't want anyone to see me over there."

"What?! No!" I snap. I head inside the truck to get things fired up, as someone approaches the window. "I'll just text Steve to drop one off, otherwise it'll be like thirty-seven dollars more just to get it delivered down the block, and someone might see you—"

"Hey, are you doing breakfast sandwiches too?"

"No," I say to the person approaching the truck, "but we'll be open for lunch—"

"THEY AREN'T DOING THEM HERE!" they shout across the street, making me wince. I watch them cross the intersection toward the Plazas truck and join some folks already in the line. Guess they came over to try their luck.

I walk out of the truck and stand on the edge of the sidewalk, glaring at Jordan and his crew. Steve catches me staring, and nudges Jordan. He waves playfully, and shrugs.

"You forget how to make cheesesteaks over there?!" I yell, and a few people turn to me and Laura lifts her phone in my direction. I glance to the side, and Mom is leaning against the truck. Her face has hardened, and she's staring across the street at the Plazas truck with all the powerful rage of a South Philly mother who is actually from Boston.

This whole show they put on. I don't get to see Mom or the Ortiz family in action all that often, since I'm usually at the truck solo. But Mom could win an Emmy with the power of her stink eye burning holes into Jordan like she didn't just have him over at the house a few days ago.

I'm going to miss this, when we hit the road. Don't get me wrong, it'll be great to finally be a normal couple, but...it's all been so much fun putting out this act.

And then you know, it got really fun our senior year.

Hiding that we were together the entire time at school was *not* fun, but sneaking around to steal some kisses behind the lockers or have a make-out session in one of the high school band practice rooms...that was fun. And all of this, here in this little square roundabout in South Philly that feels like it belongs to us, that's fun.

I wish I could just bottle all this up, and keep it this way.

"Just trying something new, Cindy!" Jordan shouts back, out of the truck. His eyes flit over to Mom, and he nods, respectfully. "Mrs. Ortiz."

"Humph," Mom huffs, playing along. It's kind of hard not to laugh. The days that Jordan's mom or my dad or whoever are in the trucks, they just don't bring the same level of showmanship that me and Jordan do. Lots of pointed glares and the occasional swear, but me and Jordan? It's a whole show.

I admit, I'm kinda worried what business is going to look like when the two of us are on the road for a whole year. People are always going to want sandwiches and cheesesteaks but… I don't know. They can get them somewhere else. Anywhere else. It's the experience that brings some people here, I think.

God, I hope Dad isn't in trouble again.

A few more phones are up, taking photos, shooting video, so I clear my throat and put on my game face.

"That's interesting, considering you and your family haven't tried anything new in years." I cross my arms, smugly. Mom chuckles.

"Come try one, you might like it." I can see Jordan's smirk from here.

"Yeah right, not likely," I jeer, and turn on my heel, heading back to my truck. Mom shoots daggers with her eyes for an extra beat. I feel like all the reality television she's been watching for decades prepared her for the show our families put on together, even if it is mostly me and Jordan. I don't think there's ever been a moment where we walked by the Union Bank of Philadelphia Building in Old City, and she didn't mention that it "used to be the MTV *Real World* house" even though that show aired before I was born.

"The two of you," Mom says, turning toward me. "We really need to talk about when you're both going to drop the act. Me, your father, and their family, we'll keep it going when you're both done here at the end of the summer. Or if, you know, you change your mind and hang around."

"What?" I ask.

"Well, I mean, have you...heard anything?" she asks. "From the colleges? From the wait list?"

"No," I say, feeling a bit surprised. "Why does it sound like you maybe don't want me going?"

"It's not that. I went backpacking before *and* after college, I'm not *that* parent. It's just...that road trip is gonna be fun, sure," Mom exhales. "But me and your father, we worked so hard so you could just enjoy being young. You could live at home, go to college here in town. You won't have to worry for much."

A flash of anxiety rushes through me. Thoughts of Boston and how weird Dad was back in the market. And now all I want to do is get right to work.

"But out there?" Mom continues. "On the road? Just... know if that boy has you sleeping in a gross motel or God, in the back of that truck..." She flashes a pointed stare at the Plazas truck, just as the generator spurts out a loud snapping noise. "Sweetheart, you can call anytime and we'll come get you."

"Mom!" I laugh, the anxiety washing away.

"I'm just saying." She raises her hands up. "I think the reality of all that is going to be a lot less romantic than you think."

"We'll see."

"Yeah, I'm afraid we will," Mom sighs.

"I'm...not sure that's the best pep talk, Mom," I say teasingly.

"Well, I'm an Ortiz. And we're brutally honest." She pats my cheek. "Alright. Let's unpack the rest of this stuff, and I'll leave you to it. Maybe tonight we can get caught up *Rit-*

tenhouse Rehab. There's a rumor the two hosts are dating but they're trying to keep it a secret."

She winks and I roll my eyes, then peek over at Jordan's growing line. Laura takes her phone and holds it up to the window of the truck, and whatever is there sends Steve and Jordan into fits of laughter when she shows them. Great. I busy myself with food prep as a distraction from whatever that video—of me, surely—looks like, courtesy of Laura's completely unbiased eye.

Getting lost in some reality television tonight sounds really good.

I hear Mom's car drive off with a friendly double beep, and I get to work slicing veggies for the day. Lunch isn't too far off, and while Jordan's line is still rounding the corner somehow, it'll be my turn to shine when folks wander over looking for a healthy sandwich, wrap, and what have you.

I get my little Bluetooth speaker situated on my countertop, a small wooden thing that Jordan bought me at a nearby boutique called Open House. It's made of reclaimed bowling alley wood or something, and it's really pretty. I put on the latest episode of *The Main Live*, a podcast that recaps a reality show set in the suburbs of Philadelphia.

I slice up some tomatoes, peppers, onions. I toss a few mushrooms into a dicer, and slam down the plastic plunger to chop them into bits for our wraps, the podcast chatting me up in the background. After prepping for a while, I can't help but notice the noise outside has gone quiet. I step outside the truck, and spot Jordan standing outside, thumbing through a pile of cash so thick that I can see it in his hand from across the street.

Jesus.

Steve is there, of course, and Laura.

"Hey!" I shout.

All three of them look up, and Laura pulls out her phone and immediately holds it up, pointing at me. She spins around, aiming at Steve and Jordan, who both promptly give me the finger.

Ugh. *Content.* There's nobody even here right now, and I wish I could just go over there and talk to Jordan. I'm sure he's so relieved to have finally figured out what to serve at the Truck Off.

But the show must go on. Everything is content, after all.

"Didn't realize you got so desperate over there, Jordan!" I yell. "Breakfast sandwiches? I thought you and your family were purists."

"Little change never hurt anybody, Cindy!" he shouts back. "Which is probably what your truck is going to make today."

"Oh *wow!*" Steve bellows.

Laura lowers her phone, laughing so hard that she reaches out to grab Jordan, leaning against his shoulder. For support. Or *something.*

"Whoa!" I yell, pointing at Laura. She lets go of Jordan and looks at me, puzzled. "What, so I don't even get a chance to retort?"

"No coming back from that one, Cindy." Laura grins.

A flash of heat flushes to my cheeks. Her crush on my boyfriend gets less and less cute the more she's around. I don't care if they're just best friends or neighbors or whatever Jordan claims they are. To her, they are obviously more, and he's too clueless and sweet to see it. A cinnamon roll that doesn't realize it's about to be bitten into.

I grumble to myself and whirl around, stomping into my truck. As much as it pains me to admit, I like when Laura shoots her little videos of us. They're fun to post from our accounts, and I know she gets a real thrill out of seeing them go viral—well, locally viral. Shared by the *Philadelphia Weekly* or *Billy Penn*. Though we have had a handful blow up a bit more than that. But man, she definitely leans toward making Jordan look better for reasons that are wildly clear to me, even if they aren't to Jordan.

I need my own videographer. I wish Eesha or Ariana lived here. They'd have my back. And as if the two of them are summoning me, I pull my phone out to see what they're up to.

Eesha: Downloads are going strong on the episode

Ariana: Did you see that one producer share the link?

Eesha: What?! WHERE?!

I smile, the thread going on and on. Every time we release an episode, it's like this until the next one. Great thing about reality television is that the seasons have a million episodes. So we've got a lot of time to work and play together.

And speaking of work.

I start to shave some carrots from Reading Terminal when there's a rapping on the shutter door to the truck.

Alright, Laura, you wanna play? I'll turn up the rage and put on a show.

I storm out of the truck and reel around it, my finger out and ready to point right in her face.

"Listen up, you—"

A woman in a blazer is standing in front of the truck, staring up at me, wildly perplexed.

"Uh…" she starts.

"Oh Jesus, sorry," I laugh awkwardly, a hand on my chest. I unclasp the canopy, which doubles as our shutter, and push it up. The woman reaches out and helps, kicking one of the poles out to support it. "Thanks for that. We're not open yet, so I thought you were someone else. I didn't realize…"

"It's okay," she says kindly, her eyes looking over the truck and then settling on me. "You're Cindy, right? Cindy Ortiz?"

"Yes?" I answer.

"Excellent," she says. "I'm Bethany Ireland. Your, uh…" She glances over at Jordan's truck, and the three of them are just horsing around, taking photos with people. "Your friends over there rang the bell for me when I ordered mushrooms on a cheesesteak?"

"Ah." I nod and lean against the truck. "You'd have to be more specific, honestly. They do that a lot."

She laughs. "Look, I want to talk to you and your family about a reality show." She smiles and hands me a business card. "Can you maybe have one of your parents reach out to me? I tried stopping by the farm, but they always seemed to be out delivering something somewhere. The line to see your nemesis was a bit out of control this morning, and I discovered his parents work some wildly late hours. Food industry folks are hard to get a hold of when you keep typical work hours."

Nemesis. I have to stop myself from laughing. Like we're in a Marvel movie.

But my heart is just absolutely pounding in my chest.

A television show?! A reality show?! About my family and Jordan's?!

Eesha and Ariana are going to lose it over this.

"Yeah, that sounds great." I nod, slipping the card into my pocket, trying to stay cool. "I'll make sure I talk to them as soon as I get home."

"Awesome." Bethany nods, and peers into my truck through the window. She squints for a moment and then turns to me. "Is that *The Main Live* playing in there?"

"Oh." I'm surprised, but then again, I guess I shouldn't be. "Yeah. I love Helen and Brittney, they've gotten me through a lot of long train rides and quiet days at the truck."

"We work with them sometimes," she says casually, and she must see my eyes go wide, because she laughs. "Selling ads and stuff, sometimes sending them swag. Pretty normal for when a podcast gets popular. Much like yours is."

My heart hammers.

"You...know my podcast?!" I practically shout.

"It's good," she says. "You and your friends are a riot."

"Th-thank you," I stammer out. My God. A producer in reality television has heard my podcast and knows who I am. This is not what I expected to happen this morning. Not by a long shot.

"But this..." She gestures at my truck and over at Jordan's. "I think this could really be something. We could shoot a pilot, or really, a proof of concept, and see where things go...

but I'm getting ahead of myself. Talk to your parents, see if they're even okay with it."

"Oh, I think they will be." I smile and rub my hands together. Mom is going to go absolutely wild. Dad, I'm not so sure…

Then again, if we're in some financial trouble, maybe this will help.

"Any idea how to get a hold of…well…" She glances back at Jordan and the gang, and Steve currently has him in a head-lock, Laura snapping photos. "That bunch?"

"You could message them on Instagram, maybe?" I suggest. "I think they've got a website for the truck." I know they do. My mom helped put it together for them, since Mr. Plazas is kind of useless when it comes to technology. Jordan's not even really into it—I think if it wasn't for the fact that so many local food trucks have an online community on there, he wouldn't touch it.

"Great, great." Bethany claps her hands and sighs. "Alright, I'm gonna head back to the office, but yes. Talk soon."

"Definitely."

She smiles and snaps her fingers at me and heads off down the block. I watch her go, and once she's well out of eyeshot, do a little victory dance. Hell yes. Yes. A television show. This could be amazing. I wonder how much reality television even pays for a pilot. Or what did she call it? Proof of concept? I've read it's not a ton, but I imagine it would be enough to help with *something*, right? The way Dad eyed up that empty stall in Reading Terminal…the nervous feeling it's left me with… thinking about those shouting matches back in Boston…

My mind races as I finish getting the truck ready for what will probably be a busy Saturday.

A reality show.

And here's my foot in the door, before I even have to go to college for television production.

I fire off a string of excited texts to Ariana and Eesha, and the two of them reply with a wide array of screaming emojis and texts. Which is exactly how I'm feeling.

chapter seven:
jordan

Sunday, Seven Days until Truck Off

"This is so ridiculous," Dad mutters as we hide behind an SUV.

"Antony, it'll be over in a few minutes." Mom tries to calm him down. But I get it. The whole thing *is* ridiculous. I peer over the SUV, parked across the street from the Ortiz family's home, a row house that looks just like every other row house on their block, with the exception of how much attention they've paid to the window trim. Dark green shutters pop against black frames, with auburn window boxes bursting with flowers. They're a blast of color on a fairly drab brick street.

Our home is the same in that way, just a few blocks over— a small row house with white siding on it, that makes it stick out from the other brick homes nearby. Dad talks about pulling the siding off every single summer, but never gets around to it.

I peer over the SUV's hood at the Ortizes' house, and I spot Mrs. Ortiz in the doorframe, her expression intense, focused on the street and sidewalk. She catches sight of me, and waves for us to come over.

"Alright, let's go," I say to my parents.

Abruptly, Mrs. Ortiz puts her hands out, her expression urgent, and points off to the side. I see a mail carrier two doors down and settle back into waiting behind the truck.

"Just a second," I say, and my dad grumbles again, so loud that I think for a minute it's the engine of the car we're hiding behind. Once the mail carrier turns a corner, a middle-aged woman comes into view walking a small dog. I sigh. This could be a while.

Every year, in the summer, it's the same routine. A picnic with the entire Ortiz family, or at least, Cindy's parents and her. One year, a few of Cindy's cousins came down from Boston, but generally, it's just them. Mom and Dad have managed to wrangle up just about everyone in our family that stayed in Philadelphia—cousins, aunts, uncles, you name it.

It was Mr. Ortiz's idea. A yearly get-together after school let out, to celebrate the success of the faux rivalry and remind one another of the reality...that we're close. That the mess surrounding the parking permits is a thing of the past.

I glance over at Dad, who now has his back to the car we're hiding behind, his arms crossed like a grumpy toddler waiting in line for a ride.

"Antony, come on," Mom says.

"No. I hate this," Dad mutters.

I try not to laugh, but I wonder, though, with his confessional about the truck…

How much of the real rivalry, the real anger, is really forgotten.

The spread dished out in the Ortizes's backyard is outrageous. Even though their home is skinny and tall, like a book shelved with many others like it, their yard is something of an urban oasis. It's about the length of the house, a long narrow rectangle of grass and small fruit trees, with container gardens speckled throughout like freckles. A half barrel containing a tangle of cherry tomato plants sits near the tables that are full of food. There are piles of wraps and skewers with crisp tofu. I poke around for something, anything, I can dip in ketchup but come up short.

Those planters give me an idea though. I wonder if I could do some kind of window box on the food truck, for the road trip. Or some cheap grow lights inside? While I'm not sure I want to grow any herbs for the cheesesteaks I'd make on the road, it could be nice for, like, anything else I might cook while we're traveling. And I bet Cindy would love it. Tending a little garden together while driving across the country? I know how much she adores her organic produce—this could be, like, a little something just for her in the truck.

I wonder what else I can do, to make it feel more like home for her. Once I buy the thing, I'm gonna figure all that out.

"I just think you guys take this a bit too seriously sometimes," I hear Dad say and turn just in time to see him taking a swig from a Corona bottle. "I mean, the mailman?"

He sure did get that beer bottle fast.

"Well, we have to be careful," Mrs. Ortiz says. "The more popular the rivalry gets, especially with the kids and those videos, the more we have to be cautious with our friendship. Though I would really like it if those two would drop it and just enjoy this summer. We can still act like we hate each other without them."

"*Cautious with our friendship,* do you even hear yourself, Maria?" Dad laughs. He glances over at me, gives me a quick nod, then looks down at the table, sighing. "Is there anything here *we* can eat?"

"It's all *food,* Antony." Mrs. Ortiz nudges him, and he rolls his eyes. "Look, I can probably find some Hot Pockets in the back of the freezer complete with freezer burn if that's what you want."

"Now you are speaking my language." He smiles, nudging her back. "Where's Daniel?"

"You'll be happy to know he's on his way from picking up burgers and…" Mrs. Ortiz closes her eyes, like the words physically hurt her "…*hot dogs,* from the deli on the corner."

My dad takes Mrs. Ortiz's hands.

"Thank you, my friend."

I nab a few grape leaves wrapped around *something* from the spread on the table. While my parents and Cindy's mom chat, I walk about, peering into the container gardens. More people make their way into the yard through the house, and soon, the backyard is pretty busy, with familiar faces from all our families.

It's just me, Mom, and Dad at home, but a few cousins have swung by from out in Manayunk. Valerie, Mary, Tommy, Doug, Ron…they wave at me from across the yard before digging into some of the picnic food. They're all wonderful, but we don't hang terribly much. I mean, they're grown with lives of their own. Val and Tommy do something in finance that I don't quite understand, and Mary and Ron are both in medicine. Doug is over in the Navy Yard. All of them worked in the diner when I was little and they were in college, but those days are long behind any of us.

I don't think I'll ever quite fit in, but that's okay.

I'm looking at another container garden, this one overflowing with multicolored chili peppers, when I hear the screen door open again. And there's Cindy.

She's beaming, as always, wearing tight jeans with tears along the legs and knees, and a wrinkly T-shirt with the band Japanese Breakfast on the front. We went to see them last year, a little after the lead singer's memoir came out, and showed up with backpacks full of our books and vinyl records to get signed. Although saying "we" went is a bit generous. The lights in the venue were way too bright so we stood on opposite sides of the concert, texting each other. She was worried we might get spotted by someone from school.

Her eyes meet mine from across the yard, and she waves at me before turning to say hi to her family. I make my way over to her.

"Hey, babe." I reach out to hug her, but she shirks away, looking around, almost frantic. "Wow, okay, what is it?"

"We don't know who's here!" she says, eyeing up the yard. "We have to be careful."

"Are you serious?" I laugh. "It's a picnic with *both* our families. They know the deal. They're all in on it."

"Yeah, but what if one of your cousins brings a new boyfriend or something?" She stares at my cousins huddled together near a cooler full of beer. "They could leak things, and then it would be all over and—"

"Whoa, whoa," I say, reaching up to take her hands, which are shaking a little bit. "What's going on?"

We spent senior year hiding our relationship at school, and we're careful around town, but this feels like a whole other level. Something is up.

"Nothing, no, everything is fine…" She looks down at her feet, wringing her hands.

"Hey," I press. "Talk to me. What's the matter?"

"Nothing, it's good, it's just…" She gazes up at me for a second, then back down again. "Look, I don't know how you're going to feel about—"

"Excuse me, everyone?!"

Cindy's father's voice booms out over the yard, loud and boisterous, silencing everybody. He's got thick eyebrows, a thick mustache, thick arms…honestly everything about him is thick, from his hair to his calloused hands from working the land on that farm in Northern Liberties and that place their family had back home. My dad and Cindy's mom join him by the steps leading into the yard, and I see my mom peak out from over Cindy's father's shoulder. Everyone towers over my dad, and I watch him hop up an extra step on the backyard stoop to compensate.

"Well, here we are," he starts. "To tradition."

He lifts up a soda bottle, and the entire yard toasts with whatever they've got on hand. I lift an imaginary glass, and lean closer to Cindy, but she nudges away a little, looking back toward the cousins.

What is she so worried about?

"A little over four years ago, on a hot summer day that we would come to learn is pretty normal for this city of yours, our family moved from the only home any of us had known, to Philadelphia," Cindy's dad continues, and I have to hold back my own sigh. Every summer picnic, him and the family like to regale us with the story of how they moved here and became friends, and I'm just not sure who any of it is for.

I glance back at the cousins, who are looking ahead, but their expressions are glassed over. They're thinking about something else, anything else.

"And well, if you had told me that the family who we fought with over parking permits would become our inseparable best friends and neighbors, I don't know. I might have laughed you out of our house."

Cindy's dad reaches over and nudges my dad, who smirks and tussles back with him.

"Back then, we realized if we pushed our petty differences aside, what with all the attention we were accidentally creating with the food truck spats in the community the Plazas family is so embedded in, we could do something magical. We could lean into it, put on a show, and make our trucks a destination."

"You kids have been a huge part of that," Mr. Ortiz says, looking up and across the yard to me and Cindy. "You gave us the idea, after the whole ketchup incident."

There are some scattered laughs, and again, I hold back the sigh. Just let them have their little moment and I can get back to finding something I want to eat and hanging out with Cindy.

"And now, the next chapter in that story is about to begin."

Cindy's father pauses and looks around at all the parents next to him, and places a hand on my dad's shoulder. Dad grins up at him, and there's just this…joy bursting from all four of them.

This is…new.

"What is going on?" I whisper to Cindy.

She doesn't say anything.

"Cindy?" I ask.

Her hand tenses up in mine.

"We've been asked…" her father continues, and Cindy squirms "…to film a pilot for a reality show!"

The cousins and everyone in the yard gasp, coming to life after the revelation, little whispers and muttering filling the air.

And I can't stop the laugh that escapes my chest.

Cindy stares right at me, as do our parents.

"What?" I ask, and then to Cindy's father. "Wait, are you serious?"

"It's true!" he exclaims, walking into the yard, my mom following him. They've all got huge smiles on their faces, and all their eyes are on me and Cindy. "They want to shoot one episode and try to sell it to the networks. A pilot. About our great family rivalry!"

Dad laughs as Mr. Ortiz grabs his shoulders, playfully shaking him. Everyone suddenly looks ten years younger, like all their stress and worry have just been washed away.

And me? I feel like I've aged a decade.

"Wait, wait, wait." I step forward toward everyone, shaking my head. "How will that even work?" I glance back at

Cindy, but she's avoiding my eyes. "We don't actually hate each other. Our families get along. We're friends. It's all… just a joke."

"Well…" Cindy's dad shrugs. "It's not like there isn't some truth to the whole thing."

"We *did* bicker quite a lot over the parking spots," Dad says.

"And there was that whole mess with the truck—" Mom starts.

Dad shakes his head at her and she doesn't finish.

"And how many years ago was that again?" I ask, knowing what Mom was about to get into. Do the families just not talk about that part? "Mrs. Ortiz bought you that shirt for Christmas *last year*, Dad."

Dad chuckles at his T-shirt, reading The Stakes Have Never Been Higher.

"I mean, we'll just keep pretending," he says, folding his arms, like he can hide the shirt and evidence somehow. "We'll be careful. Like we always are."

"What?" I laugh. "Just minutes ago, right out front, you were getting mad about all the effort that goes into this!"

"Well, there are going to be a few…inconvenient bits, I'm sure." He shrugs, and my mom wraps her arms around him from behind.

"What about me and Cindy?" I ask, a desperate edge to my voice. I know she loves this kind of stuff, these reality shows, but this feels like we're moving in the wrong direction. I don't want to hide our relationship anymore. The road trip—that was going to be the end of all of this.

"It'll be fun," Cindy says with a smile.

"Is that what you were worried about?" I ask. "Did you *know* about this?"

She winces.

"For how long?" I press.

"It's barely been a day." She waves me off. "A producer came up to my truck on Saturday and my parents got in touch with her this morning."

"Come on, kiddo, this will be a blast," Dad says, gripping my shoulder. "I thought you'd like the surprise!"

"I knew we should have said something," Mom says, shaking her head at Dad. She looks between me and Cindy, warm pity on her face.

Yeah, at least Mom gets it. She strolls off to talk with Dad, and my cousins mill about, congratulating the parents. I pull Cindy aside and take her hands.

"Truck Off is coming up, wouldn't it be better to focus on making something awesome? Winning that prize money?" I don't want to be the buzzkill here, but it's like I don't exist in any of this. "That money could pay for my truck. I don't even need all of it, we could share and set aside some of your college fund when we get back from the road. I also want to give some to Steve though…the breakfast sandwiches were his idea."

"Yeah, but like, think about what a *show* can do for our families," Cindy implores as she wraps her arm around me. "I mean, your parents could get a whole new restaurant. My parents could focus on maybe rebuilding their own business, instead of working on someone else's farm. It'll do so much for us. It's just a pilot anyway, and maybe it won't even happen."

An image of my family's diner flashes across my mind, like

a postcard. Alive again. Mom and Dad practically dancing as they move table to table...

I know that's a relic of the past. I know there's no getting that place back. But maybe...maybe getting the *feeling* back is a possibility.

"I don't know. I feel like if I won the food truck competition, or even came in second place, it would help you and me plenty. And we wouldn't have to put on a show for it. How much does a reality show pilot pay, anyway? It can't be that much, can it? Funding your family's farm and helping relaunch a restaurant? Is that...is that realistic?"

"Jordan," she says, gazing steadily into my eyes. "Trust me."

And God help me, I do.

chapter eight: cindy

Monday, Six Days until Truck Off

Mom and Dad hustle ahead of me as we power walk through Washington Square. I can't help but smile at their energy. This is the version of them I want to see all the time. Not Dad worrying about the future and Mom stressing over the bills in the kitchen. And if this works out, maybe I'll get that side of them all the time.

Usually when we walk anywhere downtown, they take their sweet time, still behaving like tourists in this city even after we've lived here for four years. But right now, they're bursting with excitement. Locals with dogs and toddlers rule the park this morning, sprawled out on the cool grass under towering oak trees older than the massive buildings that surround us.

It's a strange park. There are a lot of year-round ghost tours here, as the city-block-sized patch of land was a burial ground for yellow fever victims, and there's a big Tomb of the Unknown Soldier memorial in one corner, a monument to the Revolutionary War. Construction crews still find the remains of bodies while doing touch-ups in the area, yet folks are throwing Frisbees and making out in the grass as we walk on by.

Philadelphia is weird.

The Esco Publishing building looms at the end of the park, a large brick-and-stone structure housing two local newspapers, a magazine, and who knows what else. Their logo, a French bulldog, is silhouetted on a brass plaque. I can see the large stone columns at the end of the main path that cuts through the park, framed by rustling trees.

A busker with an acoustic guitar belts out a melody on the corner we're approaching, and I bristle, reminded of Laura. But then I remember that this one band Jordan likes has a whole song about this park. I pull out my phone and stop walking to text.

Me: Hey we're on our way to the meeting with the reality show people

Jordan: Oh boy. Let me know how it goes

Me: When's your family seeing them?

Jordan: They're swinging by the house at some point today. Apparently, they want to shoot some kind of video with my dad once we sign whatever paperwork there is

Me: Whoa

Jordan: Yep

Me: Well, their office is near Washington Square, and it made me think of you and that band you like. Don't they have a song named after the park?

Jordan: Ah, The Wonder Years. You remembered

Me: Of course I did. I remember everything

Jordan: Me too <3

"Cindy!"

I look up from my phone, and Mom and Dad are at the corner, ready to cross the street. I take a photo of the company's logo for the girls, and to post on our podcast's social media feeds at some point, and then slide my phone back in my pocket, hurrying toward the future.

"Well, well, well!" Bethany Ireland exclaims, almost the second the elevator doors open onto the tenth floor of the Esco building. She's dressed much the same as the other day, all professional, her outfit made of sharp edges that betray her gentle face. She smiles brightly, waving me and my parents over.

"I'm so glad you could all be here today," she continues, opening a large glass door for us. A receptionist glances our way before staring back at her computer at a massive front desk that's just overflowing with mail and packages. Bethany laughs at the piles. "Don't be fooled, that's all just promotional swag people send us to consider for the show."

I squint at the packages. Everything is still sealed and stacked precariously.

"That could be you, you know," she says, shrugging. "With your podcast and all. Once sponsorship opportunities start rolling in, and they will, a lot of people will send you free stuff. It's kinda like a potluck, never really know what you're gonna get in there." She winks, my parents laugh. "We'll have to send all three of you off with one or two on the way out, you know, to celebrate a little."

My dad grins like a kid in a candy store, but I'm left with a bitter taste in my mouth. They're not even going to open this stuff? I spot an elegant gift basket in the mix, books inside tucked around wine bottles and chocolate. A few vinyl records sit still wrapped in their plastic, notecards attached to the sealed edges. Feels like people put in a lot of effort and money just to be ignored.

I shake my head. This is the place I want to be. I only want good vibes right now.

Bethany leads us down a brightly lit hallway lined with framed posters of the shows the company has produced. I can feel my eyes widen as I take them in. *Rittenhouse Rehab, Manayunk Makeover, Curating Queen Village...* I've seen them all, from the ones that are very local to the shows that go nationwide.

Dreamed up here, in this place. This building.

I could learn so much.

I take a quick photo and send it to Eesha and Ariana. Their response is almost immediate, just a string of unintelligible text and various celebratory emojis.

We turn a corner, which takes us into a conference room.

Mom and Dad get comfortable on huge, cushiony chairs at a large mahogany table in the sizable meeting room. Dad rocks back and forth in the thing, a giddy smile on his face, and quickly stops when more people start filtering into the space. Some older faces, a few young ones, all sit around the table, a mix of serious hardened eyes and bright excited ones.

A boy rushes in last, a tablet and digital pencil in his hand, and stands in the corner of the room. He can't be much older than me. He's tall, white, has sandy blond hair that is bordering on reddish brown. He catches my eye and smiles, before looking back down at his tablet. I turn away just as quick.

He is...unnervingly cute.

"Jeff!" one of the older men at the table shouts. The boy startles and scurries over, a bundle of nervous, flailing limbs. "Can you grab a couple of coffees from the kitchen?"

"Oh, um..." he stammers. "It's Jared...and I'm sorry, but Ms. Ireland wanted me to take notes during the meeting."

"We can record them, it's fine." The guy waves him off.

Jared looks toward Bethany, who shrugs her shoulders and nods. He catches my eye again, looking a bit embarrassed, but also like...he maybe wants to say something to me. There's a flash of recognition on his face, and I wonder if maybe he went to our school. He wavers for a minute, and just like that, he's out the door in a hurry.

I'm guessing he must be an intern, which irks at something in my stomach. This is a snapshot of the world I want to be navigating and that is...not a great photo out of the gate. The ignored packages. The kicked around intern. Not even knowing his name. Is that going to be me, right out of college? Or *during* college?

"So," Bethany starts, and I shake off those worries, focusing. "I'd like to welcome the Ortiz family to Philly Reality, and we're here to talk about the pilot of..." She grabs a small remote and hits a button, and a projector turns on, illuminating the wall at the empty side of the table.

"... *Cheesesteak Wars!*" she exclaims. A few of the older folks in suits mutter approvingly, and others lean forward, small smiles on faces. At least they seem to be into this.

A photo of our two cheesesteak trucks lights up the wall. It's a professionally taken shot, nighttime on the horizon, the lights of Bardhan Square bright and twinkling. There are lines at both trucks, a time of day Jordan likes to refer to as "golden hour" when we both have sprawling crowds. I recognize the picture from a story in *Billy Penn* a few months ago.

"The premise of the show is simple," Bethany continues. "The cameras will focus on the drama at the trucks, and how it pans out at home and in the personal lives of everyone involved. We'll follow your family to the farm, the Plazas family as they fight to reopen a restaurant, and of course, our main characters, as they battle it out on the streets."

Hmm. The whole Plazas family fighting to reopen a restaurant bit has me a little surprised, as I know they're nowhere near ready to make that happen. But I guess if the show gets green-lit, that's a real possibility. I wonder if they talked to Jordan's parents yet about this detail.

Bethany smiles at me, and I look around to see all these executive suits doing the same. And then something else she said hits me like a brick.

"Main characters?" I ask.

"Well, yes," she says, like nothing she said was shocking.

I turn to my mom and dad, who also appear a bit worried and surprised. My heart hammers in my chest.

"So, the show is about…me and Jordan?" I ask.

"More or less," Bethany replies. "Whenever your parents are at the trucks, it's pretty calm. We've had a few scouts out to the location while we were considering the possibility of a show, and they aren't at each other's throats the way you two are. And that's the show people are going to want. Some of the drama at home, of course, but at the heart? Two rival cheesesteak trucks shouting and battling one another in the street? That's television. That's the show."

My mom worries at her lip and then meets my eyes. She doesn't even have to say it. This absolutely isn't going to work.

"Keep in mind, this is just a pilot episode. We'll shoot it, edit it, and try to shop our vision around to a few networks," she adds. "You know, we've had a lot of success, particularly on stories that are niche and hyperfocused. No one thought our show about that coffee roasting family in Hoboken would go anywhere, and now we're on season eight!"

Some of the suits clap and laugh.

"Maria, I don't know about this…" my dad says to my mom, but the entire room quiets, all eyes on him.

"I promise you, Mr. Ortiz," Bethany says confidently, leaning over the table, "disruption to the kids' lives will be minimal…though I suppose you really only care about one kid."

She grins and some of the suits chuckle, but Dad has a glowering face on. I kick him under the table.

"Oh. Oh yeah. Um, to hell with that other family."

Jesus.

"There's that attitude, but save it for the cameras," Bethany says, smiling. "And remember, we have writers, and there's a story arc that we try to build with what is naturally unfolding in real time."

There are writers? For reality television?

Huh.

I mean, I always see them during the credits, whenever I'm watching something with Mom or the girls. Those names listed alongside others that I hoped to be around, with titles like executive producer and the like. But I thought they wrote... I don't know, the bits and pieces that appear on the screen that help narrate the story. Though I suppose there's got to be more to being a writer for a reality show than writing the "last week" subtitles during flashbacks...

I'm already learning so much. I love this. Maybe being an intern wouldn't be so bad.

"Like, right now, according to social media, your trucks are preparing for Truck Off over in Camden, the big food truck festival and competition. Yes?" Bethany asks.

"Jordan's truck is," I correct. "We didn't really plan on entering."

"Well, you are now." Bethany smiles.

"Excuse me?" I scoff. "Why would we do that?"

"For one, that's the story we want to tell here," Bethany continues. "We introduce viewers to the battling cheesesteak trucks. The families. The two teenagers in the middle of the war. And it's all building up to this food truck competition. One family wants to use the prize money to open a restaurant. The other, to launch their urban farm."

"By winning a food truck competition?" It's Mom's turn

to scoff, and she gives me a look before glancing to Bethany. "I mean, how much money are we even talking about here?"

"Well, the first-place truck gets twenty-five thousand dollars," Bethany says.

Dad spits out some of the coffee he was drinking like someone out of a sitcom, and starts coughing and hacking at the table. Mom slaps him on the back.

He wipes at his eyes and clears his throat.

"I'm sorry." He coughs a little again, shaking his head. "Twenty-five grand?"

"Yeah." Bethany nods, and the smile on her face borders on nefarious. I can't help but feel like she kinda led us here. "Second place is ten thousand, I believe."

"Jesus," Dad says, turning to Mom. "Maria. That's…that's a lot of money." He looks to me. "Why didn't you bring this up?"

"Uh, I did." I glare at him, as both he and Mom stare at me with shock on their faces. "You said you didn't want to compete!"

"I didn't know it was basically a year of tuition!" Dad exclaims and runs a hand through his hair before slapping his palm on the table. "Our truck is entering."

"That's the spirit!" Bethany shouts, beaming. Her eyes flit over to mine, and she winks at me. "So, we have both trucks vying for the prize. Both kids have their own dreams. Both families have their own hopes. We can absolutely tell that story in forty minutes…or maybe ninety, if we push to do a big premiere pilot."

Some of the suits mutter with approval.

Ninety minutes?

"I read somewhere that an hour of reality television is something like twenty-four hours' worth of filmed content, so like...two days' worth of video for two hours feels like... a lot?" I venture.

Some of the suits look to one another, sharing smiles.

"This is true. You've done your homework." Bethany nods, and a little bloom of pride bursts in my chest, swirling around with the anxiety that's brewing about entering the competition. "But keep in mind, not all that footage will just be about you. We'll be focusing on your family, on Jordan, on *his* family. We'll be up at the farm with your parents. Maybe we'll chat with your friends! You never know who is going to end up being a supporting character in these things."

"I thought that kind of stuff got planned out? In like, the casting and all that?" I ask, while thinking about Eesha and Ariana. Chatting with my friends would mean a video call to them in Boston, or maybe a trip up there? Whatever the case, oh my God, I cannot wait to tell them about that possibility. They will positively lose their minds if they get to be on a reality show, even for just a minute.

"Sometimes," Bethany replies. "Sometimes the viewers end up deciding. Maybe after the pilot, people get attached to one person or another. We'd keep an eye on social media to feel that out."

"Last question," I say, and Bethany smiles, her eyes and expression warm. "Isn't this a little fast?" I glance at the suits around the table and then to my parents. "I mean, we only just chatted this weekend."

"You're not wrong," she says. "We've been talking about this premise here for a while, though, and well, it's a pseudo-

pilot. It's for shopping around, what we call 'a proof of concept.' If networks like it, if they're into the drama, into the
concept, then we'd green-light something a little fancier.
More cameras, more planning. It's a bit easier to just call it
a pilot." She looks at my whole family. "There's something
here, though, I just feel it."

"Okay, well, I hate to burst the bubble of excitement,"
Mom says, and the shift in the room is audible. Suits turn to
her, throats get cleared. "But while my husband here doesn't
watch reality television, I do. A lot of it. And I know someone is always the villain. How do you plan on dividing the
viewership?"

Bethany looks at some of the suits, and it's quiet for a beat.
Someone shuffles a stack of papers.

I get the impression no one prepared for this question.

"Mrs. Ortiz," Bethany starts. "We do have an arc in mind.
With your truck versus the other truck, leading up to that
competition while your families deal with your individual
struggles…it doesn't really matter who is painted to be good
or bad, or who wins or loses in this—"

"What do you mean it doesn't matter?" Mom snorts out a
laugh and gives me a "can you even believe this?" look. "Reality stars sometimes get painted to look like monsters, when
they're really not. And it doesn't matter who loses? What are
you talking about? Of course it does."

"Listen, realistically…the Plazas family, they aren't going
to get that restaurant back, or even launch a new one with
the funds from the competition. And twenty-five thousand
dollars isn't going to be enough to start up a farm," Bethany
says, wringing her hands a little.

"Well, sure, but we could pay off—" Dad starts.

"Shush," Mom says, but I know what he was about to go into. The family debt.

"I hate to be cold, but...let's just air some hard truths. We need a joyful conclusion in this. You're not being painted as the villain, but we did imagine the Plazas family being the victorious ones with the competition. They're from Philly, they have this intense neighborhood connection. You're the outsiders, new to town."

Mom just stares ahead at her.

"That said," Bethany continues, "we can't exactly *make* the Plazas win, we're not controlling the competition..."

She pauses for a moment and looks over at one of the executives sitting across from her.

He shakes his head slightly, and she continues on.

"But giving them some sort of victory lap is important in good storytelling."

Mom exhales, sounding frustrated.

"Fine. And how are you going to do that, drive the story, if you're not controlling the event?" Mom asks. "What if what they make isn't any good?"

"Have you seen the breakfast cheesesteaks they're making?"

"Cheesebreaks," I interject, and when everyone's eyes flit to me, I immediately regret it. "I saw them calling them that on social media."

Bethany smirks a little. "I've been at this a long time—" she starts.

"Please, what are you, thirty?" Mom snorts.

"Thirty is fifty in reality show years," Bethany says. "I've been here a while. I do my homework. None of the other trucks have anything on the Plazas truck. Or yours, for that matter. And I do genuinely hope both of you take home something, but we want to push the Plazas family here."

I can practically see the gears turning in Dad's head, as Bethany drums her fingers on the table in front of her.

But all of this is rocking me to my core.

I thought... I thought so much of these shows were real? Like, okay, I'm aware some of the scandals that have happened were a little embellished. And I totally watched all of *Unreal* with my mom and the girls—that show about producers behind the scenes of a reality show manipulating things. But that was a scripted television show, fiction. It's weird to hear it like this. A planned story from the very beginning, plotted and scouted out.

Is it *that* planned all the time? It can't be. Can it?

Mom breaks the silence, leaning back in her chair. "My second question is about compensation. There's been a lot of talk about all this potential. How much are we going to be paid here?"

"Oh. Well, Mrs. Ortiz, it might not even air. It's a proof of concept, and besides, if we do use it, the exposure alone—" Bethany starts.

"People *die* from exposure, Ms. Ireland."

I swear I hear the sound of a record scratch.

"Pilots...don't pay much," Bethany admits. "And it's kind of impossible for us to guarantee an amount for the actual show should it get green-lit. It doesn't really work that way—"

"Well, how *does* it work?" Mom asks, crossing her arms.

Bethany laughs awkwardly and rubs the back of her neck.

"Right now, I can offer ten thousand dollars for the pilot,

to both of your families. There will be other things to discuss in the contracts, like residuals, and what you make as a result of advertising. But honestly, the pay isn't high in reality television because of how much stars of programs make off the air."

Mom looks confused, so I chime in. "Sponsorships, endorsements. That kind of thing."

"Exactly." Bethany exhales. "These reality stars become influencers. But for a smaller show just starting out, ten thousand dollars for the pilot is being rather generous, if I'm being honest."

"I see." Mom nods, steepling her fingers and sucking in a breath "Ms. Ireland. Bethany. Our food truck has a small following on social media. Same with me and my husband. In fact, he basically only posts photos on Instagram of the overweight neighborhood squirrels."

My dad laughs at this and Mom glares at him. "What?" He smiles. "They're so chonky."

"You see what we're working with here?" Mom continues. "And then my daughter just does the food truck, she doesn't have a...platform."

"Well, that's not entirely true, Mrs. Ortiz," Bethany says, a little smile on her lips. "Your daughter's podcast has some significant numbers. We looked up the downloads, the subscribers. If anything, I'd say the show benefits from *her* platform, not the other way around."

"So...doesn't that mean we should get paid more?" I ask.

Dad stifles a laugh, Mom gives him a sharp look.

And so does Bethany, surprisingly.

"Your story is what we're paying for, Cindy. You and your

family's story. The platform you've got, it's an added bonus, but our show is what will boost it even further."

"Alright, well," Mom says, shifting around in her seat, "I think that amount for a pilot or proof of concept or whatever it is will be fine, I'm not going to get worked up about that. Ten thousand dollars for a week of work and cameras? Okay. But if this gets green-lit, I want to discuss strategy regarding our family's…ugh, our family's *brand*. I hate saying that."

Bethany smirks at this.

"I mean it. If our financial success from this has to ride on being on social media, on utilizing a platform in a bigger way, I expect a team to teach us how to use it. I want one of these guys—" she gestures at the executives sitting around the table "—showing my daughter how to do all this stuff with her podcast."

I've never seen Mom be so…tough and assertive. And Dad is looking at her like he's falling in love all over again.

"Deal." Bethany reaches her hand out. Mom does the same but stops just before taking it, staring the producer down.

"We still have a *lot* to discuss," Mom says. "I want to be clear here, no one is going to take advantage of my family."

"I understand," Bethany says and wiggles her fingers.

Mom smiles, nods, and shakes her hand.

I have no idea how I'm supposed to handle carrying this gift basket home, but Bethany pretty much shoved it into my arms on the way out. I have to peer around the crinkly clear cellophane wrap to get across the street back toward Washington Square, doing my best to avoid getting hit by any cars or bicyclists, or collide into anyone walking a dog.

"What did you grab?" Dad asks, striding toward me, his arms cradling a much smaller basket that I'm immediately jealous of. There are two coffee mugs inside and a bundle of bags of roasted beans from ReAnimator, a café/coffee roaster here in Philly. Looks like a totebag is folded up inside too, with a few cash gift cards tucked in with free coffee vouchers.

"I didn't grab anything. The receptionist shoved this into my arms." I move my head around, trying to get a better view. Dad peeks into the plastic, mumbling appreciatively at the wine, little cheeses wrapped in plastic, and a bunch of jars of things I can't pronounce, which means they're expensive.

"Daniel," Mom snaps as he moves to look in her basket. "Don't worry, I got the one you were checking out."

"Yes!" Dad exclaims, his basket jostling a bit. I hustle up next to Mom to see what she took, and the basket has a few catalogs for local retail spots in Midtown Village, and a ton—I mean an absolutely wild amount—of gift cards smattered about.

"We don't even shop at some of those stores. You barely drink coffee!" I say, confused.

"Sure, but the gift cards," Dad argues. "Could use them at Reading Terminal instead of at those stores. Maybe we don't need the bargain bags next trip."

"I thought there was nothing wrong with dollar bags," I grunt, wrestling with the heavy basket again. "Fights food waste and all."

"Sure, sure," Dad says, sighing a little. "Why don't you um...take a seat for a minute, we've got a few blocks to go until we get to the Broad Street Line and I want to talk to your mother."

"Yeah, okay." I shrug, and get cozy on a nearby bench, the basket by my feet.

Mom and Dad walk up a little, toward the center of the park where the paths connect, but I can still hear them talking. The concrete and brick walls that line the walkways of the park have little curves in them, and the sound travels right to the bench.

It's, like, one of the first things you learn about on field trips to places like this in junior high.

"We are entering that competition," Dad says, his voice firm, intense.

"Yeah, no kidding, Daniel," Mom replies, and I see her hoist the basket up in her arms before setting it down on one of the walls. "They said we had to. Part of the story."

"Sure, but...we're gonna win it."

"What," Mom says, deadpan.

"Twenty-five thousand dollars?!" Dad shouts, and I don't even need the curved wall to have the sound travel my way. "Look, I love the Plazas but they ain't getting that restaurant back, and Jordan doesn't need that much for his truck. You know what we need that money for..."

"That's not fair. It's your fault we—" Mom starts, but I lose what she's saying.

"Come on, we can do this. We..." His voice fades out as the two of them stroll farther away from the curving walls. Mom hurries back to grab the basket, but that's all I get out of them.

My heart pounds in my chest.

I know they've still got some debt from back in Boston,

but I didn't think it was bad enough to screw over Jordan's family. Is something else going on here?

What does my family need the money for?

And what aren't they telling me?

Pilot: Confessional Shot Transcript (Jordan)

Jordan: Trust is an important part of the whole food truck community. We look out for one another. There's a ramen truck that parks not too far away from us, Hot Noods, and I go there a lot. The girls who run it, Melisa and Ana, are these really popular burlesque performers when they aren't busy making the best noodles in South Philly.

And if I'm solo, if Steve or Laura aren't around, I can count on them to watch the truck for me when I need a bathroom break, you know? If I have to get some ingredients or something, or just need a quick walk around the block to clear my head.

Would I let Cindy and her family watch the truck? Are you kidding me?

I don't think anyone in her family can even name

another food truck other than theirs and ours. And
they only remember us because we get in their way.
I wouldn't trust them to return a bottle of ketchup.

chapter nine:
jordan

———

Monday, Six Days until Truck Off

I stride over to Laura's house—the row home right next to mine. I stop short of knocking, hearing the distinct sounds of an acoustic guitar thrumming from somewhere outside.

I smile. She's in her yard.

There's a narrow easement between our homes, a slim, bright blue arched door set in the middle of where our houses connect. You can see the seam where the siding on my house stops and the brick exterior of her home begins. The door squeaks as I nudge it open, and I shuffle my way through the narrow alley, mostly reserved for garbage cans and bicycles, but thankfully is devoid of both right now.

I reach the small concrete square patio, just like ours, maybe fifteen by fifteen feet. The Ortiz family definitely has the nicer space, as do most of the homes on their street a few blocks up. Just the luck of the draw when it comes to city planning in the 1800s, I guess.

Laura's sitting on the little stone steps that lead from the back door of the house into the yard, two large potted shrubs that have seen better days on both sides of her. She shifts to look at me, her Converse scratching against the concrete.

"Hey, Hollywood." She strums a chord hard and lays her guitar down in one of the dying bushes.

"Don't start," I groan and sit next to her. "You know, maybe your parents' plants would be doing better if you didn't use them as guitar stands."

She shrugs.

"So, how's all the uh…" she waves a hand around "…preparation or whatever going?"

"I don't know. They're shooting some of the first bits for our family today," I sigh. "This feels like a huge mistake."

"I could have told you that."

"You *did* tell me that."

"Yeah, well…" She nudges a foot against one of the pots. "When it comes to Cindy, you don't really listen." She glances back at me. "You've got a soft spot there."

"Whatever," I grumble.

"I just worry, man." Laura hops up from the step, grabbing her guitar by the neck. The shrub it was in rustles, and a few little branches snap off. "When you two are on your big road trip…are you going to just, what? Bail because she says so? Skip a town because it isn't nice enough? You've waited forever to do this. You've worked so hard."

She strums another chord, this one ominous and angry.

"Just don't let her, let *you*, get in your own way."

My phone buzzes in my pocket and I pull it out.

Mom: Where are you? The television people are here. Your dad is being embarrassing.

Dad: I am not.

Mom: You asked one of them to arm wrestle you in the kitchen!

Dad: He looks like he thinks he's stronger than me.

Mom: He is!

Oh my God.

"The producers are here," I say, looking at the fence between our homes, like somehow, I'll be able to see them through it. I honestly don't know why we bother with a fence. Her yard is just as empty and concrete as mine, only we've got a few more plants that are alive, some garden boxes, and a grill that Dad likes to barbecue on from time to time. The old decaying wood posts have enough holes in them that I can tell no one is outside right now.

"Well." Laura shrugs. "Time to go sing and dance and all that."

"Yeah, I don't think so." I settle myself on the hard step at the back door. "Shouldn't you be the one rehearsing with your show tomorrow? Time for *you* to sing and dance and all that."

"Oh God." Laura laughs, twirling the guitar around. "I didn't actually mean that."

"Well, I did," I say. "Practice makes perfect and all."

She looks at her guitar and back at me. "It sucks," she says.

"How do you know unless you share it?" I ask.

"Ugh. This isn't one of your sandwiches, you know. This is full of my…my *feelings*."

She makes a face like saying the word hurts her.

"Oh, come on, there's feelings involved in cooking," I scoff. She gives me a doubtful look. "There are. They make movies about it. Didn't you watch *Chef* with me?"

"Eh, I fell asleep when you had that movie night." She winces. "I'm sorry!"

"Look, when I cook…it's the same thing, okay?" I point at her guitar. "It is. I can't explain it that well, but it is. I just… feel it right here, you know?" I thump my chest and run my hand through my hair. "Every vegetable oil burn, every pair of jeans stained forever with ketchup and cooking grease, every smiling face when someone bites into what I've tried so hard to get right…that's the song. The food is the instrument."

I get up and walk over to her.

"The guitar doesn't matter," I say and put a hand on her shoulder. "Just the person playing it. You're gonna do great. People are gonna love you."

She stares at me for a beat, and then looks away.

"How long you been practicing that one?" she says, but there's a little tremble in her voice. I know I got through to her, and it cracks a little smile out of me.

She turns back, eyes piercing mine.

"Fine." She twirls the guitar around again and sits down on the concrete in her yard. "But I'm not singing. The lyrics aren't done yet and…there are feelings in them."

"God forbid you have any feelings, Laura."

"Alright, you sound like my moms." She shakes her head

and jostles her shoulders a bit, before taking a deep breath. She conjures a guitar pick seemingly out of nowhere and starts to play.

The song kicks off with a clean chord, and quickly moves into a bunch of little melodies on the strings, Laura plucking and strumming in equal measure, making the guitar sing. It's some kind of acoustic pop punk thing—I can tell without any of the words, the two of us having listened to enough of The Starting Line to last a lifetime.

"Jordan!" I hear my mom shout from next door. Laura wavers on her guitar, looking off toward my yard.

"Keep going!" I say, trying to duck down a little on the steps. Not like there's anywhere to hide though.

And Laura does, eventually finishing what I'm guessing is the first verse.

Whatever the song is going to be, it's already beautiful.

"See?" I nod at her. "Not so hard, right?"

"It's gonna be a lot different up on that stage tomorrow," Laura sighs, swinging her guitar down.

"Are you going to play it...you know, for him?" I ask, breaching the subject that she never wants to discuss. It's just more of those pesky feelings.

"We'll see," she says softly.

"I'm telling you, I think he's going to—"

"Jordan!" Mom's voice is suddenly loud and close, and there she is, peering over Laura's fence. "Hey, Laura."

"Hi, Mrs. Plazas," Laura says, all sunshine and sweetness. I try not to scowl at her.

"You need to come over here and get ready," Mom says, nodding back at the house. "Me and your dad are trying to straighten up the living room for the cameras. Could use a hand distracting the producers away from your father."

She disappears behind the fence, and before I can even move, she's back.

"Right now."

I peek through the window blinds in my bedroom to the street below. There's a sizable white van out there, and two guys hefting large camera equipment out of the back. I recognize one of the producers, the woman who we rang the shame bell for—Bethany, I think. But there's a trembling young guy at her side with a tablet and a large metal thermos. She plucks it out of his hand, takes a sip, and hands it back to him, all while staring intently at her phone.

Why...why can't *she* just hold it?

I check the time. I've already missed the breakfast rush this morning, where I was hoping to keep testing out the cheesebreaks, but maybe we'll get some folks wanting them in the afternoon and evening. Steve was right about that. People do like breakfast for lunch and dinner. Not only do I want to take advantage of the extra tips from morning customers, but with the Truck Off just a few days away, I need to perfect the recipe. Something is still missing.

I pull way too many T-shirts out of my dresser, suddenly for the first time in my entire life finding myself worried about how I might look. Is my shirt the right shirt or my pants the right pants and...wow.

How am I supposed to do any of this?

Be on camera?

Like, a real camera. Not just on iPhones and all that.

But between the potential income for my parents and the excitement that just seems to burst off of Cindy, I know I have to rally up. For them.

I finally decide on a simple dark red shirt with a golden logo in the middle from a local emo band, Zachary West & the Good Grief. The color looks great against my brown skin. It just feels right, after Laura played that song in her yard, to sport some local pop punk vibes. I toss on the same jeans I had on yesterday and, frankly, had on all weekend, grease and oil stains on the legs. I can picture Cindy scowling at me for the choice, but it's authentic, whatever. If I have to be on this show, I'm going to be as much of myself as I can.

By the time I'm finally downstairs, the cameramen are standing in our kitchen, and a bright light is illuminating our entire living room. I squint, walking by it, my shadow dancing over our family photos on the walls. Our house is wildly clean. It's never, ever this tidy. Dad is a short whirl-wind by nature, leaving disaster everywhere in the form of abandoned cups and plates and sneakers, and Mom honestly isn't much better. The two of them have been in a hurry their entire lives, just like me, and cleaning never really factored into all of that much.

Everyone in the kitchen turns to me, the one who disturbed the setting. Mom and Dad are sitting at our small dining table, which is now pushed to the other side of the room, both of their backs pressed against the wall, their arms crossed and leaning forward. Dad motions for me to walk on over, and I catch the producer, Bethany, eyeing me.

Her brow furrows a bit, glancing at my pants.

Good.

When I'm on the road in my food truck with Cindy, I plan to dress like an absolute gremlin. Give me the coziest, loosest T-shirts imaginable, jeans that were once light blue, now nearly black, thanks to cooking grease. And no one can stop me.

"Ms. Ireland, should Jordan be in this?" Dad asks, adjusting his seat a little. The wooden chair squeaks against the hardwood floor.

"No, it's okay," she says, waving him off. "We're going to do another interview with just him later."

"Okay, okay." Dad clears his throat. "We're ready. Are you ready?" He glances at Mom, who nods quickly, and I get the sense this has been going on for a minute. "Okay, let's go."

"Alright."

Bethany steps back and motions at my dad, who looks perplexed.

"Aren't you going to say 'action' or—" he starts.

"This is reality television, Mr. Plazas. We've been filming since we got out of the car."

Dad looks at the camera, his eyes wide.

"Oh!" He clears his throat. "Okay, okay, um…"

"Just remember, this is our way of introducing you and your family to the viewers. Talk about yourself. Where you're from, the business, how you two met…" She smiles at Mom, who scoffs and laughs. "We'll piece together our favorite bits. It's how we tell the story."

"Alright." Dad drums his hands on the table and shakes them out. "Okay, okay." He closes his eyes and takes a deep breath, and I hear one of the camera guys chuckle a little bit.

Dad. So dramatic.

He's all worked up and fidgety, but the truth is that he is simply made for all of this. From installing the shame bell on the cheesesteak truck to his boisterous energy at home, he's a walking reality show in the first place. I think that comes with working in the food business. So much of it is personality as well as how things taste. You want people to like you. You want them to keep coming back. I don't know why he's even remotely nervous to be on camera.

"Our story, our story…" he mutters. "Well, I suppose it all started with the diner."

Oh. The diner.

He deflates a little, just mentioning it, and Mom's hand is immediately on his. He gazes up at her and smiles.

Jesus. I haven't told him yet about the signs. About the fact that the diner is coming down in…what day is it again? End of the week? With everything that happened with the reality show, it slipped my mind.

"For a good thirty years, my wife and I operated The Stateside on Broad Street here in Philadelphia. A diner. It was a popular place. I started off as a busboy there in my teens, ended up managing it in my twenties, and suddenly, there was this offer from the owner. This was back when you could actually buy a building or a house in Philadelphia for the price of what a car costs now."

He chuckles a little, shakes his head.

"But, um…about a decade ago, business started to slow. More and more restaurants were opening up nearby, which was fine, of course. The Philadelphia food community is a great one, everyone always seems to have each other's backs. We had this surge in popularity again because of…" He laughs. "We hosted these industry nights, where we would stay open until, oh God…three in the morning, some weekdays? Everyone who was a waiter or a bartender or a manager…they would be in there, eating breakfast or steaks at an impossible time, downing coffee just to stay awake and be social a little longer, before sleeping away the day.

"It was a lot of things that eventually got us. We owned the restaurant, but taxes were going up. Services for food pickup really didn't work for a place like ours, where the prices were low because the food was, well…comfort food. No one wants to spend thirty-seven dollars to get a platter of chicken fingers delivered, especially when they end up being cold by the time they arrive. Doesn't matter how much you love a place, eventually cost gets in the way of your heart. Both in terms of going there and, well, owning it."

He swallows and clears his throat, looking back up at my mom.

"We, um…had to shut down about…six years ago now. It could have been worse. A lot worse. People *had it* a lot worse than we did, especially in the heat of the pandemic." He wipes at his eyes, and something twinges in my chest. Dad, the constantly happy, always bouncing-around positive man, looks like he's about to start sobbing here and now. "We took the money from the sale—which we were lowballed with, by the way."

Mom sighs, and this cracks a little smile out of me. Dad likes to bring this up for absolutely no reason any chance he gets.

But I get it. I do. And so does Mom.

When you're forced to say goodbye to something, you never

really say goodbye to it. You spend years trying to figure out how to, with no promise that you ever will.

"But that money," Dad continues. "It let us pay off the mortgage on our home. Helped out our former employees till they got on their feet. Put a little nest egg away for our son's college—"

I can't hold back a huff. This is a constant struggle in this house. I am getting my food truck and then I'm out of here. If only they would let me take that nest egg and put it toward my truck.

"Whether or not he wants to use it for college, is yet to be seen."

His eyes flit up to mine, a little smile on his face. Okay, Dad. Thank you for seeing me.

"And then...we bought the food truck," he continues. "Well, the food truck we could buy."

He glances at Mom, who shakes her head.

This is the second time he's tiptoed around something about the truck. What's going on?

"I took a job as a night manager at Wink's, an upscale gastropub that's a lot less saucy than it sounds, out in Fishtown. And Saray here is an assistant general manager at Alina's out in West Philadelphia, that bar all the Philly poets hang out at. She's always been cooler than me."

"But our goal is to get out of that truck, and out of other people's restaurants, as much as we love them, and into our own again. It feels like...like a piece of our home was taken from us. And I know, I know we can't get it back. Not the same place. It wouldn't be the same place anymore, even."

God, I gotta tell him that the diner is being torn down right after this.

"But we could make a new home somewhere else. I just know it."

He wipes at his cheeks again, and Mom puts an arm around his shoulder.

"Sweetheart," Mom says, and Dad gazes at her. "Home is right here. Home isn't a place of work. It's here, with him." She nods at me, and I smile back.

Dad sniffles.

"I know, I know." Dad clears his throat. "I just…miss it. Having something that was ours, it just…meant something."

"Me too," Mom says, patting his cheek. "I know."

"Alright, that was fantastic," Bethany says, with a clap of her hands, the sharp sound interrupting the… I don't know, soft warmth of everything that just happened. "Thank you, Mr. Plazas, for digging deep like that—that's just the level of emotion I'm hoping to bring to this show, particularly in these cutaways with you and the rival family."

Dad looks puzzled for a moment and Mom nudges him.

"Ah! Yes, yes of course," he stumbles. "The Ortiz family. Curse them!" He shakes his fist in the air.

Oh my God.

How in the world are we supposed to get through this if this show gets picked up? I'll have to stay on the road in my food truck forever just to avoid coming home and being on camera, so I don't have to dance around these lies like this.

And I don't think I can convince Cindy to be on the road with me forever. We do have to come back eventually, once she's done with her gap year. Maybe when she starts at county,

I can park my truck over there once and a while. Meet her outside of class, with lunch ready to go for her and her friends. Maybe something special, that I make just for her.

"One thing we want to make sure we get are some more details about the start of the rivalry with the Ortiz family," Bethany says, snapping me back into focus. I glance over at Dad and Mom, whose eyes are wide like deer in headlights. "Can you tell us a little bit about that? How did it start? What carries that flame, that anger?"

"Well, I wouldn't say we carry some kind of burning fire or anything like that," Dad says, laughing a little, sounding nervous. He rubs the back of his head and glances at Mom. "I guess it all started with…"

Dad's face hardens for a minute, and then he shakes off whatever it was.

"The truck," Mom interjects.

"The permits," Dad says at the same time.

The two of them look at one another, and back to the camera.

The truck?

What is Mom talking about?

Dad's eyes flit over to me and he winces.

"So…it's hard to talk about the start of things with the Ortiz family without digging into how we met." He glances at Mom, who laughs and shakes her head. "What? You're the one on Facebook."

"Fine." Mom exhales, taking over. "I run a neighborhood group, where people post about finding a cat in their yard or if they have a piece of furniture to give away…stuff like that. And one day, I get a message from someone who wants to join the group. It's Maria Ortiz. Says her and her family are moving to Philadelphia, to our neighborhood, looking to connect. I let them in."

"First mistake," Dad says, and Mom swats at his shoulder.

"And at first, when they moved here, they were great," Mom says, nodding. "Really great. But one day we're talking about our food truck plans and—"

"And that damn family bought the one we were bidding on!" Dad exclaims, and then grits his teeth, tightening his fist.

"Wait, what?" I stammer out. All this time I thought their initial spat was over the parking spaces, not an actual food truck.

Bethany and the camera crew glare at me.

"Sorry," I mutter, quieting down.

But this...this is news to me.

"The fight we had over the parking permits was the icing on the already bitter cake," Dad grumbles. "The food truck is what started it. We got stuck with a junker, while their family bought the nice one that we could just barely afford. They still use it, and every day it's just a reminder. They come here, from Boston, thinking they can just take whatever they—"

"Hey, honey." Mom says, rubbing Dad's arm. Her eyes flit to me and back.

Dad clears his throat.

But I want to hear about this.

"We made it work for all these years, but that was it," Dad says. "That created the rift."

"Did they know they were outbidding you?" Bethany chimes in, leaning forward a little.

"Oh, they knew," Dad says, crossing his arms. He sighs, but it sounds like a growl.

"Every time I see that truck, I'm reminded of how often people have taken from us. And I'll be damned if I let that family take anything away from me again."

You could have dropped a needle and heard it fall.

"Sweetheart…" Mom says, touching Dad's shoulder.

He's shaking.

"Sorry," he practically whispers. "That…that was a little off the handle."

I glance over at Bethany.

She's grinning.

"No…" she says. "That was perfect."

chapter ten:
cindy

Tuesday, Five Days until Truck Off

I usually sweat a lot when I'm working on the farm on one of my volunteer days. The sun hammers my shoulders, and I can feel the dampness trickling down my neck, the warmth on my back. But it's more than the heat of the Philadelphia summer that's making me uncomfortable.

Dad walks by, a few visitors to the farm following him like ducklings. He pats my shoulder as he passes, rambling on about the fertilizer used here. There's a tour almost every day, folks curious about making their own little urban farms in their respective tiny city yards, who want to know how to eat and grow things more sustainably.

I look over my shoulder as Dad wanders off, and Drew, the cameraman who has been following me around all day, huffs out an irritated sigh when I glance right into the camera.

"Sorry, sorry," I murmur, turning back to the dirt in front of me.

"It's okay," he says, but his tone is still frustrated. He's a slightly imposing guy, maybe in his forties, with a bald head and a friendly face that immediately wrinkles up into angry lines when I make eye contact with him or the camera. I hope I haven't ruined too much footage, but I really cannot help it. It's a camera! The urge is too great.

"It takes some getting used to," he says, his tone warming. I hear the camera on his shoulder moving around, and he groans a little. "But you'll get the hang of it."

"Yeah, I dunno..." I mumble, digging. The soil is cool against my hands, and I pluck a few twigs and pebbles out, flicking them to the side. I have to be careful, every now and again, someone unearths a piece of porcelain or an old soda bottle while digging around. Once upon a time, this was a mostly barren lot full of garbage, overgrown grass, and dying trees.

Now it's an urban farm that serves as a small fresh produce oasis in what used to be something of a food desert. At least, that's what everyone who works here says. We weren't here when they created it. But it's the story the tour guides and volunteers and part-time workers dish to people who stumble in with wandering wide eyes, lost on their way to a restaurant.

And I can understand the wonder. There are bars and boutiques just two blocks away, and people's homes line the blocks across the street. And then there's this. A farm smack in the middle of it all. It was like that back in Boston too, and while I enjoy it—the plants, the earth, the butterflies and wildlife that find their way here—the wonder has kinda faded.

I pluck some tomato seedlings out of their cardboard egg-shell cases, and plant them in rows in this particular space. With each wobble, the smell of those tomato vines and leaves fill my nose, the scent sharp and crisp. Once they're all set, I stand up, stretch, peering at the large cart full of seedlings that still need to be planted. There are a few cucumbers, pep-pers, and squash that look eager for homes too, and I reach out, coiling a cucumber plant's tendril around my finger. The leaves are soft and velvety, making a soft crunching sound when I press them between my fingers—

Someone yawns loudly.

I can't help it, I turn around and look at Drew, who winces from behind his camera.

"Sorry." He shakes his head a little. "It's early in the morn-ing and this is...not what I'm usually capturing. The name *Cheesesteak Wars* implied, you know, wars."

"What..." I glance at the plants and back at him. "What do you mean?"

"Nothing, I just..." He gazes off to the side, and I catch a glimpse of Jared, the intern-looking guy from the office, hurrying over. I hadn't even noticed he was here—when I showed up at the farm, it was just Drew waiting with a cam-era, awkwardly introducing himself to me and my parents. I brush at my pants and shirt, trying to swipe away the dirt, but...why am I bothering? I don't like the effect this guy has on me, but I also kinda do.

"What's up, kid?"

"Mr. Gormley." Jared nods.

"Oh my God, please, I've told you it's just Drew." The cameraman shakes his head. "All you interns are so formal.

Most of the time the bosses don't even know my name, and I've worked on every reality show in the area for a decade. I respond to 'you' and also 'guy' as well as 'you guy.'"

I stifle a laugh, and Drew smirks at me.

"Sorry, just…is there a problem?" Jared asks, his brown eyes flitting from Drew to me. I have to look away and focus my attention on the tomatoes, like they're up to something terribly interesting. "I saw you chatting and…well, Ms. Ireland says that when the talent is breaking the wall, chatting with the crew, it means something is off."

This time I snort out a laugh and peer back up. Jared's eyes cut to me, fully of gentle worry. A little heat flushes up my neck.

The talent?

"No, no," Drew says and then sighs at me. "Kid, this is just…this isn't television." He gestures at the plants. "It's pretty, it's interesting, for…some people, I suppose. But viewers watching reality television for drama aren't going to be terribly excited to see someone planting lettuce or whatever that is."

"Tomatoes." I scowl but feel myself softening up. "These go in the sandwiches though. Isn't that interesting?"

Drew gives me a look.

"Fine. So…what should I be doing? I can't…argue with the plants."

Jared chuckles a little and just as fast, he turns away from me. I swear his cheeks are reddening a little, but that must be from the sun bearing down on us here.

"Not up to me, kid. I figure we can use some of this footage in B-roll moments." Drew shrugs and looks at Jared. "Producers say anything, check in with you at all?"

He also shrugs, as if to say, *What do you think?*

"Of course not. Look, I've been in this business a long time," Drew says and puts his camera down on the ground. Why does it seem like everyone who works for reality television says some variation of that?

"The shows that make it" he continues. "They've got the drama that ropes people in, but also the heart. I met the other family yesterday, your rivals or whatever, and the heart? It's definitely there. Those people care."

"I care!" I exclaim. "We're on a farm! We serve the community. How isn't that heart?"

"Yeah but, who is your favorite not-selfish reality star?" Drew asks. He crosses his thick arms, which have got to be as muscly as they are from lugging cameras around all day every day.

I think for a moment of the shows that me and Mom are addicted to. The live tweeting me and the girls do while watching the various rich housewives, recording our podcast episodes of *Beacon Street* about them.

I swallow.

"Yeah, see," Drew says. "Look I'm not saying they're all selfish to the core. Plenty of them do charity work and stuff you don't always catch on television. Guy Fieri? Man is a saint. But for the most part, people don't always care about the wholesome bits. They want the gritty underbelly of it all."

"The chefs screaming at contestants," I say.

"Exactly." Drew smirks. "Keep the heart but push the

drama." He hoists his camera back up. "So. Where we going? Who we gonna go yell at?"

I laugh, but his expression is expectant. Jared seems to be waiting to follow my lead too.

"You're serious?" I ask.

"Sure," Drew replies. "It's *Cheesesteak Wars*, isn't it? Think about it. I need a water or something."

He adjusts the camera on his shoulder and heads toward the entrance of the farm, where we've got a stand selling fruits, veggies, juices, all kinds of healthy delicious stuff.

"Hey," Jared says, taking a step toward me, his movements all…strangely cautious and awkward, like he's approaching a deadly animal. "Drew is great. He's taken me to some other locations this year, like over on the *Main Line Wives* shoot in the spring. He won't lead you astray."

"Yeah, he seems like… I don't know, a straight shooter or whatever."

Jared laughs, tucking an unruly strand of that blondish red hair behind his ear.

"Is there anything I can do?" he asks, his eyes lingering on mine, like he sincerely means it, like he wants to hear everything I have to say. Suddenly I wonder if my cheeks are a little flushed. But thankfully he looks away, shuffling his feet. "To be a better…support? I mean, I'm just an intern, though I'm definitely doing the work of an actual production assistant. If you need anything, you can ask me."

"I think I'm okay right now," I say.

But I'm not.

Something about him is sending my heart racing a little. And the way he moves and looks at me, tells me that he maybe realizes that. It's surprising, and I try to shake it off, focusing on the task at hand.

There's really only one person, or rather, one family, that the show expects me to argue with. Jordan. His parents. But all those spats, they happen at the trucks. Maybe a few times in the hallways at school, and once at the supermarket, but honestly, whenever we'd see each other in public over the last year, we'd just avoid one another.

Big *Lord of the Rings* vibes when it came to our relationship.

Keep it secret.

Keep it safe.

"Just a second," I say to Jared, turning away, pulling out my phone for reinforcements. Just a few messages waiting from the girls. Nothing terribly important, some GIFs from the latest episode of *Main Line Wives* and a link to a Reddit thread breaking down a conspiracy theory about the latest *60 Days to Wed*, how one of the contestants is only in it to secure an acting career.

Me: Hey, so, the reality show folks want me to crank up the drama

Eesha: Drama?

Ariana: Don't you and Jordan have drama at the trucks all the time?

Me: That's just it. We only have drama there, and the camera guy and Jared are both saying what I'm doing is boring

Eesha: Jared?

Me: Yeah, he's an intern on the set, assisting the producers and stuff

Eesha: Oh interesting, I think I found his Instagram

A few little dots pop up in the chat window, and then vanish, and then pop up again, and then vanish...

"You doing okay?"

I startle back and drop my phone. Thankfully, one of the joys of an urban farm is that most of the ground is soil, so it falls into the patch of tomatoes I've been fussing over with a light floof, instead of a clatter with a shattered screen.

Jared picks it up for me. He's smiling as he hands it over, and I notice the little creases on the sides of his dark brown eyes. Maybe he's like me, or Jordan for that matter, operating on a constant lack of sleep.

"Thanks," I say, trying to sound like I'm not catching my breath.

"Sorry I scared you," he says, still smirking, and nods at my phone. "My Instagram, huh? What else did your friends dig up?"

"What?" I ask, looking to my phone, my heart pounding.

Eesha: Wow he is CUTE

I almost drop my phone again as I shove it into my pocket, and Jared laughs loudly, the sound melodic as he runs a hand through his hair.

"Look, I—" Jared starts.

"Whew!" Drew exhales, rejoining us, the large camera swinging from his thick hands. He hoists it back up on his shoulder and then shakes his head, settling it back down on the ground. "Nope, I think I'm done. They've got some killer snacks and drinks over there, youse two should go get something, you look all flushed."

Oh God.

Jared chuckles under his breath and I shoot daggers at him with my eyes. But that only makes him laugh harder.

"I'm gonna take a breather, maybe wander this place," Drew says. "Might not be any drama here, but it sure is nice. Anywhere I can stash my camera?"

"Oh, yeah, just go ask Kelly at the cash-out by the entrance. She'll put it in one of the sheds or something."

Drew looks at me, squinting his eyes.

"It'll be safe," I press, and he relents.

"Alright," he says, walking away, and turns briefly to point a finger at me mock-threateningly. "I'm trusting you, Cheesesteak Girl."

"Well," Jared says, watching Drew with me as he heads to the entrance with his camera. "Union does say he gets a solid hour lunch break." I look back at him—*up* at him, really, with how tall he is. "Do you, um…take a break ever?"

"Oh yeah, sometimes, it depends on—"

His phone rings, but it doesn't just ring. It sounds like an alarm, incredibly loud and insistent. He hurries to pull it out of his pocket.

"Hey, yes, hi, Ms. Ireland." His eyes flit to mine, and he makes a wincing face. "Yeah, I'm here. Drew was filming around the farm, taking a breather now. I'm not sure where we're off to next, he wasn't really liking the footage… Well, yeah, I'll..." he looks at me and mouths *I'm sorry* and turns away, back to the phone "...see what I can do, but..."

He strides off, toward the entrance after Drew.

I think...

He was about to ask me out. Before Bethany called.

I don't know how I feel about that...

My phone buzzes and I head away from the scene of the "nearly asked out on a date" crime, to a flurry of texts from the girls, and some email notifications. Probably just some messages from listeners. Lately we've been getting a few emails that we read aloud on the show, which is a lot of fun.

Eesha: Hello?

Ariana: What are you doing?

Eesha: Maybe she ran away with Hot Intern

Me: I'm at the farm, helping my parents out. Planting some tomatoes

Ariana: Sorry, I fell asleep

Eesha: More about this Jared guy, please and thank you

Me: Ugh. He SAW your text message, you know

Ariana: So it looks like WE are the drama

Eesha: Hahahah

Me: I'm losing my mind. Any ideas? Any thoughts?

Eesha: About Jared? Quite a few

Me: Oh my God stop it. You know I'm with Jordan

Ariana: And you know we're just picking on you

Me: I know. But they want me to do something interesting. Drama. Other than you two

Eesha: Hm. Why not show up somewhere Jordan is going to be?

Ariana: Yeah, just roll in, make a scene

Eesha: Where is he now, is he working the trucks tonight with you?

And that's when it hits me.
He's not working the trucks tonight.
But I know *exactly* where he's going to be.

Me: You two are geniuses. More soon

Eesha: Yeah more Jared please

Me: Oh my God

I move to put my phone back in my pocket when I spot those email notifications again. I give it a tap and the email subject line at the top of a bundle of messages to the podcast nearly stops my heart.

Congratulations from Northeastern University: Admissions Offer

My phone just falls out of my hand, again, and I scramble to scoop it up out of the dirt in front of me, brushing soil away from the screen.

I open the email up, my heart racing.

Northeastern University
Admissions and Financial Aid
Boston, MA 02115

Dear Cindy Ortiz,
Congratulations! On behalf of the admissions and financial aid committee at Northeastern University, we are delighted to inform you that you've advanced off of our wait list, and we're pleased to offer you admission starting this fall. Please, do accept my personal congratulations at this monumental achievement in your young life. Your essay about your ties to Boston, your yearning for the city streets and the connections you have there, absolutely moved this office.

We're happy to admit you to this year's class, and details regarding your scholarship are attached to this—

My mouth falls open.
Scholarship?
My God. This is it.

I'm going home.

But suddenly, my chest feels heavy, and there's this sinking feeling in my stomach. This pilot, this…proof of concept for *Cheesesteak Wars*, what happens if I'm not around if the show gets green-lit? Do I have to choose between staying in Philadelphia and going to my dream school? To being back with my friends? I mean, I guess that's part of reality television, right? People move, change jobs, careers, the cameras follow…but would it be interesting, without the rivalry in person? Just our parents? How would it even work?

What do I do about Jordan and the road trip?

With Northeastern, there's no more gap year. Especially with this scholarship. It's an offer I can't refuse.

It feels like too much. The show. My family. My boyfriend. My friends. My hopes and my dreams and the things that I want for myself, weighed against what other people want for me. Want *from* me.

Suddenly, it's all very much feeling like everything is outside of my control. I've been so focused on what I can handle, and this just sends it all into a spiral.

Okay.

Okay, okay, okay.

I look back at my phone, at the string of texts from the girls, and then shove it back in my pocket.

I have to call my parents. I have to tell the girls. Maybe I need to talk to Bethany and the production crew.

But I definitely have to talk to Jordan.

And tell him I'm not going with him.

Pilot: Confessional Shot Transcript (Cindy)

Cindy: So, when my family lived in Boston, my parents had this farm. It was a nonprofit space where they employed lots of college kids and older folks who needed a fresh start. I kinda grew up on a farm, even though we lived smack in the middle of a major city.

I don't know many people who get to have that weird dual experience. Most television shows, or the Lifetime movies I watch with my mom, it's the big city girl who moves to the country, or the timid country gal who moves to the sprawling metropolis or whatever.

I've been both my whole life.

It's...hard being two people, straddling two worlds. Not just in that space—I mean, an urban farm is a lot different from working on a farm out in the Pennsylvania countryside. I know that.

But you know, being Latinx and growing up in Boston. Moving here. Feeling American, but also not at all. Welcome at my home, but looked at strangely when standing right outside of it. Like I don't belong here.

In the movies, the city girl and the farm girl usually realize they're not so different from one another.

But I'm not sure other people ever get that message.

Pilot: Confessional Shot Transcript (Jordan)

Jordan: Ha! Of course I have a life outside the truck. I've got my tight group of friends. There's Steve, who I've been close with since high school started. And Laura, my neighbor and best friend since we were in kindergarten.

But you know, I've been pulled toward food just as long. Working in my parents' diner, sure, but also early mornings as a kid making my own breakfast before school and packing lunch, while my parents worked wildly early hours at The Stateside.

That's where I get my independence, really. I had to find it. I mean, have you eaten school breakfasts and lunches? Not great, let me tell you.

So, I got up early, cooked for myself. Started doing

that when I was... I want to say sixth grade? It became less about me too, soon after.

I had a lot of classmates who couldn't afford the meals at school. Sometimes you end up falling into this weird middle space where your family makes enough to pay for things, but also really doesn't, because you know, rent. Bills. Life.

We'd get all these extra eggs in the Italian Market, day-old rolls. Heaps of pork roll.

long pause

I'd um....make breakfast for a lot of my classmates. Became a ritual. Breakfast sandwiches, sometimes cut up hoagies at lunch.

I got pretty popular for a while too.

What?

What do you mean, what happened?

I'm still popular. Or was. Whatever.

It wasn't about that, though, you know? Being popular. Or well-liked. It was about the food. It was about bringing everyone together. It was about helping my community, something my parents did nearly every day with their restaurant before it was taken away from them.

The food truck, it's not just about me.

It's about showing up for people.

chapter eleven:
jordan

Tuesday, Five Days until Truck Off

Leaning against the cool steel of my food truck, I stare down at my phone and dodge the camera that's getting closer to me. My eyes flit up toward Frank, the cameraman who has been following me nearly all day, and he sucks a bit of air through his teeth, irritated.

"You gotta avoid looking—"

"Looking at the camera, I know," I interrupt, and he ambles off.

Cindy: Hey can we talk tonight?

Jordan: You make it sound like I'm in trouble ;-)

Cindy: Shut up. There's just a lot on my mind

Cindy: I could use the alone time, together

Jordan: Same. My dad said some wild things during the thing where they record you talking to the camera

Cindy: It's called a confessional

Jordan: Yeah, well it definitely was one

Texting with Cindy feels like an impossibility, with these reality show folks leering over my shoulder and breathing down my neck. At least when Frank and the on-site producer, Kory, decide to follow Steve around for a little while, I can get some time to myself. Though I absolutely overheard Kory muttering something about installing cameras in the food truck.

That's gonna be a hard pass for me.

Kory looks a bit older than the woman who roped us into all of this, Bethany, and has this... I don't know, just this look that tells me he's been at this a long time. His eyes are a little tired, but his face, his bone structure, makes him look like a shark.

Or a knife.

I don't trust him.

"You guys still open?"

I look up from my phone at two tipsy guys, who glance from me to the truck and back in a constant motion, like they can just teleport me inside of it with their eyes. I'll admit, it is a bit early to be wrapping up—and for these two to be as drunk as they are—but I don't want to miss Laura's show tonight at Cousin Charles, a music café across town. And I'd prefer to not show up smelling like cooking oil and onions, so I wanna swing by home first to change clothes.

"Sorry, gents." I shrug. "Closing early for a family event."

"Oh no, sorry, bro. Who died?" one asks, leaning over a little too much. His arm juts out just in time to catch his fall, and he supports himself against the truck.

"No...no one..." I grimace, taking a step back when he starts moaning. "Are you gonna—"

And then he does.

Throws up all over the side of the truck.

"Sorry, man," he says, in a tone that makes him sound years younger, like he might cry. His friend pats his back. "I was having such a nice night..."

I sigh and shake my head. At least the shutter wasn't open.

"Did you get all that?"

I turn and there's Frank and Kory, standing close to one another, grinning as they watch the camera's monitor.

"You bet," Frank says.

There's a pause as they watch a little screen on the camera, and then the two of them immediately start cracking up. Kory slaps Frank's back.

"Roll it again, roll it again," Kory says, swiping at a tear streaking down his face.

"Hey," I snap. "Are you two gonna help clean this up?"

"Well...no... I..." Frank stammers.

"Then let's not celebrate in front of me, alright?" I catch a glimpse of Dad walking down the sidewalk. He waves to me, excitedly, and Frank turns the camera to focus on him as he approaches.

Dad looks across the street, at the Ortiz food truck. It's been pretty quiet here today, since Cindy's been working at the farm to get some footage for the show. Her mother is working the truck, and when she catches my dad's line of sight, she gives him the finger.

He gives her the finger back and turns to me, smiling.

It's funny, a week ago that would have felt pretty normal. Part of the show our families put on. But now, thinking about his confessional during the taping at the house, I wonder how much truth there is here.

I wonder what he's thinking as he looks at the truck that was almost his.

Ours.

"Hey. There. Champ?" Dad says, and it's hard not to laugh, his awkwardness bringing me right back from my worry. His tone is…weirdly robotic and mechanical, and I can tell he's not used to being on cameras at all. He managed fine during the interview at home, but right now, out here in public, he's navigating it like one of those animatronic machines at a theme park. His motions are all jittery, and his eyes keep flitting up between me and the camera. Even him giving the finger across the square looked off. I really thought he was going to be good at this. He's such a showman in all other aspects of his life.

"Are you. Ready to. Uh. Head home?" he asks, and awkwardly turns toward Passyunk, away from the truck, waving me over with his arm in a perfect right angle.

I dump out another bottle of water on the street, and walk after him, the cameraman behind me groaning. And I definitely hear the sound of Kory's palm smacking his own forehead. I take a few quick hurried steps ahead of them to catch up with Dad.

"Dad, you gotta like, loosen up," I say, shaking my shoulders about.

"Sorry." He chuckles, clearing his throat. "This is harder than I thought. Cameras all the time."

"Yeah." I swallow. "Same."

"It's okay, kiddo." He reaches out and grabs my shoulder. "You're a Plazas. You're built for challenges." He let's go and we continue along the sidewalk, heading toward Broad.

"Here's a challenge for you," I say. "Can we get the truck washed?"

"What?!" Dad scoffs. "We don't move the truck, Jordan."

"Well..." I shrug. "That's not entirely true. We do for festivals, and you know, we will this weekend for Truck Off. It would be nice if it was clean for that."

"Ugh, you and that contest," Dad grumbles. "Fine, fine. I'll find a day to give it a good power wa—"

"Not with a power washer in front of the house, at an actual car wash," I interrupt.

He glares at me. "Okay."

We turn up Broad when Dad stops and looks off in another direction.

"Hey," he says. "Let's take another route." He smiles warmly. "The old one."

"Sure—"

But then it hits me like a lightning bolt.

The diner. The Stateside. Our former second home that's really just under a mile away in the direction toward home. The old route.

Does he know? Has he seen it?

I look over my shoulder at the cameraman.

Oh no. I can't let Dad get caught on camera seeing all of that for the first time.

"Actually, you know, Dad, why don't we just head straight to Laura's show?" I ask, stopping. "We could grab an ice cream or something, I don't really need to pick anything up from home or—"

"Nonsense." Dad waves me off. "You smell like a bad night out at Jim's and you've got throw-up on your shoes."

I look down at my feet. He's not wrong.

"Come on. I'm in the mood to reminisce." He keeps walking.

Oh no.

No, no, no.

I hustle to catch up and when I do, he wraps an arm around my shoulder, giving me a little side hug. He always has to reach up a bit to do this, so I lean down. He sighs loudly and clears his throat.

"About your plans…" Dad starts, and I can physically feel my expression darken. He lets go of my shoulder and tussles my hair. "I *know*. Me and Mom haven't been the most…supportive. With your food truck goals and the upcoming competition and those… breakfast cheesesteaks you're making."

He gives me a look and shrugs.

"They're creative, I'll give you that," he continues, and I can't help the sigh of relief. "But we are here for you. Whatever you choose, we'll be on board, even if we're still a little pushy about what we want. That's the whole dynamic of being a good parent. I think."

"Dad, we don't have to talk about this now," I say, the words rushing out of my mouth. I force myself to look ahead and not stare back at the cameras.

"Please, it's fine. And it's not like it's some grand secret that I want you to go to college." Dad laughs. "I've got nothing to hide."

We turn a corner, heading up Broad Street.

"Have you thought about it at all?" he asks, interrupting the quiet lull we'd just fallen into. City hall looms in the distance at the end of the large main street, cars zooming up and down, buses roaring. My heart hammers. Just two more blocks, and he'll be able to see the diner.

"No...not really, Dad." I shrug. "It's just...not for me."

"You can run your own food truck *while* going to college, you know," he presses. "We'd even help pay for the truck. Go to county, enroll in some classes. Maybe the Culinary Institute with Steve!"

"Dad, please, even *you* hate that place." I can't help but chuckle at the thought.

"Listen, if that's what it took, we'd love for you to go there. You can learn to make wildly expensive, pointless desserts out of sugar glass or frozen air or whatever the hell Steve does. It can't be too late. Don't they have rolling admission?"

"Dad, I just can't do more classrooms, no matter where it is." I sigh. One more block. The condo that rises ahead of The Stateside is coming into focus, and in a few more steps, in half a block, we're going to be able to spot the fence and the parking lot. "I feel like I learned everything I needed from...well, you and Mom. About food. Talking to people. Running a truck."

"But what if the truck doesn't work out?" Dad says. "You need to have a backup plan."

"Dad, I'm not going to Hollywood to be an actor or trying to make it as a rock musician," I point out. "It's a food truck. I want to run a food truck, and maybe have my own restaurant someday."

He looks at me, his eyes lighting up.

"*Maybe*," I stress. "Or maybe I'll write about the kind of food I make. I don't know. But my place isn't in a classroom learning…algebra or calculus or…"

I look around, but Dad is suddenly gone.

I stop and turn back, and he's standing still on the sidewalk. Staring across the street. The cameras are on him, and I can see where his line of sight is focused.

The Stateside.

It's right across the street. We were talking and I wasn't paying attention and—

It's worse now.

The other day, it was just the signs and the broken fence, the boarded windows and all that. But now…there are construction vehicles in the ruined parking lot. A bulldozer, a crane with a wrecking ball on the ground. There are a few workers milling around, near the vehicles and fence, talking to one another or staring at phones.

"Dad—" I start.

"It's time, isn't it?" Dad asks, his eyes flitting over to mine. He closes them for a second, and a lone tear trails down his cheek. He shakes his head and inhales sharply, like he's trying to suck that tear back into his eye. He glances back at the cameras and then at me. "Jordan, I don't know if I can do this," he says, his voice breaking.

"Dad, it's okay, you don't have to, let's just go home—"

"Mr. Plazas, if I may…" Kory says, walking over toward us from where he's been trailing behind Frank.

He waves at Frank, who sets his gear down, looking relieved and thankful for a break. He plucks out a cigarette and lights it in a practiced motion that almost borders on a magic trick.

"In our earlier footage, you brought so much power and vulnerability to our potential viewers," Kory starts. "Talking about how you felt losing this place, digging into the rivalry with the Ortiz family, how they took that truck out from under you."

He looks at the diner and then back at us. "I can see why it was so special."

He smiles and I want to punch him in his sharp face, but Dad seems to warm up.

"Let's just take a minute," Kory continues, "and sit with some of these feelings. Maybe we can walk over to the diner, find out what's going on. Capture the place and its…well, final days. Isn't it worth having that on film, forever?"

"Yeah," Dad says, surprising me. "Yeah, I think you're right, let's go."

A flash of heat rushes up my back. How can Dad not see that he's just being…manipulated by this guy?! Is this how these shows work, producers poking and prodding folks into whatever situation they want? But before I can even properly object, Dad's hurrying across the street thanks to a lull in traffic. I rush after him, and based on the worn-out grunts

I can hear behind me, Frank has hoisted his gear back up to follow us.

Dad immediately slows down once he hits the sidewalk, like a character in a film moving in slow motion.

"Mr. Plazas, how are you feeling?" Kory asks immediately, before I can protest again.

"So, this is really it," Dad says, his voice something of a whisper, echoing what he said earlier. He looks so heartbroken, and I'm filled with rage that these people who don't know him are taking advantage of him in this way.

I'm going to have to talk to Cindy tonight, maybe after Laura's show.

This isn't going to work. I'm not gonna be able to do this. Not with these people.

Maybe...maybe we can just hit the road earlier than planned. I've got a decent amount saved up from tips. I won't be able to afford the best truck in the world, definitely not something like Big Red, but it would get us out of here. Out of this. Neither of us really *has* to work the entire summer.

"You know, when you were younger..." Dad begins, and I can tell he's launching into a *thing*. Whenever he has a family story to tell, there are a lot of pauses, a lot of long looks. It's one of the reasons why I thought he might actually do okay with this whole *Cheesesteak Wars* thing, but so far, every time he's tried to fake his way through, he's been mechanical and robotic.

But when he's leading with how he actually feels...everything seems so real.

Maybe there's a lesson in that.

"Your mom and I couldn't really afford a babysitter when

we first took over the place." He walks closer to the fence, catching the brief attention of the construction workers before they look away again. "So this was it. In you'd go, running around the place on your little legs, bumping into tables and chairs and people. You had more bruises on your cheeks and forehead and arms than I can count." He laughs a little. "It wasn't great, but I think it toughened you up a little."

He glances over at me, a wistful smile on his face.

"I'm sorry, Dad, I should have told you when I saw the signs," I say, nudging against him.

"Ah, I knew," he replies, throwing an arm around me. "I saw it in the neighborhood Facebook groups, that it was coming down. Nothing to be done. But seeing it in person…"

He sighs, but it's more of a shudder. And I think he might really start to cry. I want to scream at Frank to turn the camera off, but I'm frozen to the spot.

"Your mom was right, earlier, you know," Dad continues. "Home isn't a place, it's the people around you. I'll miss seeing it here but…we've got the memories. All the restaurateurs we touched throughout the city will remember where they got their start and talk about our little place for years. It'll live on, in its own way."

"Should we…" I look at the construction equipment, at the people there in the parking lot. "I don't know, ask if we can go inside or something?"

"I don't want to think about what it looks like in there. Dusty and broken." He taps the side of his head and smiles at me. "I like how it looks in here a lot better. The day we left it behind. Still clean from the final dinner. You remember that?"

I chuckle. How could I forget?

"It's the only time I've ever seen you try to make a lobster."
I smirk, and Dad emits a loud belly laugh, swiping at a tear.
Everyone knows you never get the lobster at a diner, doesn't
matter if they say it's a specialty. You just don't.

But everyone was there. Our family, neighborhood friends,
a lot of them from the bars and restaurants and coffee shops
in the area. I remember sitting at a back table with Steve and
Laura, the three of us all in eighth grade, sipping coffee and
trying to be cool. Mom and Dad tried to cook every single
thing left in the freezer. God, the meals were piled up so high
and just kept coming out of the kitchen, with lines sprawling out of the diner.

Afterward, Dad took me out to a soup kitchen in West
Philly, where he kept serving people food from the diner.
Mom told me later it was because he didn't want to watch the
diner empty out one last time. Well, that and doing something good for our community.

Dad starts to sniffle but waves me off when I turn to him,
concerned. "It's okay," he says. "We'll make more memories
somewhere else. And we've still got all those little mementos.
The terrible diner art framed in the bathroom. The toaster
your mom hates, that burns everything. And the shame bell,
of course."

"The bell?" An image of Steve ringing it madly outside the
truck this past weekend flashes through my mind.

"Used to hang above the window where servers would grab
food," Dad says, looking wistful. "When it was extra busy,
the cook would ring it when plates were good to go. I hung
it up in the truck to remember all that." He smirks. "And to
shame some people for mushrooms."

That's where the bell is from.

I hadn't connected the dots. Now I like it even more.

Dad takes out his phone to snap a few photos, but the fence is in the way. He takes a few steps forward and angles the phone into the chain link, trying to line up a photo in one of the holes. But the phone tumbles out of his hand.

"Ah, dammit," he mutters, picking it up, and the screen is completely shattered. A picture of the diner is there, though, the cracks in the screen making it look like the diner is breaking apart.

He sputters out a sob and is suddenly hunched over his phone, crying. He grabs at the chain-link fence, like it's the only thing holding him upright.

"Dad…" I start, feeling helpless.

"It's okay." He lets go, sniffles and wipes at his face. "Can't believe I broke my phone. Stupid, so stupid." He crams it in his pocket and starts to walk in the direction of home.

"Dad!" I call, but he doesn't stop, and I can see him still wiping at his face.

I hear footsteps rushing, and I reel around to see Kory and Frank hurrying after my father, camera still rolling.

"Hey!" I shout, blocking their path on the sidewalk.

"Come on, kid—" Kory starts, looking like he's gonna run me over.

"Are you happy?!" I snap, and he backs down a little.

But in the way that he glances at Frank, it's very clear that they are.

chapter twelve: cindy

Tuesday, Five Days until Truck Off

Mom always likes to joke that I treat my phone like it's burning a hole in my pocket since I take it out all the time, a quip that frequently annoys me.

But right now, I feel like I finally get it. I can't stop looking at the Northeastern email. I keep sliding my phone in and out of my pocket as I walk home, like that email isn't real. Like I dreamed it up, and I have to check to make sure it's still there.

By the time I get to my house, my battery is practically drained. I look at the front door, and exhale, centering myself. I need to tell my parents, tell the producers, and tell Jordan. Keep it all under control.

I reach for the door just as it swings open, and I stumble into my own home, colliding into my mom. She wraps her arms around me, with an "oof" and laughs in my ear.

"Hey, sweetheart," she says, steadying us both and pulling back. "You're home early, is your dad still at the…whoa, whoa, whoa…what's wrong?"

She's staring at me intently, and that's when I realize I'm crying. She wipes away a tear on my cheek.

"Darling? What is it?" she asks again, her voice sounding more urgent.

I laugh, palming the tears off my face.

"It's okay, they're good tears," I say. "I got… I got into Northeastern. I'm off the wait list."

There's a pause as surprise washes over her face, and I watch as her expression shifts from shock to joy to joining me in crying. She pulls me in tight.

"I'm so proud of you," she says, letting me go and stepping back. She nods her head toward the inside of the house. "Cameras are here, come on."

Oh. Okay. Well, looks like I can maybe strike that second thing off the to-do sheet.

"We were just wrapping up one of those confessional videos, where I talk to the camera and all that?" Mom says, excitement bubbling off of her as we walk into the living room. "Can you believe it? Me. Doing those talks to the camera like…like I'm one of those Housewives we watch."

She laughs giddily, and swipes at a tear under her eye, looking back at me with warmth.

I glance over at the camera crew.

They're absolutely filming.

"So," Mom starts, sitting on the couch and motioning for me to join. "What happened to your gap year? Your county college plans? Have you told—" She clearly stops herself be-

fore she says *Jordan*, thank God. "Have you mentioned anything to your friends?"

"Not yet, I thought...maybe it would be fun to break the
news to them on our next recording, you know? Or maybe
I will tonight. I don't know." I shake my head. This is good,
sharing this with her, but I'm not sure this is the thing I
wanted to get off my chest right now. I was hoping to get
her advice on how I'm supposed to tell Jordan. His big plans
for our road trip, and really, our relationship, are hanging in
the balance there.

But because of these cameras, because of this show, I can't.

I don't really have to wonder how much the reality stars I
watch hold back from the shows they're on. I know it's a lot.
Massive scandals somehow happen off camera, away from the
viewers, only to come out later in hugely embarrassing ways.

Are me and Jordan going to become that kind of scandal
if the truth comes out? Will our whole families come under
fire?

Have I...not totally thought all of this through?

"Well, it's a reason to celebrate, that's for sure," Mom says,
grabbing my hand.

"You're not mad?" I ask.

"Mad?!" she laughs. "Why would I be?"

"Well, you know, it would mean I'm moving," I say, gazing down at our hands. "Back to Boston. Away from you and
Dad and the truck and the farm and, you know...the potential of this show..."

"Cindy, Cindy..." Mom says, squeezing my hand and stopping me from unraveling. "We both know your heart is there,
studying what you want to study. It's what, four hours on the

Amtrak to get to Boston from here? I'm not worried about it. And it's a city you've been in and know. It's not like you're jet-setting off to LA or something." She pauses with a smirk. "Not yet at least."

Mom stands up and claps her hands together. "Okay, we should find a way to celebrate tonight." She smiles.

But a shock zaps through my system.

Tonight. Laura's show.

How am I supposed to have a heart-to-heart with Jordan about Northeastern when I'm supposed to give the camera crew that splash of drama they've been asking for?

I guess the conversation can wait but... I just feel the anxiety building in my chest. And there's no way I can tell him just via a text message. He's going to be devastated.

"I, uh... I can't, I'm going to a local concert. Couple people from school are going to be there, thought it might be fun."

"Oh!" Mom exclaims. "Well, okay. Tomorrow, then. Do you want me to tell Dad, or do you want to wait to let him know?"

"Let's surprise him together." I smile, and so does she. I lunge into a hug, and Mom laughs.

This is good.

This is going to be good. It won't hurt to hold off on telling Jordan until tomorrow. I can still navigate all of this.

"I'm gonna go change." I gesture at my farm-stained jeans and shirt before hurrying upstairs. The sound of Mom talking to the camera guys echoes up the steps after me.

By the time I come back to the living room, there's a new voice chatting in the living room.

"Hey, Cindy."

He smirks.

Runs his hand through his thick sandy-blond hair.

It's Jared.

Jared takes a seat in front of me, placing two mugs of hot chocolate on the table before us. The atmosphere at Wark's, a café not too far from the place Jordan and his friends are going to be at later, is warm and cozy, a sharp contrast to where the founder of this place came from.

Buffalo.

There are all kinds of Upstate New York kitsch decorating the space: big, beautiful illustrations of Lake Erie, vintage bottles of hot sauce, an old-timey sign for a place called "Mighty Taco," pictures of pine trees. It weirdly makes the space feel like it should be cold, but instead, the heat is always blasting in here.

"So…" Jared says, leaning forward, smiling. I notice there's a dimple that collapses into the corner of his mouth. For some reason, that detail makes a swarm of butterflies take off in my stomach.

What is happening. What am I doing here?

"So." I shrug, taking a sip of the hot chocolate to distract myself. I sigh loudly and slap a hand over my mouth, embarrassed, but Jared laughs kindly. I forgot how this place just overloads their hot cocoa with a staggering amount of syrup. It's perfect.

This was one of my safe spots with Jordan, where no one from school visited. I mean, it's a café themed around a city that isn't Philadelphia. Not even anyone in the food community would set foot here. It was a refuge.

Until it wasn't.

Two juniors at school landed jobs here in the spring. I haven't been back since, and it feels more than a little strange sitting across from Jared right now.

"Are you doing okay?" he asks. "You know, with the show and all? I know Bethany... Ms. Ireland, she can be kinda intense. But the crew, the camera guys, they're all good people. Even some of the executives are pretty nice..."

"Oh yeah?" I ask skeptically. "They didn't even know your name when I was in your office."

"I mean, I did say *some*." He smirks, and there's a silent beat between us at the table. The Goo Goo Dolls come on over the café's speakers, reminding me just how Buffalo this place is, and also how overly romantic this situation is starting to feel.

"Jared, what...what are we doing here?" I ask, feeling my cheeks flush a little. I should be figuring out how to break my college news to Jordan, but instead I'm killing time with some other boy before creating pointless drama at Laura's café concert.

A very cute boy whose eyes are just awash with concern for me.

Who also doesn't know that I'm hiding something from him.

"We're just, you know, having a coffee. Waiting for the crew to shoot at that music place." He smiles and I squint at him, and he deflates a little. "I'm sorry, it's just..." He sighs and gazes around the room for a minute before settling his eyes on me.

"I love reality television," he says, a small smile cracking on his face. "And I know you do too. I, um...had a bit of a fanboy moment when you came in the office last week. I've been listening to that podcast of yours for like a year now."

"What?" I gasp, and again, feel myself blushing a bit. "You're kidding?"

"Nope, totally serious. I felt like you three really hit your stride around like... I don't know, ten episodes in?"

"Yeah, those first few were just us talking."

"But afterward!" Jared exclaims. "You had the commentary on social media stuff, the things you found on Reddit—you figured out a structure. Reading listener emails and their theories at the end of every episode? Love it." He grins. "I dunno...not to be weird or anything, but listening to your show, I felt like I met someone who really got me."

Oh my God, my face must be bright red. Jordan can't really be bothered with the podcast, even though it's something I pour so much of my time into. I mean, sure, reality shows and the drama around them aren't really his thing, but then again, a yearlong road trip in a food truck isn't exactly mine. Yet I've been all-in, for him.

Why can't he be all-in for me?

"I couldn't believe my luck that the girl who ran that cheesesteak truck near Passyunk was the same person on the podcast I listened to every single week... I just had to get to know you. I kinda pleaded with Bethany to let me work on *Cheesesteak Wars* with her."

"Really?" I ask, my heart fluttering a little in my chest.

"Yeah." He shrugs. "So...there's my awkward confession. And I didn't even tell you how many listener emails I've sent the show."

"Oh my God," I laugh, tucking a wild curl behind my ear.

"I'm just, well, a huge fan. Maybe have a...slightly huge crush. And I'd just...like to get to know you better some-time."

He pauses, looking down into his coffee and then back up at me.

"Is there...a someone?" he asks, worrying at his lip in the same way that I do when I'm anxious. It's terribly cute.

But then his question registers.

Oh.

Am I really about to lie to him? Am I...doing this because I need to keep up the feud for the show, or because there's something about him that I feel wildly drawn to?

What would Jordan want me to do here?

That's probably the wrong question. He'd tell me to for-get about the show, maybe flip over this coffee table, declare it all a lie, and run right into his arms. But it's more compli-cated than that. This show, there's all this potential to help our families. To help Jordan fund his truck.

The one I'm not going to be traveling in.

What is it that... *I* want?

"No." I shake my head, a spike of anxiety rushing through me at the lie. "I'm just...too busy with the truck and the pod-cast and all that. It takes up a lot of time."

"I get it," he says. "It's my first year at Drexel, and this internship has been a lot. I thought I'd get the summer off but that is not the case. 'You don't get days off from reality,' Bethany always says. I heard you're going to Northeastern?"

"Yeah. I'm excited. They have a great program there for television and media." God, I can't believe I haven't told Jor-dan yet, and here I am telling Jared. I wish all these cameras would just leave us alone for an hour so I could talk to him. To Jordan. Oh God.

Between Jordan and Jared and my future and the show… it just feels like a lot all at once. How do reality stars do this? Hide so much? Constantly hedge what they're saying depending on who is listening.

"That's awesome," Jared says. "It's too bad you're not staying here. I'd have…liked to try to hang out sometime. There's a great television production program at Drexel. Penn too."

"We can still hang out." I shrug, but immediately want to put my hands over my mouth. What am I saying? This boy has a crush on me. "Sometime."

"I'd like that a lot. I really would," he says. "That concert tonight, the one where your cheesesteak rival is gonna be. Is it far from here?"

"No, no, it's just a few blocks up Walnut." I glance outside the front window to the café, it's definitely dark out now.

"Great," he says, getting up and grabbing his jacket. "I'll message Drew. Let's go make some television."

Pilot: Confessional Shot Transcript (Jordan)

Jordan: I feel like everyone has friends that other people insist have to get together. Like, they're just too perfect for one another to not wind up in love. When I was really little, my parents and Laura's parents would sometimes joke about the two of us getting married. And we'd laugh and talk about how gross that all was. Because it was. It is—that's just not us.

It's not me she's had her eyes on all this time. And after tonight, I think all that talk from our family will change.

What's going on?

Oh, you'll see. It's going to be a perfect evening.

chapter thirteen: jordan

Tuesday, Five Days until Truck Off

I exhale as I step out of the SEPTA subway and into the West Philadelphia evening. It never really matters what time or day of the week it is, it's always busy up here, and not because of tourists. It's all students, from Penn or Drexel, out enjoying the nightlife or studying or whatever it is college students with dorms do when they've got that first big taste of freedom.

I mean, I've watched movies and read books. I know what happens.

But I don't really see the freedom in it. All that student loan debt if you didn't get good enough grades to nab a scholarship, or if your family is in that weird position where you can afford college, but you actually can't, because _life_. I'm not quite sure what I need a degree for when the things I already know how to do—drive a truck and handle a short order grill—are what I need for my career.

Still, a part of me wonders if I'm missing out on anything, as I see a bunch of people so close to my age walking down the sidewalk with their arms linked, laughing. Steve's going to do so well at the Culinary Institute in Center City. I know Laura will too, up at Arcadia in Glenside.

And maybe I should be making more of an effort to stay here. With my friends.

Would Cindy be happier if we stayed? Instead of doing the whole gap year thing?

I need to talk to her about it. Maybe tonight, after Laura's show, like she said.

I hurry past restaurants and pubs that are overflowing, dimly lit coffee shops that still have people reading and talking inside, despite the fact that it's nearly 10 p.m. Cousin Charles, the café Laura is playing at tonight, comes into view pretty quickly, tucked away between a small rare bookshop, Azantian's, and a microbrewery.

A chalkboard sign sits outside, advertising tonight's show. Acoustic Night! in big white outlined lettering, a list of names below. Thankfully Laura is closer to the beginning, because Cindy wants to talk tonight, and I still gotta keep testing out the breakfast cheesesteaks for the festival. It's this weekend. The clock is ticking.

Steve knows it as much as I do. There's something not quite right about the cheesebreaks yet. People are inhaling them in the morning, but something still feels like it's missing. Something to really push them over the top.

I'll figure it out.

I nudge open the door to Cousin Charles. It's this heavy, old wooden thing, probably as ancient as the building itself.

So many of the structures in West Philadelphia are over two hundred years old and still standing.

The door nearly slams behind me as I make my way inside, music blasting over the café speakers. I recognize the voice and the chords almost instantly. It's impossible not to, considering Laura plays Dashboard Confessional all the time. I wonder if she's doing covers tonight or—

"Jordan!" Laura shouts and barrels into me. I stumble back and something collides with my face. The end of her soft guitar case, slung over her shoulder. "Ha! Oops, sorry are you okay?"

"I'm fine, it's fine," I laugh. "Anyone else here yet?"

"Just… Steve," Laura says, curtly. Her eyes drop down at the floor.

"Hey," I say, reaching up and grabbing her shoulder. "It's gonna go great."

"Yeah, we'll see." She glances back toward the inside of the café. It's a cute place, big snuggly couches and large wooden tables lined up with multiple chairs, big enough to fit maybe two dozen people all at once. There are a few folks sitting at individual tables and lounging back in small sofas, but for the most part, it seems like everyone is situated closer to the small stage.

Laura's eyes widen as she takes in the crowd. "Ugh, okay. I'm gonna get some air," she says before rushing for the exit.

"Hey—" I start.

"It's okay, I'm okay!" she exclaims without turning. Her guitar case *thunks* against a table, and then against the doorframe, and just like that, she's out.

I know her though. She'll be back.

I make my way toward the stage. It's not like being at a concert, like any of the shows I've gone to with Cindy over the last year. Like at Fillmore or the TLA, catching Motion City Soundtrack and All Time Low in a dark venue, splashes of red, blue, and purple dancing across our faces in the dark to the sound of power chords and synthesizers. Where we could be together and invisible. Where our relationship could be kept a secret, to protect the rivalry or whatever.

I'm so tired of it. I want to be someplace like this. Bright lights, holding hands in front of everyone. Will we even be able to do any of that with the show happening? If it actually takes off?

I nudge my way through a few people my age and find an open couch, a small table in front of it. I shrug off my jacket and sit down, just in time for Steve to spot me. He's not hard to miss, considering he's about a head taller than everyone else here. He quickly weaves around everyone.

"Hey!" he shouts and leaps onto the couch like it's a piece of furniture at his house. The whole thing shakes and I swear I almost fly off it like we're on a seesaw in a playground.

"Dude!"

"Sorry!" he laughs, reaching an arm around to give me a strong side hug, squeezing the hell out of me. "You doing okay? How are you holding up? Where are the cameras?"

"Eh, they didn't think this was going to be particularly interesting." I shrug. "Acoustic guitar open mic night in front of a few dozen people from school? Not exactly reality television gold."

"I dunno, Laura's pretty great," Steve says, looking up toward the stage, as if she's already there. I can't help but smile.

"Where's your dad?" Steve asks, turning back to me. "I thought the whole family was coming out."

"Oh yeah, he…" I exhale. "He saw the diner." Steve's expression drops. "He knew it was coming, but he hadn't seen it in person yet, you know? They got it all on camera too."

"Oof." Steve shakes his head. "That's rough. I'm sorry."

"It's alright. I wonder when Laura is going on—"

The speakers in the café screech, and I swear I can feel a collective wince from everyone in the crowd, as they all turn to the small stage at the same time. The stage isn't much, I mean, this is a coffeehouse, but there's still a somewhat decent sound system and pretty lights that cast everything in a soft glow.

"Okay, okay!" a voice says, and someone walks onto the stage—I'm guessing the MC for the evening. "Welcome to Acoustic Night here at Cousin Charles. It's pretty simple. Each performer gets a ten-minute set on the open mic, two songs, and then right into the next person. What you do with that time is up to you, but ideally, you're playing music. First up is the one and only Emily Anders!"

There's a smattering of applause as a red-haired girl takes the stage with a black acoustic guitar in her hands. She looks a bit nervous as the MC adjusts the microphone on its stand before scurrying off, leaving her staring wide-eyed out to the audience.

"Um, hi, I'm Emily…" She bumps the mic with her chin, and there's a small bit of reverb. She laughs nervously, and the crowd laughs with her. It's all kinds of wholesome. This isn't the sort of place where you're going to get a bunch of boos for little hiccups. "Sorry, I'm Emily Anders, and well, this is 'September' by Neck Deep."

There's a collective murmur of approval, and she launches into a cover of the pop punk song that's breathy and beautiful. I lean back on the couch and can practically feel Steve sigh as he does the same, and, wow, this is good.

I'm so glad those cameras aren't here to ruin this.

She launches into the chorus, and a few people start singing along, some are waving their phones in the air, bright blue light casting a glow around the room.

"Hey, Jordan!"

I look up, and there are a few kids from school standing near me, right to the side of the couch. They're from my graduating class, but no one I'd really consider actual friends. I've been to their house parties, but I couldn't tell you the name of any of their siblings or whatever.

"How's the truck, man?" Kyle, a guy I remember from honors English, asks. Maureen, his girlfriend, is leaning against his shoulder. They were up for prom king and queen, but I'm not actually sure who won. I left prom early. Probably was them though. They're cute.

Prom though. I just couldn't stand not being able to talk to Cindy.

Not being able to dance with her.

"It's good!" I reply, trying to speak loud enough so they can hear me, but I don't want to talk over the girl on stage either. "Rolling out some new things for the big festival this weekend."

"Oh yeah, I heard about that," Maureen says, turning to Kyle. "We *have* to go."

"What is it?" Kyle asks.

"Food trucks," I say. "Right over in Camden along the waterfront. Bunch from all over are gonna roll in. Some trucks from New York even."

"Oh, cool." Kyle's attention immediately wavers.

Sometimes I forget that, like, food truck culture isn't something most people are even remotely into. Cindy barely gets excited about it, and she *works* in one. Whenever I gush to Steve about a new truck I've come across or one going viral on social media because of a new creation, his eyes glaze over a little bit too. His heart isn't really in it the way mine is—he's focused on inventing wild new flavors using food chemistry or whatever. For him, the truck is a fun way to hang out and make extra money, and that's okay.

It's fine. It's not their world.

But you know, they could *pretend* a little bit.

Hell, I'm pretending all week for this reality show pilot. Our families have been pretending since right before we entered high school—at least, I think they have. I still haven't quite processed the whole food truck purchase drama that Dad unleashed on the cameras. How much of that was real? And when did it shift from... I don't know, real to a playful act to garner more business? And I've been pretending for over a year now to not be dating Cindy, even though she's the only person I want to be with at any given moment. Even though we're in love.

Well, I'm in love. I think Cindy feels the same. Maybe?

Why can't anyone just pretend a little bit, for me?

"You and Cindy still fighting?" Maureen asks, which snaps Kyle's attention right back. People at school were always far more interested in the faux rivalry than, like, the actual trucks or us as people.

"Yeah, you know, the rivalry burns bright." I shrug.

Steve chuckles and I shoot him a look.

"She's just the worst," Kyle says, rolling his eyes. "I saw how she carried herself around school, thinking she's better than us because she's from Boston."

"I...don't know about all that." I try to laugh a little to diffuse the tension, and Steve nudges me. Fine. I probably shouldn't be defending Cindy, but I don't like the way Kyle's talking about her.

"How did you deal with being in that truck all day, seeing her across the park? At least school is over and you don't have to worry about that anymore," Kyle continues.

"Yeah, well, I *like* my truck, thanks," I grumble, trying to steer the conversation away from Cindy.

"Oh no, I mean of course," Kyle says. "But I bet you'd enjoy it a lot more without that...that...what's the word for, like, a girl who just complains all the time? We read that Shakespeare play..."

"Shrew?" I mutter.

"Yes! *Shrew.*" Kyle snaps his fingers.

This is why you did so bad in English, Kyle.

"Yeah, I don't think I'd go that far," I nearly growl, and Steve is full-on glaring at me now. Trying to tell me not to blow it. But what's it matter? The cameras aren't here. School is out. I'll probably never see these two again once summer is over. Hell, once this little coffee shop concert is over.

"Whatever, this is a safe space, man." Kyle reaches out and

punches my shoulder in a harmless bro-y way. "Are you still doing that road trip after the summer? With the truck?"

"Well, yeah, but I'm buying my own truck. My parents are gonna keep the current one at—"

"We can't let that bitch win, am I right?!" Kyle shouts.

I jump to my feet.

"You need to stop talking about her like that!" I yell, leaning into him.

It's then I realize the room has gone completely silent.

My heart sinks in my chest, and it feels like the air was just sucked out of the room.

"Dude," Steve whispers.

Everyone. I mean *everyone* is looking at me.

I glance at the empty stage—Emily's set must have just ended. Of course, I chose to scream at this guy when the entire café had gone mostly quiet.

"What do you care?" Kyle asks, hands raised in front of him. He and Maureen are both peering at me, clearly confused. "That girl makes your life hell. I've seen it on social media. At school. Screw her, man."

Before I can lunge at him, Steve's hand is on my shoulder.

The pressure is just enough to calm me down.

He knows me.

"Don't," Steve says.

"Ohhhhh-kay," a voice chimes in over the café's speakers. The MC has returned to the stage, and he's looking around, grimacing in a playful way while nodding at me. Kyle sucks at his teeth and he and Maureen tuck into the small crowd. "It's time for our next performer of the evening. Everyone give it up for Laura Lim!"

There's a smattering of polite applause, but Steve goes absolutely ballistic.

I cheer with him, but I want to just sink into this chair and disappear. I'm just…so angry. I can't even defend my girlfriend. Between Dad's breakdown outside the diner and now all this, I'm having a hard time feeling like any of this is worth it.

Cindy really wants this though.

And despite all the conflict brewing in my chest, I gotta keep pushing forward.

I've watched Laura take the stage before. She's played at a few coffeehouses here and there, and at our school's various talent shows and a battle of the bands. But right now, on the stage, I swear she looks like a different person.

She's up there with a tight pair of what look like pleather pants—I know there's no way they are real leather—paired with a purposefully ripped band T-shirt fraying along the edges. The group The Summer Set in a bold, neon font across the front. She looks like a real performer, like the girl who plays covers outside my truck is completely gone.

"Hi, I'm Laura. And this one…well, he should know it's for him."

My heart catches in my chest, suddenly nervous for my best friend.

She's finally going to say it out loud.

She closes her eyes.

And rings out a chord.

I know, I know
You see a lot, a lot.

But what about me?
How much longer do I have to be stronger
And stand here, looking at you the way that I do
To see that flash
Flash
Of understanding in your eyes
When you finally see me?
There are friends who are close
And then there's whatever this is
Leaving me wondering
When I can be yours.

There's another verse in there, but it's lost on me. Because I can't stop looking at Steve.

I watch as Steve's eyes stay focused on Laura, go wide, and then his warm, supportive smile turns into the absolute goofiest grin I have ever seen on his face. It's like one of those TikTok videos where someone says they've written a song for their best friend, and play it in the car, capturing their surprise on camera. Not entirely sure I buy into all of them, but standing here, right now, maybe there's some truth there.

Maybe I should believe in magical moments more often.

Steve grabs my shoulder and shakes me.

"Did you know?" he asks.

"Steve, Jesus," I laugh. "You're the only one who didn't."

He looks back at the stage, and I swear, I think he's about to cry.

Laura sings out the chorus one last time at the end of the song, and everyone in the little crowd erupts into applause—

"I *knew* it."
I whirl around.
And there's Cindy.

chapter fourteen: cindy

___

Tuesday, Five Days until Truck Off

I knew Jordan would be here.

It's his so-called best friend's concert or whatever.

But this? *This?* I don't even know what to say.

I thought this would be an easy opportunity to catch some of that rivalry on film. Yell at somebody, like Drew said. He and another cameraman are trailing behind me, and Jared is right next to me, staring right ahead, oblivious to the truth of the situation. Afterward, when the cameras were off, I was hoping we could finally talk about everything. I could tell him about school, about how I can't do the road trip, how I can't...just give up on what I want, for what he wants.

But this.

What I didn't expect was Laura to finally make tonight the night she unleashed all those feelings for Jordan in front of, what, a whole bundle of our senior class? All her friends, probably. And there's Steve, Jordan's eternal sidekick, just egging him on.

I saw him, just grabbing Jordan's shoulder, jostling him around.

Like two frat bros or something.

"Cindy," Jordan says, leaning forward on the couch. "What are you doing here?"

His eyes flit to the cameras and back to me. He looks wildly concerned. But I'm furious.

"Heard there was a little concert," I reply casually, nodding at the stage. I cross my arms, ready for our showdown. Laura's watching awkwardly, like she isn't sure whether or not she should play another song or run off the stage. "Thought I'd see what all the fuss was about."

The words feel ridiculous coming out of my mouth. Fuss? Who am I right now?

Jordan's eyes flit to the cameras again and onto Jared and back to me.

Everyone is staring at us.

"What are you *doing*?" Jordan asks through gritted teeth, and it feels like a really loaded question. He's not just asking what I'm doing here. He's asking what I'm doing with the cameras, approaching him like this far from the trucks.

"What, I can't just come to enjoy a little local music?" I ask and wave up at Laura. "I mean, you seem to be really into her."

Jordan leans into the couch and huffs.

"Is that what this is about?" He glares at the cameras. "Get out of here, turn the cameras off—"

"What?" I ask, trying to grab his focus, get him back into

our spat for the cameras. "What's so wrong with me being here and listening to an open mic? We can't be in the same room?"

He squints at me, as if trying to figure out my angle.

"Hey, we need to get a mic on you," Drew says, and I turn around to see him nudging a little microphone toward Jordan.

"Yeah, I don't think so." Jordan swats the microphone away. Drew huffs and turns to Jared, who moves toward Jordan. My heart absolutely pounds in my chest at these two so close to one another. It's not like either knows about how I feel about the other...but then again, the fact that I'm even worrying about that seems like a sizable problem. Because I definitely feel something for Jared. I can't help it. He gets what I'm so passionate about and, God, it was so nice being somewhere in public with somebody without all that fear of being caught.

That is what I want.

"Look—" Jared starts. "We need to—"

"Why don't you just leave?"

It's Kyle. I recognize him from school. His girlfriend, Maureen, is standing nearby, and they're glaring at me. Really, it feels like everyone is right now. Just staring lasers through my entire body.

"Why don't you make me?" I say, taking a step forward. Jared shifts so he's in between us, and Kyle immediately jostles back. I can't ignore how Jared just...jumped in like that, like those security guys do on every reality show when a fight is about to break out. "That's what I thought." I look back up at Laura on the stage. "Go on, keep playing."

I smile at Jordan, and he just scowls. He turns around to watch the stage, and I take a step forward, standing next to him. Jared stays back with the cameras, which I can *feel* in back of us.

Jordan glances at me, and then wrestles his phone out of his pocket.

Mine vibrates.

Jordan: What is this? What are you doing?

Me: The producers said they needed a little more action, so I thought I'd come here and stir things up. Jared and Drew thought it would be a good idea

Jordan: Stir things up

Me: Didn't realize you'd actually be here swooning over your other girlfriend

Me: That song was something

Me: Feels like a real two birds one stone thing. I get the drama the producers wanted, and finally get the truth out of you

Sure, maybe I'm hiding a silly little crush on some college freshman intern, but that's nothing compared to unearthing this. I hear Jordan groan loudly and suck through his teeth. He opens his mouth and shuts it again, like he desperately wants to say something but knows he can't. Not with the cameras and mics here.

Jordan: Are you kidding me? This? This still?

Jordan: That song was for STEVE

Jordan: Laura has been in love with STEVE forever

Jordan: She wanted to finally tell him before they both left for college

Oh.

I can feel my heart in my throat as I read the texts. I can see the light from the cameras getting a little closer, so I hurry and cram my phone into my pocket. I step away from Jordan, who barely looks at me as I do, and push my way through the crowd toward the exit.

"Cindy?" Jared asks as I brush by him.

"Hey!" Drew the cameraman says, following after me. The sea of my former classmates parts as I hustle my way out of there, finally wrenching the heavy door open into the Philadelphia evening.

"Cindy, hey, come on," Drew says, lowering his camera. "What's going on? That was good stuff."

"Nothing..." I manage to say, sniffling. "I just... I'm just too tired, it's late."

"Okay..." Drew says, his eyebrows furrowed in confusion. "We'll get production to send a car, get you home. Don't burn yourself out with this, kid. It's a lot, but you know, you should have some fun too. Cause some trouble, but find some joy, you know?"

"Yeah..." I nod. "Yeah, I know."

My phone buzzes.

Jordan: Where are you going?!

Jordan: You're just going to ruin the evening and bail?

Jordan: What is getting into you?

Me: Sorry, sorry. I'll explain. When we talk tonight. We can still talk tonight, right?

Me: Tell Laura I'm sorry. And Steve

Jordan: Tell them yourself at the trucks tomorrow

Jared walks out the doors of Cousin Charles.

"You alright? What did he do to you? What did he say?" Jared asks, his arms out, and I can't help myself. I fall into them, and he hugs me while I cry into his shoulder. When I start to calm, he pulls away and bends down a little, looking right at me. "What did he do?" he repeats, his tone urgent.

"It's okay," I say, my voice stuffy. "It's nothing."

"It doesn't look like nothing," Jared says, his eyes hardened. He glances at the door to the café, where I can hear music pouring through its cracks. "I'll be right back."

I grab his arm, stopping him from going inside.

"No, no, don't." I swallow, shaking my head. "It's okay, it's just…the usual rivalry stuff. Sometimes…it gets kinda hard."

Jared pauses for a beat, looking back and forth from me to the café.

"If he hurt you—"

"No!" I shout, surprised at the force of my voice, and Jared flinches a little. "No, really. Thank you though."

Jared steps toward me again, and cups my cheek with his hand, wiping away a tear with his thumb.

"I should go," I say, hurrying the words out. Afraid that if I don't say them, I won't. This is all spiraling right out of my control, and not just things with the show and Jordan and everything but…whatever feelings are swirling around in my chest right now.

And considering I just finished fighting with Jordan over thinking there was something going on with him and Laura, of thinking he was hiding something from me, yet here I am with all these secrets…my worry over Dad's debts, the acceptance to my dream school, and now this smitten intern who seems to really hear me…

I feel like a walking hypocrite right now, and the control I like to hold on to is slipping.

But goodness, being with someone who I wouldn't have to hide, who would stand up for me like that…

The guilt is swirling inside my chest, but I feel like I want this.

"Alright, I'll…see you tomorrow," Jared says, his face full of conflict. His mouth opens like he wants to say something else, but he exhales and shakes his head.

"You're trouble, Cindy Ortiz. I would have ran in there for you. No question."

Pilot: Confessional Shot Transcript (Jordan)

Jordan: Huh. That's an interesting question. I'm not sure what it would take for me to just forgive the Ortiz family.

It's not like they've ever done anything, I don't know, violent or truly awful to us. Cindy and her parents are just annoying. The videos are sometimes embarrassing, their insults occasionally get a little too personal, but it's never completely awful.

I guess forgiveness isn't out of the question. But then what does that look like, afterward? Are we going to hang out together? Eat doughnuts in the basement of the local church on Sundays, like we haven't been horrible to each other for years?

I don't know.

And then after listening to my dad the other day, the way he was talking about everything with the trucks.

How we almost had the nicer one? How do you ever really let something like that go?

I don't know if you do. I don't know if my parents ever really have.

Hmm.

The idea of forgiveness is nice, but why bother when you can't really see the point of it?

Wow, that sounds really messed up coming out of my mouth when I say it out loud.

I'm not a monster!

chapter fifteen:
jordan

———

Tuesday, Five Days until Truck Off

I'm home. It's nearly midnight. The cameras are gone. And I have no idea how I'm supposed to get to sleep.

What was that?

Who was that?

I can hear Mom and Dad downstairs, their voices full of excitement, loud and joyful over the drone of the television. Ever since the picnic, ever since we signed on for this nonsense, they've been watching all kinds of reality shows. Dad is studying them like he'll be able to figure out exactly how to behave on camera, and Mom's determined to unlock some kind of secret hidden on the screen.

I've been texted more internet memes of reality stars in the last forty-eight hours than I've ever seen in my life. Usually, it was just Cindy sending me them, followed by lengthy explanations detailing who these people even were. But now it's my whole family.

I stare up at my ceiling, off-white and pocked, and reach to turn off the lamp on the desk by my bed—

Plink.

I turn toward the window, squinting.

Plink, plink.

Under the golden glow of the nearby streetlamp is Cindy with some pebbles in her hand. She waves at me as I open the window, the frame rattling against the wood and brick.

"What…what are you doing?" I ask and glance at my phone to see if it's dead. It's not. "Why not just text me?"

"You're not answering my texts!" she says.

"Because I'm mad at you."

"Still?" Her expression wavers. "Just…come outside, I need to talk to you."

"Listen, this whole thing isn't going to—"

"Shh!" Cindy hushes me. "Not so loud. Someone might—"

"Oh, someone might what?!" I ask, loudly, my voice reverberating into the night. "What's the worst that could—"

"Okay, we'll see you tomorrow!" Dad exclaims, and I hear the front door open. Cindy bolts away from the house as two cameramen from the show walk out, hefty gear on their shoulders. That Drew guy who has been mostly following Cindy around, and someone else I don't recognize.

Okay, I guess we should be more careful. It seems like these reality television people keep just as wild hours as me and my parents do from working in the service industry. What were they doing? Watching television with my parents while I was lying down up here?

Once they leave, my eyes sweep the street, but I don't see any sign of Cindy, so I close the window. I flop back onto my bed and pull out my phone.

Me: Hey where'd you go?

Me: They're gone

Cindy:...

A few dots pop up and disappear, pop up and disappear, like she's writing something but deleting it. Eventually all the activity stops, and I hear the plinking of rocks against my window again.

I groan and get out of bed.

This.

This is my life now.

I open the window, just in time for one of the pebbles to hit me in the face.

"Ow!"

"Sorry!" Cindy winces. I can see her hesitant smile, bright against the growing Philadelphia evening, shining even in the pale orange hue of the lamps lining the block. I shake my head and hurry out of my room and down the stairs. Mom and Dad are back in the living room, basking in the glow of whatever reality show is on right now. It's hard to make out, but the people are very beautiful and very angry at each other.

"Be right back!" I shout, tossing on a jacket.

"What?" Dad peers over the couch at me. "It's late, where are you going?"

WITH OR WITHOUT YOU

"Cindy's outside. Probably just a walk."

He pauses for a beat, and my mom turns to me, concern marring her face.

"Oh, come on, the cameramen are gone," I grumble. "What were you even doing down here?"

"Filming another confessional," Mom says.

"With the television on?" I ask.

Dad laughs and shakes his head.

"The camera guy... Drew, he was showing us examples of how people act on the shows. I'm trying to get it down." He adopts an incredibly melodramatic expression and says to Mom, "No, who do you think YOU are?!"

"Oh my God," I groan as Mom laughs.

"Just keep an eye out, okay?" Dad says.

I hate this.

I really, really hate this.

I swing the door open, ready to see Cindy, ready to just be caught up in her arms no matter how upset I am with her right now...and she's across the street, ducking behind a car the way me and my parents were just the other day, outside her family's house.

"No one is watching us!" I shout, my voice echoing a little on the quiet street.

"Shh!" Cindy says, slowly standing up. "You can't know that."

I run my fingers through my hair, gritting my teeth, and take a breath. It has only been...what, three days? What if this thing actually gets green-lit? What if Bethany and her people take this to the networks and someone decides they want to

buy it? How am I supposed to keep doing this? In what world
is any of this even possible for the two of us, and our families?

Am I the only one who already feels like they're about to
fall apart?

Breathe.

Think about Mom and Dad. The diner about to be torn
down. The pilot money. Their dreams. How much all of this
means to Cindy.

I can do it. I can rally. It's all for them, it's all for her.

Maybe…maybe my truck can wait.

I walk around the car Cindy is tucked behind, and after
she looks up and down the street, she leans in and gives me
a kiss. I feel like my entire body sighs.

"Let's take a walk." Cindy grabs my hand, and for the first
time in a while, I feel… I suppose the way she does, about
holding hands in public. I have to force myself not to tighten
up when her fingers lace through mine. I'm upset, I'm hurt,
I don't know if I want this but also I absolutely do and oh my
God feelings are the worst.

I could go for some mozzarella sticks right now. Just some
comfort food in my face to forget about everything swirling
around inside.

I catch a glimpse of Mom and Dad through the front window. Dad is gesturing wildly about, Mom is laughing, col-
lapsed against him. I swear, the joy reverberating off them in
the light of all this television nonsense has them looking as
happy as they did when they owned the diner. Maybe whatever hurt was there, with losing the restaurant and having
their dream truck swiped out from under them, is healing
from all of this.

I grip Cindy's hand a little tighter.

For her. For them.

Dickinson Square Park is illuminated by the nearby streetlamps that hug the row homes that circle it, casting the fields in an orange-red glow reflecting off the old bricks. A few people are playing wildly late-night games of basketball on the well-lit blacktop court, but otherwise, it's quiet. Just locals walking their dogs or sitting on benches, chatting with one another. Night owls, much like me and Mom and Dad.

"Are you doing okay?" Cindy asks, breaking me from the reverie.

No.

I'm not.

"I'm...good." I shrug, and she immediately shoves her shoulder against mine.

"I know when you're lying." She smiles and walks her fingers along my arm before pulling me in closer as we stroll. "You're gonna need to work on that. For the show and all."

I grimace.

"Really though," she continues. "Are you okay? Are...we okay? Do we need to...talk about what happened?"

"Well, no." I clear my throat. "I mean, no I'm not okay, and yes, we need to talk about that whole incident... Look, I know it's been a day, but it's really easy to see how this ends, right? This whole *Cheesesteak Wars* thing? It's going to be terrible, and I'm just... Cindy, I'm trying so hard, for you, but how am I supposed to keep it together?"

"It's for our families," Cindy presses.

"Is it?" I ask. "I know how much you love this stuff. The

drama. You were willing to ruin Laura's show tonight. Her big grand gesture for Steve. Because you couldn't get over the idea that she supposedly had a crush on me, even though I told you so many times—so many times!—that we're just friends. And you did it in the name of this…this *thing!*"

"That's because whenever I want to talk about it, you just… shut down."

"No, I shut it down because there's nothing to discuss!" I exclaim. "And now, now you really know there isn't. Do you finally have enough proof?"

We keep walking, despite the tension hovering in the air.

"What's the deal with Jared?" I ask, the words tumbling out quick and short.

"The intern?" Cindy laughs, but her tone is…awkward. "What do you mean?"

"Nothing." I shake my head. I'm not about to start acting the way she does, assuming something over nothing. But the way he looked at her, stepped in front of her when Kyle was making a scene, I don't know… I can't shake the fact that he's looking at her the same way I do. "Was just surprised to see him tonight."

"He's only a year older than us and is already working in TV! That could be me, right out of college, thanks to this show and my podcast and all that. Or even *in* college! I could snag an internship while I'm at…county…"

She trails off. I exhale.

"Jordan—"

"Cindy—"

We both start into something at the same time. We stop walking and face each other.

"You go ahead," she says, glancing away like she's guilty of something.

"Look. Tonight was really bad," I say, glancing up at her. "Us bickering at the trucks is fine but that... I don't like *that*."

"Me either," Cindy says, reaching out and grabbing my hands. The streetlamps that illuminate the park are buzzing above us, casting the two of us in a pale gold. Little shadows flutter around her face, and I peer up to see a swarm of moths dancing around the light.

She worries at her lip, her hands squeezing mine.

"There's something else," I say, tilting my head to get a better look at her. She keeps turning, more and more, until she let's go of my hands and takes a few steps away. "What's going on? What is it?"

She looks back, her eyes glistening.

"Cindy?"

"I'm..." she stammers. "I'm going back to Boston at the end of August. I got into Northeastern."

"What?"

"Honestly, I didn't think I'd get in. It was just...a little dream, I guess."

"What about our dream?" I ask. "The road trip, being to-gether, coming back here after—"

"Jordan, that's your dream. The road, the truck." Cindy shakes her head. "You've got your whole crew that you've grown up with here, who have been around your whole life. My friends, my people? They're in Boston."

I stumble back and sit down on a bench.

"Say something," she pleads, squatting down in front of

me. She cups the side of my face and wipes a tear away with her thumb.

I shirk away and stand up.

"So, you were just...lying to me this whole time?" I ask, my mind reeling, trying to piece everything together.

"No, no." Cindy shakes her head. "I didn't even think I'd get in."

"But you applied."

"Yeah, you know, just in case."

"Boston," I huff. "So, we have to spend this last summer together pretending like we aren't together, for this show. And then you'll just be gone."

"You'll be on the road!" Cindy exclaims. "You'll be gone too."

"I was supposed to be gone *with you!*" I shout, surprised at how... I don't know, I guess how angry this is making me. How hurt.

"Well, what about what I want?" Cindy asks. "I mean, what I really want? Working in television, doing my podcast with my friends—"

I exhale sharply through my nose, and I immediately know that was a mistake.

"Right, right," Cindy rasps. "Dismiss the thing you've never bothered to listen to."

"Oh, come on, reality shows just aren't my thing."

"You're filming for one!"

"Yeah, for you!"

"It's for us!"

"IT'S FOR YOU!" I shout. "All of it is for you. I hate this. I hate pretending that the one person I want to spend every waking moment with is someone I can't stand. And for what? To sell some sandwiches? To help our parents and their finances? Their mistakes don't *have* to be our responsibility."

"Oh?" Cindy crosses her arms. "Is that why you're getting in a truck and driving away from all of it?"

"You're moving to Boston to get away from it!"

"That's different. Your parents scrimped and saved to give you a better life," Cindy says, stepping toward me, her eyes glistening. "Mine went into debt, ruined any chance of supporting me."

"Then why help them out?!" I reply.

"Then why not help yours out?!" Cindy cracks back.

We both stand there, quietly, the streetlamps buzzing.

I don't like this. Any of this. Real fighting instead of the fake stuff.

"Nothing?" Cindy asks. "You don't have anything else to say?"

I have a lot to say. How she hid this from me, let me plot this whole thing when really, she was planning for a way out. How I've kept up this rivalry because I knew how much it meant to her, and now it's like none of that even matters.

Hell, I'm even thinking about the awful nonsense her parents pulled, leaving me with the truck I've been in.

"You know what, I'll save it for the trucks," I snap. "That's what you want, right?"

And I make my way home, alone and in the dark.

chapter sixteen: cindy

Wednesday, Four Days until Truck Off

I throw a T-shirt on, and the second I look in my bedroom mirror, I immediately wrestle it off. Mayday Parade, the band on the shirt, is one of Jordan's favorites. I dig around in my dresser for something plain, and once dressed, fight with my hair a little, then exhale.

Everything this morning has already felt like a battle. Last night, the whole day really, was so horrible. The look on Jordan's face when I told him I wasn't going on the road trip just kept playing itself out over and over again on the back of my eyelids as I tried to fall asleep. And he hasn't answered a single text.

I slept in, but it's a truck day, and the cameras are waiting.

I double-check my phone, just in case, maybe Jordan's finally answered something, anything, but there's nothing but a thread of my messages to him asking to talk. It feels…almost embarrassing. I flip over to Instagram to check the notifications and comments on the truck's account, when I notice an unread message from someone I don't follow in the "requests" folder on my personal account.

I huff. It's probably someone complaining about an order or checking in to see when we'll be open or...

I gasp.

Jared Loves TV: Hey, I hope this is okay, but I just wanted to make sure you were alright

Jared Loves TV: That event last night, you and that guy fighting and that other kid

Jared Loves TV: It just seems like it might have been a lot, is all

I look away from my phone, like someone might be watching, and then focus back on the little glowing screen.

Cindy's Reality: Hey. No, it's fine

Cindy's Reality: Thank you for checking in. That means a lot

Jared Loves TV: Good. I'm glad

Jared Loves TV: <3

Oh God, that heart.

My own thunders in my chest. Is this...what normal people do when they're like, flirting and talking? They just get to do it, instead of avoiding one another at school or pretending like they can't stand each other at their jobs? Or in the case of how it's been the last few days, ducking video cameras?

I try to shake it off, and hurry downstairs. But a familiar sound stops me in my tracks at our second-floor landing at the top of the steps. It's coming from the kitchen across our home.

It's my parents.

And *they're* fighting in a way I haven't heard in years.

"Daniel...what *is* this?!"

"Maria, please, it's nothing!" Dad replies, and I can imagine him waving his hands around dismissively, in that animated way he talks.

"It's not nothing," Mom presses as a bunch of papers rustle somewhere. "Another credit card? *Another* one? Are you kidding me?!"

"We needed some upgrades to chicken coops on the farm—" Dad starts.

"No. No, we didn't," Mom says, firm. "Just like we didn't need to fix the apiaries that have no bees in them or the sprinkler system when everyone waters the gardens by hand."

"But—"

"Daniel," Mom says, silencing him. "That is not our farm. It's not the same one back in Boston. You're spending *our* money, ruining *our* credit, again, but this time for some nonprofit that doesn't care about our finances. That isn't going to reimburse you."

"Sweetheart—"

"No." I try to creep down the steps a little more as Mom's voice gets lower. "We're still swimming in debt from how careless you got with the farm back in Boston, and I will not see the same thing happen to us here. This was supposed to be our chance to start over, to work off those mistakes. *Your* mistakes."

Her words hang In the air for a few moments until she says, "Are there more?"

"More?" Dad asks, scoffing. "Come on."

"Daniel," Mom says, her voice like a bullet point. "Are. There. More."

Dad exhales loudly.

Mom swears in Spanish.

And the stairs creek loudly under my feet.

I hold my breath—it's quiet, and I can barely hear the two of them muttering to one another.

"Cindy?" Mom ventures.

Darn it.

"H-hey…" I say, walking down the rest of the stairs. Mom's lingering in the doorframe between the living room and the kitchen, and I can see Dad in there, rubbing his forehead. "I'm gonna head to the truck…"

Mom's expression softens. "How much of that did you hear?" she asks, and Dad peers up from behind his hand.

"I mean…" I shake my head and sigh. "I guess all of it."

"Great," Dad grumbles.

"Hey," Mom says, sharply, turning to him. "It's your fault we're back in this mess." Her eyes flit back over to me. "Darling, it's nothing for you to worry about. It's just…grown-up problems."

"If we win Truck Off, though, that would help," Dad mumbles.

"Daniel, I swear to God, do not put this on our child,"

Mom says to the ceiling, exhausted. "Ignore him. Go have some fun, and you know, do your whole show."

"Okay…" I say, hesitating. I don't really want to just leave right now. I want to know more about what's going on, I want to know just how bad it all is. I want…to talk about what happened with Jordan. But she shoos me with a hand, turning back to the kitchen. I can see her reach for a stack of angry-looking envelopes, red stamps and other bits of text that feel like a warning, as she shuffles through them.

I open the front door and take a deep breath of the summer air.

Between me and Jordan putting on a show for the cameras and our trucks and our families, and now the reveal that Mom and Dad have been hiding things… I can't help but wonder what it might be like to have a relationship, any kind of relationship, that was simpler in my life.

I glance back at my phone, another notification from Jared blinking up from Instagram.

There's still no answer from Jordan.

So… I answer Jared.

The air smells of bacon, Jordan knows the truth, and I guess, in some new way, so do I.

Dad's eagerness to grab those fancy baskets at the TV offices, the things around the farm I know the place couldn't afford, the new outfits as the show came together, how he looked at that farm stand in Reading Terminal…

And the way Mom brought up the old farm, the debt from back there.

I think my whole family is in trouble, all over again, and

no one told me. Hell, no one told Mom. Dad was keeping secrets from her, again.

Jordan's got a line around his truck, people still eager for those breakfast cheesesteaks he and Steve have been serving up. I know this is good for him, that all these tips will go toward his truck, but I can't help the wave of jealousy and anger that crashes over me, his words repeating in my head from last night.

Our parents' problems aren't ours to solve. They're not our responsibility. But if I don't help take care of them, with what little I can do, who will?

I give his setup my fiercest scowl as I make my way to my own truck.

After all, the cameras are on.

Focus on the rivalry. Focus on being upset about that. On what I can control.

Not because the more money he saves, the more likely it is he'll get that truck before the end of the summer, and he'll be on the road. Without me. Not because we had a huge fight last night and he hasn't answered a single text. Not because there's trouble at home, and maybe the one way out of it is winning that prize money.

It's easier to pretend it's just because of a rivalry.

It's hitting me how much I didn't want that road trip. The food truck life is fine for this moment in time. It's just a job that allows me to explore my real passion—reality TV. It funded my equipment for my *Beacon Street* podcast with the girls and gave me a glimpse of my own drama with the rivalry we document on social media, which became the actual very real show that's happening right now. I've been able to pay for all the things I've wanted for myself, without worrying Mom or Dad as they've chipped away at their past in Boston.

But I don't want the truck life. I just...want him.

I shake my head and reach for my truck's canopy, and one of the cameras gets a little too close to me. I shirk back.

"Sorry," the cameraman mutters. It's not Drew or any of the other guys I've met so far, and I wonder just how many folks they've got working on this. "Trying to capture some montage footage of the truck getting setup. Don't mind us."

"It's okay." I shrug and get back to it, climbing into the truck to prep.

"All by yourself today, Cindy?" a voice shouts, and I glance up from my cutting board to see Steve leaning outside the Plazas truck, smirking at me. Jordan is inside, moving around furiously while Steve takes a few steps toward me, his arms crossed. There's a camera on him, one of the actual ones from the show, not a tourist or Laura, and he's carrying himself with this odd...swagger, I guess. Some newfound confidence he's wrangled up. I wonder if it's due to Laura's confession at the open mic night.

I'll admit, the new aura suits him.

"Don't need the help!" I yell across the way and wave my spatula at him from inside my truck. I can't get out and wander about, not yet, anyway. There's too much to do to prepare for folks who want a healthy option for their breakfast. And besides, now *I* want to brainstorm ideas for Truck Off. I grab the plastic chopper for my mushrooms and it slips, tumbling right out of the truck's main window and onto the sidewalk.

"Could have fooled me." Steve's grin gets even bigger, just

as Jordan's line seems to sprawl even longer, spilling onto the park *across the street.*

"Whatever," I grumble. I storm out of the truck, grab the chopper, which now has a thin crack through the clear plastic container, and focus on my prep. I glance up and Steve is still there, outside his truck, his hands on his hips. "What?!?"

"Okay, okay." Steve lifts his hands in a faux surrender, walking away.

I am...not in the mood for any of this today.

I shred some carrots and chop up cabbage to make this house-made coleslaw people seem to love so much as a side with our sandwiches. I wonder if something like that could put us over the top at the competition. There are more than a few trucks around town famous for sides as opposed to their actual meals. Like the food truck equivalent of Thanksgiving.

I'm getting into a groove when my phone buzzes.

Steve: Hey let me know if you need me to tone it down or whatever

Steve: I just know the cameras are out, and the two of you are mad at each other

Steve: I don't know

Steve: I just want to help. I'm on both of your teams

Steve: Make me the villain today, I can take it

I sigh and put the phone back in my pocket. Steve. You tall cinnamon roll.

"Cindy, do you have a minute?" a voice asks, and there's Bethany Ireland, dressed in her usual smart blazer with her makeup entirely on point, at my ordering window. I still feel a little heated from the exchange with Steve, even after his apology. Something about all of it seems...different, when we aren't getting along. After last night, after Laura's concert, and with the silence treatment Jordan's giving me right now...it actually feels like the feud between us might be real. And I don't like that.

And I can't shake the way Jared looked at me outside that café, the urgency in his eyes. His sweet messages this morning, full of concern and worry. It feels...less complicated.

Even though it actually is more complicated. He has no idea what I'm hiding from him and the rest of the production crew.

"Yeah, what is it?" I ask, dicing up some peppers, maybe with a bit too much force. Bethany winces with each pound of the plunger against the counter. "Sorry."

"It's fine, it's fine." Bethany waves me off. "In fact, if you could bring that same energy and passion to your next interaction with the Plazas family, with Jordan, I think it would be really compelling."

My eye flit up to her.

"What do you mean?" I ask. "Me and Jordan had a whole... thing, last night, at a local concert. Isn't that enough?"

"Well..." Bethany shrugs, examining her nails. "That was good, or so I hear. I haven't had a chance to check out the footage yet, but I will later today. My question this morning is...have you tried one of their breakfast cheesesteaks?"

"No?" Where's she going with this?

"They're not bad. I had Jared grab a few for the crew."

Bethany looks at me, and I swear her eyebrow went up when she mentioned Jared. She does know? I shake my head—nothing has even happened between us, save for those texts and a hug, so there isn't anything to know. "But my opinion doesn't matter. *Yours* is what's going to get folks' attention."

She jerks her head toward Jordan's truck.

"Oh," I say as it hits me.

"Oh, is right." Bethany grins, and there's something...kind of nefarious behind it. "I'll keep an eye on the truck here, so why don't you go see what all the hype is about? And then when you inevitably find it to be disappointing, say something about it."

"I don't know..." I wring my hands a little. "That seems a little more than just yelling stuff at each other."

"Hey, we're just trying to make good television here," Bethany says. "If you don't want to do it, you don't have to. We can just focus on his lead-up to the competition and how good Jordan's food is—"

"Wait, wait..." I scurry out of the truck. Considering everything going on with Dad, with the family debt and whatever he's done to make it worse... I need this. Hell, I don't just need this for them, I want this for me. This show, this reality television show connection. I need these producers to like me for when it's my turn to give this a real go. And as everything keeps spiraling out of my control, this is something I can lock on to and handle. "Okay, I'll do it."

Bethany smiles.

And I make my way across the square.

I figured I'd go to the back of the line, but as I get closer to Jordan's truck, something I didn't really expect happens.

The folks waiting on the sidewalk part ways for me to pass. I turn and look at the cameras that are following right behind me, even though I'm not supposed to, and catch Bethany over by my truck, giving me a quick nod.

I wink right into the camera and feel a rush of...something like excitement.

Jordan stares at me through his window, confusion all over his face and Steve's. Then I'm right there, up against the countertop, at the front of the line. The steel is hot against my arm.

"So. Let me try one of those breakfast cheesesteaks," I say, trying my best to sound tough.

"The cheesebreaks?" Jordan asks, smirking.

"I am *not* going to call them that." I scowl.

"If you want to order one, you're going to have to use their actual name." Jordan shrugs and slowly starts turning away.

I close my eyes and sigh.

"Fine." I clear my throat. "I'd like one of your...*cheesebreaks*." I mumble it out.

"What was that?" Jordan asks, holding his spatula up to his ear, like it's going to help him hear me.

"A cheesebreak. I want a cheesebreak!" I snap.

"Why didn't you just say so?" Jordan asks and then looks at Steve, smiling. The two of them are enjoying this way too much, but even so...maybe it means things are back to normal? We didn't text all night, and I can't tell if he's just on for the cameras of if the air has cleared between us.

"It's on us." Jordan smiles, his eyes flitting to the cameras for a moment as he slides one of the sandwiches toward me. "I want to know what you think."

I glance down at the sandwich.

It's just as perfect-looking in person as it is in Steve's photo. The runny egg, the sliced, medium-rare rib eye… I inhale, and yes, it's cheddar that he's using on the sandwich, and everything is just salt-and-peppered just right, speckled across the egg like freckles. I won't insult this creation with a spray of ketchup, no matter how badly I want it there.

"Go ahead," Jordan says, and I glance up to see him leaning on the counter. He nods at the sandwich, and Steve jabs him with an elbow.

I take a bite.

Oh my God.

The runny egg dribbles over the bread, and the yolk is just perfect, the ideal blend of gelled and liquid. The meat is outrageously good, and the cheddar… I'm not sure where Jordan and his family picked it up, but it's sharp enough to cut glass.

"We're planning to enter these in Truck Off across the river this weekend," Jordan says, and for a second, I don't even realize he's talking to me. I mean, I know that's what he's doing. But this version of me, the one who hates him because of the rivalry, that person has no idea. Or does the fictional version of me know? I'm not even sure, but he's hamming it up a little bit for the show.

"Are you entering?" he asks, knowing fully well that I am, even though I don't have a sandwich planned yet. The producers want us to lose so they can focus on the Plazas story arc at the festival, but it sure did seem like Dad wanted to win regardless of what the producers said. And knowing what I do now, what *Mom* knows now, I'm sure he's going to be extra determined.

Still though. Jordan's playing along.

"What do you think?" he asks.

And with the spectacular taste of that sandwich lingering on my lips, I clear my throat and put the breakfast cheesesteak back on the truck's countertop.

Jordan and Steve peer down at it, and I slide it across the metal surface toward them.

"It's terrible," I snarl, and all the guests still waiting in line gasp. The few who were taking photos and videos start to put their phones away.

"Eggs are cold."

Not true, they're amazing and warm and delicious, and I can still feel the yolk on my chin from where it dribbled.

"The cheese is barely melted."

False, it is gooey and blended. It's lingering on the back of my tongue.

"The meat is tough and unseasoned."

No, it breaks apart like butter in my mouth.

"So. Good luck with all that."

I move to wave them off, to dismiss the sandwich, but I reach out a little too far. My fingertips graze the paper wrapped around the sandwich and send the whole thing flipping off the countertop and onto the ground, splattering the sidewalk with eggs and cheese and meat. For a moment, I'm not sure what to do. I want to stop and pick it up and apologize, but...the cameras are on, and...

I turn on my heel and stride back to my truck across the street. The camera crew hurries after me, and there's a rush of emotions stewing around inside of me. That was hilarious and horrible and challenging and...oh my God.

I loved it.

It was awful and I *loved* it.

I can hear the people at Jordan's truck shouting insults at me as I make my way across the square, but I tune them all out. Bethany is leaning against the truck still, and as I get closer, I can see that she's smiling with all of her teeth showing.

"That was perfect, Cindy," Bethany says. "Just perfect."

"Thanks." I laugh and rub the back of my head. "It was so intense."

"It was good television." Pride swells in my chest at her words. "I think we got what we need today. We'll get out of your hair, and swing back around later. And if you think of anything else to hitch the drama up, let me know. Or just do it. Shows like this, reality television in general, a lot of it is about going with your gut. Your instinct."

Bethany looks me up and down, nodding.

"And I think you've got it," she says approvingly.

My heart soars. I hop into my truck and look out the window, toward Jordan's. I can't see him, but Steve is out there, chatting with customers. For a moment, his eyes meet mine, and he quickly turns away.

Hmm.

I pull out my phone to message Jordan, who still hasn't responded to my texts from last night.

Me: Hey, I hope that wasn't too much

Me: It's all for the show, you know?

Me: Jordan?

I peer back at the truck. Jordan has moved into the window, and he's looking down at his phone.

He shakes his head and shoves it in his pocket without answering.

So I message someone back who does.

Pilot: Confessional Shot Transcript (Jordan)

Jordan: I feel like there's this slight misconception that my family only does like, salt and pepper and that's it when we're cooking. My father ran a whole diner! Have you ever seen a menu for a diner? If you've seen a novel in your local bookstore, you've seen a diner menu. If you've seen a CVS receipt, you've got an idea.

They're massive. Because when you're working in a diner, you have to be more than just burgers and chicken fingers, despite that being the staple diet of most of the college kids around us.

My dad, he can pan sear a steak with the best of them, poach a perfect egg, bake a pie with a ribboned crust that would make you weep.

When he opened the truck, though, when the diner shut down, I don't know. Something broke. He stuck to the basics because I think, in a lot of ways, he's been afraid to take a chance again. And I stuck to the same things in the truck all through high school because it worked.

But it doesn't really work for this, you know?

I think...me and Steve are gonna surprise people at Truck Off with our sandwiches. The breakfast cheesesteaks. I just...gotta find that one thing that'll put them over the top.

I'm not sure what it is.

But I'm gonna figure it out.

Chapter seventeen: jordan

Thursday, Three Days until Truck Off

"Can you calm down for, like, just a second?" Laura asks as I rush around my parents' kitchen. The camera guys are hanging back in the doorway that leads into the living room, watching as I scour the cabinets.

"I'm fine, it's fine," I grumble, my fingers flipping through some small jars of spices.

"You're not," Laura says, leaning against the countertop. My family's kitchen isn't anything wild, just your typical small Philadelphia row home kitchen space. No one's having a family dinner in this nook, most meals quickly devoured on the couch and coffee table, or once upon a time, at the old diner.

"You're digging around like a madman in here." She grabs my wrist, stilling me. "Relax."

I exhale.

"You're right, I just…" I glance up in the cabinet, tiny jars painstakingly labeled by my dad staring at me. We've grown plenty of herbs over the years, haphazardly sprouting in the backyard or window boxes and dried out in the microwave on paper towels, leaving our home smelling of whatever spice for days and days. Oregano. Basil. Thyme. Lemon basil. Mint basil. Chocolate basil. Why are there so many flavors of freaking basil but nothing I can actually use—

I take another deep breath, my hands on the cold kitchen countertop.

"I just…the cheesebreaks are still missing something," I stress, squinting at the jars.

"Are you kidding me?" Laura laughs. "All week you've had lines up and down the block, taking over the whole square. What could you possibly need?"

"I don't know." I turn around and lean against the counter. "I'll know it when I see it, I think."

"Is this because of…" Laura stops, and I see her eyes flit to the cameras and back. "Is this because of the Ortiz family? Don't let Cindy's little scene knock you off your game. You've got something special going on, right here. If she can't see it, that's her own problem."

I can't help the smirk on my face.

Some excellent double speak there, Laura.

"No, no it's not just that," I say. "Look, a lot of trucks make breakfast sandwiches around Philadelphia. Including breakfast cheesesteaks. It's not some wildly original idea. Granted, the ones we're making are just a little…better, than the others. Better cheese, better meats, eggs cooked just right…but that doesn't mean it'll stand out against the competition."

"You think some spice is going to change that?" Laura asks, scoffing. "This isn't *Dune*."

I stare at her for a beat.

"It's a very famous sci-fi novel and a movie...for the love of God find a hobby that isn't just food," Laura says, frustration radiating from her. "A magic spice isn't it."

"It might be though. The right dash of something can change everything. You ever use rosemary on chicken? Or lemon pepper on popcorn?" I sigh and glance back at the spices. "I don't think whatever it is, is going to be here though."

"You're letting that family get in your head," Laura presses again. "You have what, three days? Relax. You already have the sandwich. You've got it, people like it. You'll figure out what that little thing is later, and if you don't, it's *good*, Jordan. Chill out."

"Okay, okay." I clear my throat. "I'm trying."

I lean back against the countertop, letting the comfortable silence wash over me.

chapter eighteen: cindy

Thursday, Three Days until Truck Off

It feels bizarre, waiting outside of Reading Terminal Market in order to go in. Whenever Dad and I come here, or whenever I make a trip myself for just, like, lunch or to find some good snacks to inhale while watching a show with Mom or the girls, it's right in and a beeline to whatever it is I'm looking for.

But right now, I'm waiting for the cameras, leaning against a large window that reveals a produce seller behind me.

I suppose that's another eye-opening thing about reality television. I thought so much of it was immediate, right there, happening in the now, but that's only what's on camera.

I stare down at my phone, and the flurry of unanswered texts I've sent to Jordan, the array of supportive ones from Eesha and Ariana, all the notifications flooding in from the latest podcast episode. But I can't really enjoy that because of the Jordan-shaped hole in my life. And then there's all this… whatever it is, happening with Jared. His cute, kinda flirty messages. The way my heart hitches up in my chest whenever a new notification blips up on Instagram, and the disappointment I feel when it's not from him, and is just an alert about the truck or something.

God, what am I doing.

Truck Off is in three days and I don't know what my sandwich is going to be. I wonder if Jordan's figured out what he needs. It feels like we need each other.

I flip over to Instagram, just as a notification bubble pops up.

Jared Loves TV: You look cute today, you know.

What?

I look up from my phone, and I spot Drew shuffling my way, the Hard Rock Café over on Market Street looming behind him…

And Jared following, his phone in his hand, a little smile on his face.

I feel a blush creep up my neck.

While Drew huffs with the camera on his shoulder, Jared strolls leisurely, and waves at me awkwardly, sliding his phone back in his pocket. I haven't seen him in person since that moment outside of Cousin Charles, or been alone with him since that confession. How he likes the podcast. How he likes…me.

Even from here, I can see his eyes lighting up as he gets closer.

Part of me wants to duck right inside Reading Terminal and disappear among all the people who I know are filling that place up. Weave in and around everyone so no one can find me. But I see the way Drew is really hurrying with the bulky camera of his, and I can't just bail on the guy. And something about Jared keeps pulling me toward him.

Especially now.

He gets me. Gets what I love about these shows. Listens to my podcast. Knows what I want to do with my life.

Is it so wrong to want to be around someone who can understand my passion?

"Hey," Jared says, reaching me first, having overtaken Drew and his camera. His voice is warm. "You, um…doing okay?"

"Yeah, yeah." I swallow. "I'm fine."

"Okay." He wrings at his wrists. "I hope…me messaging you was okay. I just… I had to know you were okay. But I feel like I'm breaking even more professional boundaries than I already was before."

"Before?" I ask, tilting my head.

"Well, you know." He flushes a little bit. "Not supposed to have crushes on the talent."

He smiles again, and I feel myself blushing even more.

"Alright, you two," Drew says, practically appearing next to us, startling me a little. I feel embarrassed, like I've been caught doing something I shouldn't, and Jared puts his hands in his pockets like he maybe feels the same. Drew lets out a disapproving grunt and nods at the door to the market.

"Come on now," he says. "Let's get some of this footage in. Though God help me, I don't know how this is supposed to be interesting television. Groceries? Last month I filmed a millionaire heiress throwing a table at somebody."

"How the mighty have fallen," Jared says.

Drew glares at him.

"You can go first, smart guy," Drew says, gesturing at the door. "See if you can clear some room before we walk in."

"Fine, fine." Jared shakes his head and walks toward the door, and then looks back at me. "See you in there."

My heart flutters. I am in *trouble*.

He disappears into the crowd inside, and Drew sets his camera down.

"Alright, time to mic up," he says, fumbling with some gear in a crossover bag slung around his waist. He pulls out a small microphone but seems distracted, pauses to look into the market where Jared disappeared.

"What's going on, Drew?" I ask.

"Nothing it's..." He exhales deeply. "Kid, I see this sort of thing often. Talent falls for a producer, or a good-looking boom mic operator. When someone has a camera and all the world's attention focused on them, it can be hard to... oh, what's the word, I don't know...tell the difference between real feelings and what's actually just work for everyone involved."

"Drew, come on, I'm not..." I start, and he gives me a look.

"Listen I've been at this for years. *Years*," he repeats, and it's that line again that every reality person seems to spout. I wonder if Jared would echo that, even though he's only been an intern for what, a semester? Drew attaches the wireless microphone to my jacket. "Just be careful. I'm not supposed to interfere, but I've also seen what happens to kids in this space.

You might be outta high school, and he might be a freshman in college...but still. You're kids."

I try not to roll my eyes at him, and he definitely sees it.

"I mean it, kiddo," he insists. "Let's go. You can get the door."

Normally I would be squeezing my way through Reading Terminal Market, like I was with Dad just earlier last weekend, but right now, with Drew and his camera behind me and Jared leading the way, people just...move. They part as I walk by, looking curiously at me, at the camera, attempting to figure out what's happening.

It feels...strangely powerful. Like how I felt when I approached Jordan's truck yesterday.

But, ugh, Jordan's sandwich. That whole scene at his truck. The way his face turned away so sharply. How he played along through the entire thing. It's been another full day of him not texting me back, and I really don't know how I'm supposed to function at the truck today.

At least the trucks will be closed for the competition on Saturday and Sunday. One day to prepare, another day for the actual event. And then all of this will be over. They'll put the pilot/proof-of-concept thing together for *Cheesesteak Wars* and we can figure out the next steps and everyone can get paid. Mom and Dad can fix whatever debt is being stacked up against them right now, whether it's from back home or whatever Dad has been doing since we got here...

And Jordan will get his truck and drive off...

Without me.

I guess it's all coming together? I don't know. And Jordan's words keep echoing in my head, about how that pilot money isn't really enough to fix anything. And I'm wondering if I'm doing all of this for the right reasons, or just for myself.

"Hey, Good Morning America, let's go," someone says, shoving past me. That's when it hits me that I've just been standing in the middle of an aisle in the sprawling farmers market. I shake my head and keep walking.

"You need a break, hon?" Drew asks, lowering his camera down near his leg.

"Oh no, I'm fine." I shake my head. "Just…distracted."

He pats my shoulder and lifts his camera back up onto his. "Just let me know. The Baby Suit is lost in the crowd somewhere anyway."

I laugh a little at his nickname for Jared then push ahead. It's still busy and bustling, but not completely slammed with tourists and folks doing their Friday evening, end-of-the-week grocery runs. I see Sparowanya Farm, but Christine and her buzzed red hair aren't there today.

Eventually, I find the place I've been looking for. A spice and herb stand enclosed in large panels, almost like a cubicle. The aromas grow stronger as I get closer, blending with the nearby Chinese food and seafood bar. It's overwhelming in the best way possible, like sticking your face into an everything bagel, all the garlic, salt, pepper, onion, and more wafting over me.

I push a small curtain aside and peer around the space. Large spinning racks holding little bags of soup mixes sit right at the entryway, with jars upon jars of elegantly labeled spices on the left. And on the right, olive oil. So much olive oil. In every imaginable flavor.

I set my eyes on a bottle of black truffle oil, Drew and his camera swing around next to me, I'm guessing to capture all the bottles. I dip a little piece of sampler bread into a small dish, and oh my God, it is amazing. If only I could cook something with this. Maybe I could use it in a sandwich or something. It would be so—

"Cindy."

I glance up, sharply, nearly knocking over the sampler dish.

"Jordan," I practically gasp.

"Oh boy, buckle up," I hear Drew whisper.

"What are you doing here?" I ask, hands on my hips, trying to get… I don't know, into character, I suppose. I'm trying to shake off all these swirling emotions from seeing him here, talking and texting with Jared moments ago, but I just can't. There's this bloom of anxiety in my chest.

"Same as you, Cindy," Jordan grumbles, and I try to get a look at what he's browsing. "Big weekend coming up. Maybe keep your eyes on your own paper?"

"Please, like you have anything for me to cheat off of," I snap back. He stares daggers at me, but I don't budge.

"Hey, we're gonna have to mic you up here, Jordan," Drew says, interrupting the silence. He walks over to Jordan and attaches a wireless mic from his bag to Jordan's jacket. There's so much that I want to talk to Jordan about, but he just stands there avoiding eye contact. Saying nothing.

"Alright, looks like the battery in that one is dead." Drew sucks at his teeth, standing back, hands on his hips. "Any idea where Jared wandered off to? Did you see him when we got in here?"

"No…" I clear my throat, feeling…strange, talking about him in front of Jordan. "Kinda lost him in the crowd."

"Ugh, okay," Drew mutters. "You two try not to kill each other while I run out and get another mic and a battery. Wasn't expecting this."

He reaches out and turns off my microphone on my jacket, and much to my surprise...

He winks at me.

"Be right back."

My heart slams in my chest.

That...wink. Leaving us here to talk alone.

Does he...know?

There's an intense silence in the shop, interrupted by the clinking of the spice jars. Jordan is rustling through a few little containers marked "for sale," focusing so intently I worry his gaze might break the glass. Meanwhile, it feels like my entire throat has gone dry.

"Okay, one of us has to say something." I force myself to speak up. Jordan sighs in response and turns to look at me.

"Where do you want to start?" he asks, crossing his arms. "The part where you threw my sandwich on the ground—"

"It was for the cameras!" I protest. "You know that! And it was an accident—"

"Or the part where you've been lying to me...what, all summer? All year?" His mouth turns into a thin line. "All I've been doing is preparing for *our* plans."

"No, *your* plans," I stress, taking a step toward him. "You've been acting like this is entirely my fault, like I'm some villain here, but you've never stopped to ask if it's what I really want."

"You never said otherwise!" he shouts. "A gap year isn't forever, that's why it's called a gap *year*. Afterward you'd start school and I'd—"

"You'd *what?*" I ask. "You'd give up your life on the road and settle back down in Philadelphia or Boston or wherever I'm at for school? After a *year* of seeing the country? You'd be fine with that?"

"As long as I was with you, yes!" he yells. He takes a deep breath, and his voice is calmer when he speaks again. "Listen. I know you love your reality television. These cameras. The social media, the attention, the podcast—"

"Yeah, how would you know about that?" I mutter.

"Look, I don't need the adoration of tens of thousands of strangers," he continues, though I can tell that jab hurt him a little. "I just need...you."

He reaches out to grab my hands, just as I catch a little movement at the entrance to the shop. I shirk away from Jordan just in time...

Just as Jared walks in.

His eyes settle right on Jordan, and he slows down his walk, clearing his throat.

"Everything...okay here?" he asks.

My heart is like a hammer.

"We're fine," Jordan says, his tone firm. He steps away from me, toward Jared. "I was just leaving."

Jordan makes his way out of the shop, and for a minute, for a horrible minute, I really think he's going to check his shoulder against Jared. But he doesn't, and takes a long roundabout way past him. As he reaches the exit he stops, and looks back at me, before disappearing into the crowded farmers market.

"He's gone," Jared says, walking hurriedly toward me. "Are you sure you're okay?"

"Yeah, yeah." I can't quite meet Jared's eyes. He's looking at me so intensely, like if he turns away, I might disappear. My phone buzzes in my pocket, but I ignore it. "He was looking for a secret ingredient for this weekend's competition. Same as me."

I turn back to the spice jars and the olive oil, fighting back the tears that are trying to make their way out. I feel like I'm being pulled in two directions.

"Oh dammit." I hear Drew's thick Philly accent, and turn to see him strolling in, hefting up his camera. "Did he leave? Did I miss him?"

"Yeah, he…" I stammer, and Drew's eyes settle on Jared before returning to me. "Nothing exciting happened."

"Better not have." Drew glares at Jared, who fidgets awkwardly. "Jared why don't you go get in line for some coffee? The La Columbe over near the entrance there."

Jared looks at me and then back to Drew, before nodding and hustling off.

"Drew, look, I…"

"You don't gotta say nothin'," he says, once Jared is out of the shop. "I've been in this business a long time, too long." Oh my God, there it is again. "There's always something else going on under the surface. You gonna be alright?"

"I think so." He digs into his camera bag and pulls out some tissues for me, and I can't help but laugh a little at it. "Thanks."

"Gotta be prepared," he says simply. "How ah…friendly are youse two? You and the Plazas kid. Really."

"Oh." It hits me that he doesn't know the whole truth. "We just…know each other from school."

"Right, right." He nods. "Well, don't let the show ruin whatever is there. Whatever is genuine. Lot of these reality stars, they get along fine off camera, but on it? It's all rage and insults. Eventually, that stuff bleeds over into the real world, and it's hard to tell the fact and the fiction."

"Yeah." I swallow. "Yeah, I can see that."

"Alright, what's next? You find what you're looking for?" He looks around the whole shop one more time, and then turns to me, puzzled. "Does no one actually work in here?"

"Just gonna look around a little bit more, and then we'll head out." I laugh, grabbing another piece of sample bread. Drew reaches out to try a few himself, and I take my phone out of my pocket.

The buzzing earlier. It was Jordan.

Jordan: Listen, tonight is going to be hard for everyone. For my family

Jordan: But despite everything that's going on, I really need you there

Jordan: And I hope when all of this is over

Jordan: We can find a way back to each other

I blink at the screen.
Tonight?
What's going on tonight?

Pilot: Confessional Shot Transcript (Cindy)

Cindy: *laugh* look I know people love it when actors who can't stand each other team up for a movie or a television show or musicians that have a rivalry do a song. It's a thing, right? People get excited.

That's not a thing that's going to happen here.

We're not gonna do some reunion special where we all bury the hatchet and make, I don't know, a brisket together or something.

Honestly, I don't even think Jordan is capable of making something like that. A brisket takes time, hours upon hours. His family doesn't put that level of care into what they do.

Hmm? Have I had their food?

Well, I can't say I've ever eaten at the Plazases' diner. I mean, when could I have? By the time we moved here, it was closed, and their family was running the food truck and managing some restaurants around town. A poetry café and some bar, I don't know. We haven't gone to any of those either.

Look...okay fine, I had one of their cheesesteaks once, and I wasn't impressed. If you can't even cook a proper sandwich out of a truck, how can you make a real meal in a restaurant with all the gear you actually need to make it happen?

I'm good, having never experienced it.

I doubt I missed out on much.

chapter nineteen: jordan

Thursday, Three Days until Truck Off

I head downstairs, where Dad and Mom are sitting in the living room, cameras at the ready. Dad is worrying away at the sleeve of his dress shirt, which in itself feels completely odd to say. He *never* dresses up. But here he is, impossibly wearing a button-down and some slacks, with a pair of shoes that look like they have been through absolute hell. Maybe they were black once, but they are scuffed and scratched to the point that they're a fading gray.

Mom already has a large body-length peacoat on, so I can only see jeans and bright red dress shoes peeking out near the floor. My phone vibrates and I pull it out of my pocket.

Steve: People are gathering

Steve: They're not going to start until your family gets here, but I'd still hurry

Steve: I'm sure they've got limits

"Hey," I say.

Mom and Dad both look up at me. Mom's smiling gently, but Dad, his eyes are glistening. It's quiet enough in our house that I can hear the audible shift of the cameramen turning to capture me on the steps.

I clear my throat.

"It's time."

The walk to The Stateside takes longer than it ever has before. And to live in Philadelphia is to understand the meaning of long walks. When it snows, a single city block can feel like you're crossing the entirety of a neighborhood. In the summer, when the sunlight reflects off the glittering skyscrapers in Center City and lands on sidewalks like a second grader holding a magnifying glass over some ants, the heat becomes unforgiving. Each step, a little bit of torture.

And when you're walking somewhere to say goodbye, it doesn't matter where you are. What city you're in, or which neighborhood. It feels like a funeral dirge.

Broad Street isn't that dark in the evening—there are street-lights and windows illuminated along the way, cars and buses zooming up and down Philadelphia's busiest city street. But even with all the artificial light, the atmosphere is dour and dim. There's more trash littering the sidewalk than usual.

The air seems thicker. The lights on the nearby homes shine less bright.

I know in my heart none of that is actually possible. But that doesn't change the way it feels.

Mom and Dad are fast city walkers. You have to be here. Even though you hear newcomers ramble about how Philadelphia is slower paced than New York City, you'll still get mowed down by a local struggling to connect their Bluetooth headphones to their phone.

But right now, I'm at least several feet ahead of them.

I really hate this.

But I have to be here.

I turn around to check on them again, and they're still making their way up the sidewalk, the cameras a few feet away from them. I can't help but wonder what the footage is going to look like on our end versus whatever Cindy and her family are up to right now.

Cindy.

I try to shake her out of my head, but God, I can't. It's spectacularly ironic how this reality TV show has revealed the reality of our relationship. How much we hid from one another, how all we didn't talk about only made everything worse, even when it seemed like we were fine. It was just a powder keg waiting to explode.

Did some part of me know that? Is that why we avoided talking about what would destroy us? Did I spend all this time talking over her, about my hopes and dreams and the truck and the road trip…when really, she needed some room to speak?

I wonder if she'll show up tonight.

We cross the street, arriving on the diner's block. I hear Dad suck at his teeth and mutter something as we walk past one of the new build condos. I can see Steve, and he waves excitedly and power walks toward me. "Hey, man," he says. "The construction crew is getting anxious. Everyone held them off for as long as we could."

"Everyone?" I ask, glancing back at my parents, who are still strolling.

"Yeah," Steve says, a soft smile on his face. "You'll see."

"Wait, so did Cindy actually make it? She's here?"

Before he can answer, I hurry a little ahead of him. My heart pounds in my chest, anxiousness ebbing and flowing through me. I don't care if the cameras are here. I don't care if the microphones are on. If she showed up, it's all off the table.

But what if it's not that? What if it's something that's going to make this whole thing hurt even more, for me, for my parents?

"Wait, Jordan!" Steve calls out.

I keep going. If something horrible is about to happen, I want to be ready. Maybe there's still time for my parents to turn around, to avoid whatever is about to go down. It's bad enough this show has thrown a spotlight on their grief, on the ways our family has been struggling, on some of the real friction between our family and the Ortizes. It's bad enough that it's ripped me and Cindy apart.

I round the corner into the parking lot, colliding with the wobbly fence that blocks it off from the street.

And it's…

"I told you to wait, dude," Steve says from behind me.

My God.

"It's beautiful." I choke the words out.

And it is.

The first thing I notice are the candles. And then slowly, the people come into focus. Some are holding onto candles, a few are scattered about the sidewalk. But there are dozens upon dozens of people. Maybe a hundred, most outside the fence, a few inside near the construction vehicles.

I hear someone say something, and everyone out there in the lot turns their attention toward me. But they're looking at something behind me.

I whirl around and there's Mom and Dad. And Steve, leaning against the nearby building, that same gentle smile on his face. He shrugs at me, and I nod back. Neither of us has to say anything. This is absolutely incredible.

"What's...what's all this?" Dad asks, walking forward, his steps cautious and careful.

"It's a candlelight vigil," someone in the crowd says, stepping forward. Whoever he is, he looks a little bit older than my dad, and his face is familiar and kind.

"Michael?!" Dad asks and exclaims at the same time. "What are you doing here—"

"Everyone is here," Michael replies, and that's when I recognize him. Michael Wink. Owner of the restaurant my father's been working in since the diner shut down. I watch as my dad and mom look over the crowd, their eyes growing brighter and mistier as the seconds push by. Steve hefts himself off the wall and strolls over to me, wrapping an arm around my shoulder.

I spot Gina, the manager of Alina's, and even Alina herself, the famous Philadelphia and Russian poet the place is named for. Some servers who I've definitely seen out and about at restaurants, familiar faces whose names I can't quite recall but with instantly recognizable mustaches or piercings or tattoos. Artists who sling hash over a short order grill and chefs who create art out of flour and sugar. Many of our regulars at the truck have come out too.

Mom and Dad seem to hug every single person, and I can't quite make out what anyone is saying anymore, save for lots of thanks mixed in with gasps and cries of surprise and awe. Lots of big hugs and powerful handshakes all around.

I take the candlelit parking lot in, Steve's arm around me. The little flames flicker gently, swaying back and forth as buses zoom past. Somewhere in the crowd, which seems to be growing now, a guitar chord thrums out loud and a light voice starts singing a song by Philly's own The War on Drugs.

I stand on my tiptoes and spot Laura over the heads of the crowd, close to the diner. There are a few candles around her guitar case, and some people start singing along with her.

"How did this happen?" I ask Steve.

"My dad said someone on Facebook organized it. You know there was a candlelit vigil for a Wawa a few years ago?"

I snort out a laugh. "This is Philadelphia. I don't find that even remotely surprising." I glance up at him, and he's smiling. "Saying goodbye really sucks."

"Yeah, well." He sighs. "That's something you're gonna have to get used to, you know."

"Oh, come on, this is different," I scoff, watching as someone relights a few candles that have blown out in the city breeze.

"You say that, but…" He shakes his head. "I'm just gonna miss you, man."

"I'll be back!" I exclaim. It's the same conversation I've had with Cindy. Or, well, didn't really have with her. Just mostly danced around. "I just want to, like, find myself a little bit out there, you know?"

"I don't know what you're gonna get out there that you can't find right here," Steve presses. He glances over at Laura rocking out on her guitar, the crowd now fully singing along with her. "You have people who love you here. Me and Laura, and your family. And…"

He doesn't say it. Cindy.

But why does no one understand that I'm not leaving them? Not forever, at least.

There's some movement by the diner, and I watch as Mom and Dad walk over to the entrance. Laura sets her guitar down as my parents, holding their own candles, face the crowd of friends and family in our little restaurant community.

"Thank you," Dad says, his voice shuddering a little. "Just, thank you for showing up for us, for our family, today and all those days before." He looks at my mom, who beams at him before taking a step forward.

"We'll miss this place, and the memories we made here," Mom says. She looks off to the side, and I see the cameramen there, filming all of this. Something about that roils my stomach for a minute. This isn't their moment, it's *ours*. "But it'll live on in all of you. And no one can take that away."

Dad wraps an arm around her shoulder and nods at the construction workers who are leaning off to the side against their vehicles. As my parents walk away from the diner, engines roar, the smell of exhaust filling the air more than usual on this busy street. Dad and Mom join the crowd with their candles, and everyone pushes back, closer to the sidewalk and the fence, finding a safe distance.

I turn to Steve as a tear trickles down the side of his face.

"I can't believe she isn't here," I say, my throat hurting.

"I really think she wanted to be," Steve says. "I do."

The bulldozers come, some of their treads running over the candles glowing on the pavement. I see the flames extinguish, the white wax creep through the metal slats...

And oh my God. My heart feels like it's breaking.

I want her here with me so badly.

chapter twenty: cindy

———

Thursday, Three Days until Truck Off

I watch from across the street. Steve texted me, telling me to come but... I'm not entirely sure it's my place. I don't know if Jordan really wants me here. I don't know anymore. And if any of the cameras caught me, the show would just want me to make a scene out of all this.

The bulldozers. The construction crew. The candlelight shimmering, defiant little lights in the roar of the destruction.

I see Jordan holding his parents, their shoulders shaking.

And I'm here, in the shadows.

But I'm here, Jordan.

I'm here.

Pilot: Confessional Shot Transcript (Jordan)

Jordan: Can you...can we not do one of these right now? Seriously, I'm not in the mood. Tonight was really hard and...
LISTEN GET THAT CAMERA OUT OF MY FACE.

microphone feedback

Pilot: Confessional Shot Transcript (Cindy)

Cindy: Hmm? What?

Oh, no I'm still not sure what I'm making for the Truck Off competition. It's just...there's a lot on my mind right now.

Maybe a sandwich wrap?

Hummus...

I'll figure it out.

Can we do this later? I'm sorry, my head's just not in it right now.

chapter twenty-one:
cindy

———

Friday, Two Days until Truck Off

I wave the cameramen off and head inside my house, my parents still off at the farm.

Friday.

I can't believe it's Friday.

Truck Off is in two more days, and I barely have an idea for something to make in the truck. If I'm going to beat Jordan and win that prize money for my family, I have to come up with something amazing. I head into the kitchen and dig around in the fridge, looking for any kind of inspiration or ingredient, but it's all more of the usual. Organic greens and root vegetables, fruit from the trees in the yard and small paper baskets full of little hot peppers.

Maybe...a salsa?

Would people eat just salsa out of a food truck?

Or maybe I could do some kind of a special wrap? Put some hummus in there or something—

A rapping on our front door interrupts my latest terrible idea, and I hurry over, simultaneously scrolling on my phone. Just searching for "recipes including tiny hot peppers" and "sandwiches featuring persimmons" as I swing the front door open and—

"You should have been there."

It's Laura.

"Oh." I sigh and have to fight the urge to slam the door in her face. "It's you. And for your information, I was there. You just didn't see me."

"Yeah okay," Laura scoffs, clearly not believing me. "Look, I'm the one who should be mad at you. You're the one who came to my performance and ruined my whole plan. You literally have no reason to *not* like me."

I cross my arms. She isn't wrong, but still.

"What do you want?" I ask.

She looks around the entryway to my house, still not coming in.

"Are there any cameras?" she asks.

"No, why?"

"Do you have a microphone on?"

"Laura, ugh. No. What's going on?"

"It's this…show of yours. You and Jordan." She sits down on the stairs, the stoop, and then looks up at me, her brow furrowed. She nods at the step, and I groan, sitting next her. Philly people and their stoop hangouts, I'll never get it. There's a couch right inside within eyeshot.

"Look, I don't pretend to understand your relationship

and how it's even managed to work for so long with all the fake fighting and sneaking around." She goes on. "I know... I know it has to hurt. I held back the way I felt about Steve for... I don't know. Way too long. Hiding those feelings, when they were only mine, that was rough. I can't imagine what it's like to hold them back knowing you both have them, if that makes sense."

I blink, surprised.

"Well, yeah." I clear my throat. "It does."

"But what's happening right now? The way you two are falling apart and tearing into each other... I can't just..." She groans. "Listen, that show is setting you both up."

"What? What do you mean?"

"Cindy," Laura presses. "They *know*."

I laugh and shake my head, but she stares straight at me, her expression unchanging. My mind flashes back to Drew and his surprising kindness, turning off the microphone so Jordan and I could talk privately...but it didn't seem like Drew really knew the extent of our relationship. Just that we weren't exactly total enemies.

"What do you mean they know?" I ask. "How much?"

"About you and Jordan! About the families! About how the rivalry is fake." Laura leaps to her feet and gestures around wildly. "I've been trying to piece it together since the open mic—the one you ruined by the way—and what your producer friend told me."

"Who?" I ask. "Told you what?"

"The lady, the one in the blazer. Bethany," she continues. "After your little stunt at the café, she came to talk with me.

She mentioned using the song in the pilot episode of the show, the one I wrote, you know, for *Steve*."

I roll my eyes at her emphasis.

"Just making sure," she says.

"Get on with it," I grumble.

"So Bethany had this idea, for me to tell Jordan the song was about him. In some public fashion by the trucks, with you in earshot. She said that if I did this, they'd use the song in the show, instead of cutting that segment." Laura starts pacing a little and shakes her head. "I told her no way, that I would just put the song on my Bandcamp and hope people find it, that I didn't want the show. She said it would help maintain the story arch or whatever."

"So?" I ask, my eyebrows furrowing. "A lot of reality television is scripted. What's the big deal if—"

And then it hits me.

All of it, all at once.

"See?" Laura nudges, clearly seeing the realization wash over my face. "If she didn't know you two were in a relationship, if she didn't know this was all just a big act, then why in the world would she want me to come onto Jordan where *you could hear it*? If you weren't a couple, you wouldn't care. But she *knows* you would care."

"Oh no." I run my hand through my hair. "One of the cameramen...he turned off my mic and shut off the camera yesterday when I ran into Jordan. He said he knew that we weren't exactly enemies, wanted to give us room to talk... but I don't think he *knows* knows. What does this all mean?"

"I'm not even sure, to be honest," Laura replies. "I know it means you and Jordan need to figure things out. 'Cause if

Bethany knows, and this camera guy knows *something*, more people have got to know, and this whole facade is about to come crashing down."

"Wait, did you tell Jordan about this?" I ask.

"No." Laura shakes her head. "I've been trying to get him alone to talk to him about it, but the cameras always seem to be there and I don't trust texting it. I see them watching over your shoulders, shooting your screens and stuff."

"Yeah, good call—"

"Hey."

Laura startles, an arm swinging and colliding with my chest, like a parent acting as a human seat belt when hitting a sudden stop. She shakes herself off and we both whirl around.

At Jared, walking toward us, a curious expression on his face.

Does *he* know?

"I'm...surprised to see you two hanging out," he says, his eyes flitting back and forth between us. "I thought, um...you didn't exactly care for one another?"

"We don't," Laura says curtly. She brushes herself off, like she's trying to rid herself of being close to me. "I was just seeing if she was really entering the competition or not. Heard rumors."

"Why would you care?" Jared scoffs, and from his tone, it's so clear he's on my team. It all at once warms and breaks my heart. Everything has gotten so tangled up in all these lies.

"Well, I have to make sure I have some of her favorite songs ready to play outside the Plazas truck." Laura smirks at me, and then gives me a cold glare. "See you this weekend, Ortiz. Hope you're ready. Two words. Acoustic Nickelback."

Laura shoulder checks Jared on her way down the stairs and onto the sidewalk.

"Geez," Jared mutters, watching her go as she gives him the finger. He looks to me. "She's a lot, huh?"

"Yeah." I swallow as he comes closer, wringing his hands nervously. "What are you doing here?"

"Ran late. I was supposed to be with the crew earlier, and then head off to the trucks."

"What happened?" I ask.

"Nothing specific," he says, sitting down on the steps next to me. "I'm in college. Like, as much as I enjoy this internship and want to make this a part of my life, I have two summer classes. Homework. It's a lot, but at least it allows me to stay on campus in the dorms while interning."

"I didn't realize you were dorming," I say, biting my lip. "You're not...from here?"

"No." Jared shakes his head. "I'm not from far away though. Just up in Jersey. There's a lot of fun facts about me we could discuss if we hung out more, you know." He smiles and peers down the street and then back at me. "Are you off to the trucks?"

"Yeah, in a little bit. Just waiting for my dad to get back from the car wash, drive it down to the square together. Now that we're entering the competition, he's got this whole thing. Truck has to sparkle. Ingredients have to be flawless and fresh—"

"You mean to tell me the urban farmers don't always use fresh ingredients?" he asks, grinning.

"Shut up." I swat at him, and he laughs, his eyes warm. "Just, you know, extra, I guess."

Jared takes out his phone, looks at something on it, and then flashes a mischievous smile at me.

"What time is your dad gonna be back?" he asks.

"Why?" I counter.

"It's just…" He smiles. "Maybe I could walk you there instead? Squeeze a little of that get-to-know-you time in?"

"Jared—" I start.

"No cameras. No microphones." He reaches out and tucks a wayward curl behind my ear, and I swallow, fighting the urge to lean my cheek against his hand. "Just you and me."

I reach up and take his hand, and I notice how different his hands are from Jordan's. While Jordan's are calloused and full of small bumps, discolored slices of skin from burns and cuts, Jared's are smooth and soft. Gentle.

Don't I…deserve this? Someone who understands me, who gets my world and wants to be a part of it? A real part of it?

I'll just text Dad, tell him I'm at the park already…

"Sure," I say, the word just tumbling out of my mouth like an exhale. "Let's go."

chapter twenty-two:
jordan

Friday, Two Days until Truck Off

Friday. Forty-eight more hours until the competition and then it's all over. At least, I hope so.

I hurry by the remains of The Stateside as I work my way toward Bardhan Square, but God, it's hard to avoid completely. I can smell the construction, the broken bricks and concrete particles lingering in the air. The bones, broken for everyone to see.

I need a pick-me-up.

I keep striding down the block, ignoring the street that I'd need to take to get to the truck. Eventually the tall chain-link fence of the used car lot comes into view. I pass a few cars in various states, some brand-new, some looking like they've been through it, and then eventually...

Oh.

Oh no.

The food trucks are there but…

Big Red.

She's gone.

I grab the fence and give it a little rattle, frustrated. It's too early for anyone to be here—I don't see the used car lot manager or any of the people I've noticed working in the space. It's all still locked up and quiet. It's the perfect time for early morning breakfast cheesesteaks, which is what I'm off to serve. I shouldn't waste the day mourning the loss of a truck that wasn't really mine to begin with.

I give the fence one last angry shake and make my way to the square.

I'm still gonna find a way out, with or without that truck.

Chapter twenty-three: cindy

Friday, Two Days until Truck Off

"So..." Jared starts, his hands shoved in his pockets. His eyes are on the sidewalk, at his feet, as though he's walking on eggshells.

"Northeastern," he says finally. "Why there? What's your story, Cindy Ortiz?"

He turns to me, grinning, and my heart thrums in my chest.

What can I tell him?

What do I *want* to tell him?

"I dunno, I feel like you know a lot of it already," I say hesitantly.

"I could always know more," he replies. "Like...okay, why reality TV?"

"You first." I nod. "You're the one already working in it."

"Excuse me, you're also already working in it." He playfully nudges my shoulder with his. "Beacon Street? You know, I listened to the new episode twice already."

"You've been at it longer," I counter, feeling myself blush and trying to skirt by that podcast note. "And speaking of, why is it every single reality show person I've met says some variation of 'I've been at this a long time' before explaining something to me? You all make it sound like you're in a war or something."

"I'm just ten days away from retirement..." Jared says, making his voice sound grizzly and ancient.

"Exactly," I laugh, warming up a little. "The cameramen, Bethany, they all talk like they're one slipup away from being taken out."

Jared shrugs. "I mean, I'm not saying they are," he says as we cross the street, heading toward Bardhan. "But it can be a pretty intense space. Television in general, not just reality shows. I mean, look where we are. Philadelphia isn't exactly the hot spot for television or movies."

"Doesn't M. Night Shyamalan shoot here all the time? What about that *It's Always Sunny in Philadelphia* show?" I ask.

"Psh, a lot of that show gets filmed other places," Jared says, waving his hand. "It's a small market here, for a lot of people with big dreams. Why do you think I scored an internship my freshman year?"

"'Cause you're a nerd?" I ask, swatting at his arm.

He grins back and my heart flutters.

I need to dial things back.

We walk for a little while in silence until Jared sighs, digging his hands into his pockets again.

"Okay..." he starts. "If we're going for hard truths, then

maybe it's my turn to do a little reality show confessional."
He glances at me. "Audience of one."

"Sure." I smile.

"My family is…well-off," Jared says, his tone hesitant,
meeting my eyes. "I'm pretty aware of all my privilege. I'm
here at Penn, interning over the summer, not really worrying about money or student loans while most of my friends
have part-time or even full-time jobs to support them through
undergrad."

He kicks a small stone on the sidewalk, sending it clattering up the street. We're not too far from the square now,
and he slows down a little. Like he doesn't want our time together to end.

"Here's the thing about money though. It doesn't make you
happy. All those people you see on those TV shows, they're
fighting all the time over absolutely nothing. He said this,
she said that." He shakes his head. "I watched a lot of reality television throughout high school. Even though the rich
people on TV were infinitely better off than my family—
we are not on that level—I saw what it did to my family, to
my home. All that wealth…it couldn't bring them any joy."

"Yeah, well…" I chime in, thinking about Dad and Mom
and the debt. "Not having money doesn't equate to being
happy either, you know."

He sighs and stops walking, gazing ahead to Bardhan
Square, where the camera crew is busy getting ready.

"I think there's just gotta be a happy in-between, where
I can show people being a little less shallow and how being
open and honest can be glamorous. How being real can be…"

He turns back to me, staring deeply into my eyes.

"It can be beautiful."

"Jared, I—"

"I wanted to get into television like this to tell other kinds of stories. Real ones. With real people. Like what Anthony Bourdain did, you know? He won a Peabody, showing real things. Teaching people. *Real* is what I want."

I can't even look at him right now.

He's pouring his heart out to me, about his family and his dreams, and I'm just...hiding. Lying. He's asking for real, and I don't think I've been giving him any of that. What I'm feeling right now for him, it's real. But everything else...

I'm not being the real person he thinks I am.

I'm not being the real person anyone thinks I am.

"I have to tell you—" I start.

And before I can finish what I'm saying.

He kisses me.

chapter twenty-four: jordan

Friday, Two Days until Truck Off

Cindy's truck isn't here yet.

But she sure is.

With that intern.

And they're kissing across from *our* park.

I stay close to the brick exterior of a nearby corner boutique, which sits on the side street I was walking down when I spotted them. Fresh off the pain of losing Big Red, and now this? I thought... I don't know what I thought, but I didn't think things were *over*, over between me and Cindy. Maybe after this ridiculous show, this... this *Cheesesteak Wars* nonsense, we'd find a way back.

I knew that intern was looking at her a certain way at Laura's concert. I knew it.

I walk up the side street, hurrying along the brick sidewalk, all of these conflicting emotions swirling around inside me. Big Red is gone, my plans for this year along with it. Cindy's family clearly did some damage to mine, hurt that Dad is still clinging to even if he won't admit it. And I lost her. I've really lost her.

I should have listened more. I should have paid better attention.

I stop in the middle of the sidewalk and whirl around, heading toward the square. I take a deep breath and peer around the corner of the shop, but Cindy and the intern are already gone.

I slam a fist against the brick, the edges nipping at the flesh on the side of my palm, already calloused to all hell from cooking burns and every other thing I love that hurts me.

chapter twenty-five:
cindy

Friday, Two Days until Truck Off

"I… I have to go." I say, pulling away from Jared. "I just… I gotta get to the truck…"

"Wait!" Jared shouts, and I risk a glance over my shoulder. He just stands there, shoulder slumped, looking defeated as I rush away.

Oh God, he doesn't deserve that.

And Jordan, he doesn't deserve any of this. Everything that's going on here.

I gotta talk to him. I gotta figure out how to make this right. Find a way back. Get things in control. Talk to Jordan, figure out what's going on with the show…

My phone buzzes, and my heart nearly skips a beat. Jordan maybe?

Dad: Hey, truck's ready. You home? I'll pick you up. I want to get some new ingredients at the Italian Market before the day starts.

Me: Yeah, on my way back

Dad: I figure maybe I can work the truck with you today, and we can come up with something to beat the Plazas family at the Truck Off.

I sigh, shoving my phone back in my pocket. I don't want to beat Jordan's family. I don't think I want any of this anymore.

chapter twenty-six:
jordan

Friday, Two Days until Truck Off

I walk around Bardhan Square and make my way up Passyunk and back, but... Cindy and Jared are nowhere to be found.

People are starting to line up at my truck. It is Friday in the summertime, which in tourist season, means it's the weekend. Folks with weary eyes seem to light up when they spot me rounding the circle toward the truck. A few people nudge one another. I try to smile and wave to them, as I move to climb inside the truck...

And I stop.

Across the square, where Cindy's truck usually sits, is nothing but an empty corner. The road and sidewalk that the truck covers is darker in color, from years of protection against the hot Philadelphia sun.

Hmm.

It only takes a moment for me to decide what to do next.

I climb in the driver's seat of the truck for the first time since... God, I'm not even sure when I drove this thing last. Or anyone did, really. Dad's not a fan of moving it for any reason, but right now, there's an opportunity too good to pass up.

I turn the ignition, the truck rumbles to life, and I peer outside the window at a few folks in line that immediately start muttering to one another. I should be driving off in Big Red at the end of the summer, but nope. I know I'll be able to buy something else, and it'll be fine but... God. My heart was so set on it.

At least now I can get some of that frustration out. If Cindy's just gonna hurt me, if her family has this rolling history of hurting mine, well...

I guess I can dish a little myself.

"Just a second!" I shout over the engine as it grinds and putters. I put the truck in Drive.

"Hey!" The camera crew and Jared, that intern, are staring at me. "What do you think you're doing?!"

I smile at him.

"Just giving the people what they want." I shrug, glaring at him. "Drama."

I drive around the roundabout surrounding Bardhan Square and reclaim the spot that should have belonged to my family.

Pilot: Confessional Shot Transcript (Jordan)

Jordan: The difference between the two corners on Bardhan? That's hard to say. On the side my family's truck usually is, there's the bars and a bundle of condos behind us. Over on the Ortiz side? They're closer to the boutiques and cafés.

This isn't to say only people from the bars want a regular cheesesteak instead of their healthy salads, but the cliché is sometimes a cliché for a reason.

Why move?

Why fight for each other's corners?

Why not?

chapter twenty-seven: cindy

Friday, Two Days until Truck Off

"Ugh, I can't believe this," Dad grumbles as the truck inches its way through the Italian Market, narrow streets made even narrower by people busy shopping, stocking, and bartering. A guy pushes a pallet in front of us piled high with cardboard boxes, and on the sidewalk near me, two women throw massive fish into a meat distributor from the back of a truck.

"I told you the truck was fine," I start. But honestly, I'm grateful for the traffic. The longer it takes to get back to the roundabout, the longer it'll be until I have to see Jared. Or Jordan. Or face any of what's happening here. I still haven't figured out how to talk to anyone about what Laura seems to have uncovered.

"Presentation is important," Dad insists. "People come to our truck for the organic food and an element of class."

"You sound like a character from *Downton Abbey*." I roll my eyes.

"I don't know what that is."

"Whatever." It's my turn to grumble. "We really didn't need to get more ingredients, you know." I peek over my shoulder at the boxes in the back, piles of different veggies we've definitely never used in the food truck. "I mean, Brussels sprouts? In what world are those going to work in the food truck?"

"I'm convinced television and movies poisoned the world against Brussels sprouts," Dad says. "They're delicious. Roast them up so they're crisp? Drizzle a little maple syrup on them? Or lemon pepper? Forget it."

"Yeah, forget it is right. It takes, like, half an hour to roast them. It's a food truck, Dad."

Dad sighs. "Okay, I'll give you that one. It's just…making the right thing, coming up with the right snack at the truck for this weekend…it's important, Cindy."

"Dad…" I start.

"No, don't." He shakes his head. "That's why I wanted to help in the truck today. It's my fault the family is in the mess, it's up to me to get us out."

"How…how bad is it?" I ask.

Dad's grip tightens on the steering wheel, and he swallows.

"That bad?" I ask.

"You know, I firmly believe kids should be oblivious when it comes to their parents' struggles but…" He hesitates, his expression wavering, and my heart breaks a little. "Well, look. It's not world ending. But it is embarrassing. And your mother is right, it's my fault."

"The competition is *this weekend*, Dad. I just, I don't think you're gonna magically come up with something to beat the Plazas family."

"Yeah, we'll see."

Eventually we break free of the traffic, and the opening in the road sends my anxiety reeling. Whatever confrontation is coming, it's just going to get here sooner now. And Dad hits the gas a little too hard for the truck, which emits an array of strange noises that sound...not great. I give him a look that he must notice, because he waves me off, his eyes firm on the road. "It's fine. It's not like we drive it that much anyway."

"You drive it every week to get cleaned!" I exclaim, and he laughs a little.

"I'll take it for a tune-up soon, nothing to worry about right..." He trails off and squints, the truck slowing down. "What. The. Hell. Is. This."

"Hmm?" I glance out the window, and... I'm a little baffled at what I'm seeing.

Jordan's truck is parked in our space. People are lined up outside it, which isn't a surprise, since they've been going wild for those breakfast cheesesteaks of his. But his family never moves that truck. Ever.

Dad's face is turning an alarming shade of red as he parks our truck on the opposite side of the square, where Jordan's family truck usually is, the break grinding as he yanks it up, and he practically jumps out of the driver's side seat.

"Dad!" I shout, scrambling out of mine. By the time I'm around to the other side of the truck, he is storming across the square.

I have...never seen Dad like this before.

"Hey!" Dad shouts across the park. Jordan pops up in the window of his truck, and for a moment, looks genuinely scared. The cameras near his truck spin toward Dad, and also me, and everyone on line for a cheesesteak stares.

I can't help but notice Jared isn't here. There's a small wave of relief in all the mayhem.

"Mr. Ortiz—" Jordan starts, a smile on his face.

"Don't you *Mr. Ortiz* me, you little..." He looks around at everyone and then at the cameras, talking through gritted teeth. "What do you think you're doing?" He points at the truck and the street. "Is this some kind of joke?"

"Hey, you left it open." Jordan shrugs, his eyes flitting to me. He's got the smuggest face on that I've ever seen and I'm...actually not sure if this is him just playing along for *Cheesesteak Wars*, or actually being a jerk right now.

Dad is up at the window now, encroaching onto the steel counter, practically leering at him.

"Move it. Now," Dad growls.

"Now why would I do that?" Jordan asks. "Maybe when I move it out of the way for cleaning or something, you can take it back—*oh, wait a minute*. I'll just wash it here like a normal person."

"Hey..." I start, wanting to cool down the situation.

"Stay out of this, Cindy," Dad snaps without turning to me. "We spent too much money getting the permit for that space for you to just feel like it's okay to come in here and take it away. We're on this corner because—"

"Because your family outbid mine on the truck they wanted." Jordan glares at my dad.

"What?" I ask, looking from Jordan to Dad. "What are you talking about?"

"Like you even care." Jordan's eyes flit over to me, cold, and then back to my dad. A cameraman works his way around to the left of me and Dad, like they're flanking us.

"Why don't you tell her all about it? Hmm?" Jordan continues. "How you outbid my family, who were struggling while you were just taking advantage of being in a new city? Stealing the spot they wanted, in a community they were a part of? You and your family never really cared about the food scene here."

He looks at me again.

"Not even a little."

"Listen you…" Dad says, his skin turning even redder. "Our customers are closer to this side of the street, closer to the businesses and—"

"Maybe they'll just be my customers now."

Dad slaps the steel countertop. The noise rings out like a gunshot.

People stagger away. Even the cameraman near us jostles back.

"Dad," I plead, trying not to look at the cameras.

Something seems to click and he steps backward.

"This isn't over. I'll have you towed! I *will* have our family spot."

"I'll trade you for the truck," Jordan snaps.

With that, Dad turns on his heel and stomps toward our truck. The cameras follow him so I wait and peer at Jordan. I examine his face for any hint at what's going on in that head of his, but he shrugs, returning to whatever it is he's doing in his truck. Like what just happened wasn't even a big deal. Like he doesn't care.

And I...don't think he does. This doesn't feel like a game right now. It feels like actual spite.

"Dad... Dad!" I hurry after him. He's in the truck, staring ahead angrily, his hands on the steering wheel. I hop back in. "Hey, what was that?"

"That parking permit was expensive," Dad declares, turning to me. His eyebrows are furrowed. "I know it's all a fun game to you kids, maybe to your mother and his, but the fight over those spaces and those trucks was actually very real, you know."

"Wait, what?"

Dad sighs. "Our truck is the more expensive one. I mean just look at that thing he's in. Jordan's family had their eye on ours, and it came down to a bidding war. The amount we offered was...a little excessive. And...well, contributed to some of the debt we're in. But it was *ours*. And it's not okay for them to think they can just take the good parking spot too just because we got the better truck." He pauses, breathing heavily. "Our families are fine now, obviously, but that?" He points out the window. "That is not okay."

"I'll talk to him," I mutter, taking out my phone.

"Let's get to work," Dad grumbles. "We have to beat them."

He walks into the food truck, and I can hear him angrily chopping up some vegetables.

Jordan.

Jared.

My family.

The show.

I've completely lost control of everything. I need to find a way to take it back.

Pilot: Confessional Shot Transcript (Jordan)

Jordan: *laughs* Mine now.

chapter twenty-eight: jordan

Saturday, One Day until Truck Off

The truck rattles and sputters and coughs as I pull it into the massive, sprawling parking lot outside the Riversharks stadium in Camden. This is the first Saturday the truck hasn't been parked in Bardhan Square in... I'm not even sure how long, and while my heart sinks at the thought of the business we'll be losing today, at how happy the Ortiz family will be at getting their parking spot back, how my dream truck is gone, how Cindy is probably spending time with Jared...

Okay, wow, my heart is sinking at a lot of things right now.

But the promise of tomorrow has me wildly excited.

I need this. There are plenty of other great trucks out there, and the prize money will get me one.

I can do this.

There are a seemingly endless number of food trucks here, lined up next to picnic tables and empty whiskey barrels as tables. They've even got some string lights strung between the streetlamps, already lit in the late morning.

The smell is amazing. The trucks that are already here are already frying and roasting food, the aromas mixing with exhaust from those having just driven in and still showing up. This is going to be the best weekend, and I refuse to let it be anything less than that.

I just need to stay focused. I can win this tournament, still do this reality show pilot for my family, win the prize money, and then that's it. I'm out of here.

And despite how angry and heartbroken I am over Cindy, I know I'm still doing some of this for her. I can't help it. I can feel devastated and keep pushing despite these swirling feelings. I can contain multitudes.

A man wearing a bright orange safety vest strolls up to where I'm idling at the entrance to the parking lot, carrying a clipboard and a walkie-talkie. He looks over my truck and winces.

"Do you want me to take this truck behind the barn and shoot it?" he asks, smirking.

"Wow," I laugh. "The chop busting begins already?"

He flips some papers around the clipboard, before his eyes widen and he glances back up. "Oh. You're the reality show truck. *Cheesesteak Wars!*" He points his pen at me.

"I mean, I guess. That's not really what I'm all about though. It's the food for me."

"Alright, well, we've got a special spot…" He looks out into the lot, squinting, and then points with his pen in the distance. "Over there. See the tables and barrels that are in the corner back there? We set up a few extra for the camera crew. And the attention it's likely going to draw—you know, television."

"Oh." I swallow. "You think more people will check us out because there are cameras around?"

"Probably." He takes a backpack off his back and starts digging around in it. He pulls out a lanyard with a plastic square attached. "Your festival pass. Be sure to keep it on while you're wandering around. Other trucks will likely give you a discount too."

"Awesome, thanks." I take the lanyard and hit the gas, the truck groaning again.

"Offer still stands!" the security guys yells, and he makes a gesture like he's loading a shotgun. I wave and drive around the lot to where I'm meant to post up all weekend.

I feel more than a little irritated that the place reserved for our trucks is in the very back corner of this festival, but if it's really going to get more attention due to the cameras, I suppose it's not all bad. I park the truck, which I swear seems to be physically relieved by that fact as I turn off the engine, and maneuver into the back to clean up whatever has inevitably fallen off a shelf or spilled and what have you.

It's funny, I don't think I really saw how rough a shape this truck was in—I mean *really* saw it—until Dad's reveal that he wanted the truck the Ortiz family drives. That this was the one our family had to settle on. If my parents had just a little bit more money, they wouldn't have spent all these years trying to keep this thing together. They could have maybe been a little more comfortable. Maybe they could have been closer to their goal of opening a new restaurant.

But now it's the only thing I see. The rust around the

frame surrounding the wheels, eating away at the metal. The floors inside, coated in grease and salt and pepper, trapped there like it's been glued on. All the dials and display on the dashboard that require a little bit of slapping to get them to move and operate.

I don't like that I'm viewing everything through this lens now.

All the ingredients that I traveled with look secure, but there are a few kitchen tools smattered about inside. Spatulas on the floor, some containers too. Nothing that bad, but I still make some mental notes. If I'm going to be hitting the road with my own truck in the coming months, I should probably have some gadgets in place to hold everything. Clips and magnets. I don't want to arrive in a new city, ripped and roaring to go, only to discover everything is in pieces. I feel like maybe I'm channeling a little bit of Steve in all of this, the organization and cleanliness. He'd be proud.

Once everything is cleaned and back in order, I stand back and survey the space.

I picture my own truck, what the inside might look like. The kind of grill, the refrigeration units, the tools I'll need, and the storage containers. God, I'm probably the only eighteen-year-old who daydreams of The Container Store, something my mom talks about like it's a paradise. But I can see it all, how everything will fit in my own small six-by-eight-foot space, and all the ways I'm going to figure out how to make it a home.

Even though this was a home I was hoping to share with Cindy.

But I shake that thought free. It's not what she wants. It's never been what she's wanted. Hell, *I'm* not what she wants. And I should have taken more time to listen.

I test the grill and the sink, making sure everything is still working after the drive from South Philadelphia over the bridge into New Jersey. It seems silly, but I don't know. This truck isn't made for the road anymore.

It feels like...one of those things guidance counselors awkwardly warn you about. Not to plan where you're going to college around someone that you're dating. Which, like, no one listens to. I feel like every other couple in our circle of friends paired up and are off to whatever university. I wish them luck, I do.

But now I think I understand what she was talking about. Our old guidance counselor, Mrs. Birch. You should make plans for yourself, not for someone else. Especially not when that someone else might not be interested in those plans and aren't sure how to talk about it.

Dammit.

I lean over the counter and take a few deep breaths.

None of this was supposed to get this hard.

There's a rapping against the metal shutter that startles me back, and I knock over a few kitchen tools. I scramble to pick them up and head outside, ready to dance for the cameras.

But it's Steve.

"Hey?" I look around. "You're way too early, man. The festival is tomorrow."

"Dude, I came to get you," he says, urgently. "You haven't been answering your texts."

"I was driving, you don't look at your phone when you're

driving..." I pull my phone out, and there are a bundle of missed calls and messages, all from him, Laura, and... Cindy.

"Oh."

Huh.

"What's going on?" I ask, shoving the phone back in my pocket.

"Laura found out something about the show. All of us are meeting at Cindy's house. It's sort of an all-hands-on-deck situation."

"I don't understand." I pull my phone out again. "Over what?"

"Dude," Steve groans. "They know. Everyone knows. The producers, the cameramen. They know that the rivalry is fake. They've *been* known, I think."

I read the texts. Lots of please call me back, please respond, this is urgent from just about everybody, but only one from Cindy.

Cindy: It's over. It's all over.

I look back up at Steve.

"Let's go."

Pilot: Confessional Shot Transcript (Cindy)

Cindy: No, I still don't know what I'm making for the Truck Off. Are we done for the day? Is this a wrap? I really need to focus, and I'm not sure how helpful that same question is going to be while I'm rummaging around in my fridge.

Ya'll wanted television that was entertaining, and this isn't it. Right?

I'll see you at Truck Off tomorrow.

chapter twenty-nine: cindy

Saturday, One Day until Truck Off

"So," Mom says, pouring out glasses of iced tea for everyone. Jordan's parents are sitting on the couch in our living room, my dad is pacing around near the door. "What's the plan? What do we even do?"

"I don't know," Dad grumbles, stopping to lean against the wall. "I feel like maybe this is something we should have ironed out, you know, before we said yes to this."

"Wow, you think, Antony?" Mr. Plazas huffs.

"Hey, you're in this too, Daniel," Dad bites back. "Both our families and kids are caught up in this mess and now we need to figure out what we're going to do about it."

"What is there to figure out?" Mr. Plazas asks. "They know it's all an act, so we apologize and that's a wrap, isn't it?" He takes a sip of the iced tea on the table and nearly doubles over, a few drops dribbling from his mouth. "What did you put in this?! Besides nothing?!"

"You don't need sugar in iced tea!" Mom shouts.

"Jesus, Antony, you're being rude," Mrs. Plazas says and reaches for her glass. She takes a sip, and immediately coughs.

"I told you," Mr. Plazas says.

"Sorry, sorry," Mrs. Plazas replies, putting the drink down. "Sugar would be...very welcome."

"My God, you people." Mom grabs the glasses and hurries into the kitchen, just as the front door to the house opens. Steve hurries in, looking a little bit frantic, followed by Laura, and then...there's Jordan. His eyes immediately settle on me and leave just as quickly, as though they need to focus on absolutely anything else in the room. Like I'm a car crash he feels guilty for looking at.

"Ah, excellent," Mr. Plazas says. "Everyone's here."

"Great," Dad says. "Maybe first we can talk about why your son stole our parking spot yesterday."

"What?!" Mr. Plazas asks, laughing. "You did what?"

"It was nothing, it was just for the show—"

"It was not *just* for the show!" Dad shouts. "I saw that look on your face, you were enjoying it."

"Yeah, so what?" Jordan scoffs. "It was funny. Not like it matters now anyway. I'm parked up in Camden so you can have it back."

"Great," Dad huffs and then goes back to pacing around the room, like his feet might dig holes in the floor.

"Antony, can you just...sit down?" Mom suggests. Dad stops and flops onto a love seat, hunching over, and I swear you can just see the anxiety vibrating off him in waves, like he's an old radiator.

"I mean, honestly, what are we even going to do here?" Jordan's Dad chimes back in. "They release the pilot, and what happens? The whole rivalry is unmasked as a big lie? Who cares? It's not like someone is gonna die. What do we really have to lose here?"

Dad grumbles something into his hands, and Steve chuckles a little, standing next to Jordan. But Jordan just looks ahead, his expression cold and unmoving.

I just want to know what's going on in his head. Mine is just swimming with…guilt.

"Well," Mrs. Plazas interjects. "The whole thing isn't really a lie. Just the kids."

"Isn't that the same thing?!" Mr. Ortiz continues. "That's what people have cared about all these years. What they found so amusing."

"Eh, I don't know," Mrs. Plazas says. "Won't they just think it's like…a cute Romeo and Juliet situation? The families didn't know of their great love and—"

Jordan laughs miserably.

Everyone turns to him. His dad stops talking.

"Sorry, sorry," Jordan says through a final chuckle.

It feels like the eyes of everyone in our families are on me, and I look down at my feet.

"Sweetheart?" Mom ventures. "What happened?"

"Nothing." I shake my head.

There's a long silence that makes me want to scream and run out the door, but I press my feet to the floor, like I can plant myself in this house.

"We, um...we broke up," I say, the words feeling trapped in my throat, like I have to wrestle them out. I try to make eye contact with Jordan, anything, but he just stares ahead into the living room. The quiet that follows feels even worse, weighing on me like a blanket.

"Okay..." Jordan's dad starts. "Okay, I think this has all gone far enough, then." He glances over at his wife and the rest of the living room. "Let's just go come clean. Call up Ms. Ireland. See if we can salvage—"

"Not so fast, Daniel," Dad interrupts, looking up from his hands. "You're shrugging all this off, but we need that rivalry. This little—" he waves at me and Jordan "—spat between these two. It brings the trucks attention. Makes us money."

Jordan's dad gives him an incredulous look.

"Don't give me that, you know it's true," Dad continues.

"Antony, come on," Mr. Plazas says. "Yeah, I mean, sure, we make a little extra, and that truck has helped support our family through some tough times, but we can get on without the fake battle. You know that."

"Every dollar counts in this business," Dad presses, jamming a finger into the coffee table. "You'd know that if you bought better ingredients for your sandwiches."

"Excuse me?" Jordan's dad says, inching forward in his seat.

"Uh-oh," I hear Steve whisper.

"You guys barely *try* when it comes to your sandwiches. And you make so much in profits, but it's all gone so quickly. You should be investing it in better ingredients, in—"

"We invest it in our son's college, you entitled prick!" Jordan's dad shouts. "Giving back to the community! And unlike you, I'm not making my kids pay off my debts!"

"How DARE you!" My dad leaps to his feet.

Jordan's father gets up, his leg knocking against the coffee table hard, and he swears before swiping at the iced tea on the surface. "And your iced tea tastes like hell!"

The glasses hit the floor, the soft, way-too-thick rug cushioning their fall in an anticlimactic way.

There's a pause.

A lingering moment of tension.

And then everyone starts screaming at each other. Mom is shouting at Mr. Plazas, my dad is scrambling to pick up the glasses while Mrs. Plazas yells something at me that I don't quite make out. Laura is trying to get Steve to leave, but he's staying put.

And for the first time since I showed up here, Jordan is looking at me.

He nods toward the door.

And I follow him.

I can hear the fighting inside the house from where we end up on the sidewalk. Steve and Laura are sitting on the stoop, holding hands and clearly eavesdropping on our parents.

"Well." Steve breaks the tension outside first. "Guess there was a little more truth to the rivalry than we thought?"

Jordan doesn't say anything. Neither do I.

I feel like I should.

"Oh my God," Laura snaps, practically jumping off the stoop. "What the hell is going on with you two? I know you're fighting over all..." something crashes inside the house and all of us flinch at the same time "...well, this. And this ridiculous show. But come on. That isn't exactly the example to follow here."

I look at Jordan and he stares down at his feet.

Just tell him. Just get it over with.

But what is he going to do? Say? Everything feels so unpredictable and out of my control right now, and I hate it. I want to say the exact right thing and I'm afraid there isn't a right thing to say here.

"What is it?" Steve asks, getting up. "Something else is going on here."

Jordan exhales and looks over at me.

And in the same way he could tell that I wasn't going on that road trip with him anymore, under the streetlights in Dickenson Square... I know that he knows.

I swallow.

"I, um...kissed Jared." My throat feels dry, like I ate a giant piece of stale bread without any water. "The intern on the set." I glance back to Steve and Laura, and Steve is making an "oof" face that looks like something out of an internet meme. "Well, really, he kissed me. And I stopped it. Right away, but..."

"I know," Jordan says, sniffling back something. "I was heading to the trucks and saw you both."

"I'm sorry," I say. "For all of it. The road trip, pushing you into this show, the whole Jared thing..." I shake my head. "But, Jordan, you don't understand, he gets me and the podcast and the reality television stuff and...it felt nice that someone was really hearing me."

"*I* hear you," Jordan presses, his eyebrows furrowing. "Just because I don't quite get your podcast and this reality business, I listen. *You* don't hear *me*. I did this for you. The show, even the show at the trucks, I kept it going for you. Everything has been for you."

"Not your road trip," I say. "That wasn't for us. That was for you."

"Whatever." He looks away from me.

"Fine." I cross my arms.

There's a beat of quiet, and Laura and Steve shift uncomfortably.

"So," Laura starts, interrupting the silence. "What's the plan?"

"Plan?" I ask.

"Um...yeah?" she says, hands on her hips. "There's no way you're just going to, what, *just* tell the reality show what's been going on, right? Or keep the charade going, only for them to do some grand reveal on their own? One way, you lose the show and the potential income. The other way, the pilot gets made, but there's no actual rivalry, and they win and tell the story how they want to tell it."

"It feels kind of lose-lose there, Laura," I groan and hang my head.

"It's not though. Not if you reclaim the narrative," Laura suggests. I don't really know what she's trying to get at, and it doesn't seem like Steve or Jordan do either. "Listen, I know you and me don't really get along and all that, but I know you enough. You like to be in control of things, and when you aren't, it becomes a problem."

I open my mouth to protest but stop. She's right. And she gives me a look that says she knows it.

"Honestly it's probably why you'll be good at reality television someday," Laura continues. "But you can't do everything by yourself. These television people have, like, I don't know, assistants and aides and producers and annoying interns who aren't nearly as good a catch as some people."

I cross my arms, though it does get a little chuckle out of Jordan.

"Alright, too much." Laura holds her hands up. "You need your crew. Can't you call your annoying friends?"

"My what?!"

"Those...girls, the girls you talk to about your reality shows on social media all the time. With your podcast."

"How do you even know about them?" I ask.

"For one, I follow you on Twitter—thank you for never following me back, by the way." Laura snorts. "Two, you date my best friend."

"Dated," Jordan corrects, and it's like a dagger in my chest.

"Alright, alright." Laura waves her hand at Jordan dismissively. "You're making snippy comments like you're not gonna get back together and make out the second you're alone in a truck."

Steve laughs, and I glare at him. He stops.

"Listen, you think Jordan hasn't talked to me about you and your reality shows and how you and your friends are on social media and Zoom talking about this stuff all the time? How you're fighting because you're heading back to Boston to be closer to your pals? Let's get them on the phone and see what they think about this."

"Fine. Sure." I shrug and take my phone out. "But I don't see what that's going to do."

FaceTime rings. And rings. And rings.

Eesha appears on screen, and quickly after, so does Ariana.

"Hey what's…" Eesha squints at her screen. "What's up?"

"Is that Jordan?" Ariana asks.

"Yeah, so…here's what's going on," I start. And then I explain the last few days to them, the bits and pieces I've left out of our texts. The cameraman who let us be for a while so we could talk. The producer who wanted Laura to act like she actually wanted Jordan, so her song could be on the air. The fact that it seems like they do, in fact, know this is all an act.

Ariana stares ahead, wildly gripped, while Eesha's brows furrow, like she's deep in thought throughout the entire conversation.

"We're trying to figure out what to do next," I say. "Our families are inside and…" I stop, listening, and sure enough, someone swears loudly. "They're still fighting and bickering over all of this. And me and Jordan…"

I look up at him and he turns away.

"Yeah, I don't know what we are right now."

"Oh no," Ariana offers. "I'm sorry."

"Okay, okay," Eesha says, putting the phone down on something. She steps away from the screen, and claps her hands together, rubbing them against one another. "Okay, okay… Here's a thought. Remember when that one woman on *Married at First Slight*, was about to be unveiled for embezzling from her husband's business?" Eesha asks, her hands steepled together. "What did she do? Instead of letting the show do it for her in a story line…"

"She did it herself," I say and bite my lip. "But what's that have to do with—"

"Think about it," Eesha presses. "Instead of giving the reality show this story arc, this reveal where it turns out you've been together this whole time and the families have been lying...and letting them frame it the way they want, why don't YOU frame the story?"

"How?" I ask, looking up at Jordan.

Jordan nods, and it's like I can actually see the gears turning in his head.

"We find a way to take the story back," Eesha says. "Find a way for the two of you to work together on something. Take back control."

I look at Laura and she flashes me a smug smile.

Fine. You get me more than I thought you did.

My mind flashes back to Reading Terminal, to Jordan poking around the spice shop, to all the stress he's been carrying over this competition. All of it leads up to one thing.

That magical ingredient he thinks is going to make or break his sandwich.

"I think I know what we should do." I look around at Steve, Laura, Jordan, and back at Eesha and Ariana in their little video box. "We need to make the sandwich tomorrow, together, and shoot our own footage."

I glance at Jordan, his mouth turned up like he's trying to consider what I've just said.

"Let's figure out what's missing from those—" I wince "—cheesebreaks."

Laura lets out a lone "ha" in response, and I groan.

I'm gonna hate this.

But I'm taking control of this story.

Pilot: Confessional Shot Transcript (Eesha & Ariana via Zoom)

Eesha: Ah! I can't believe we're on television!

Ariana: This is amazing!

Eesha: Amazing!

Ariana: How many shows have you worked on? Like, have you met any of the Housewives? Any people from the 90 Day shows? We want to hear all your stories.

long pause

Ariana: What can you, like, not talk or something?

Producer: *says something muffled*

Ariana: Oh. That sucks.

Eesha: Well, we're excited to be here. We've known Cindy since we were all...what, how old, Ari?

Ariana: Oh, when we were six, I think. First grade. Or kindergarten? Wait. Doesn't that one Housewife on Beacon Hill have a kid just starting pre-K?

Eesha: OH MY GOD you're right, Kristina Marie! Is that really why she left the show? I know the wrap-up last season said it was to focus on family, but I heard she was moving to another town.

Ariana: Is she going to be on a new show?

long pause

Eesha: I promise we won't put this on our podcast. Unless this can be on the record? Can this be on the rec—

transcript cut off for length and time

chapter thirty: jordan

Sunday Morning, Three Hours until Truck Off

The security guard who told me I should put down my truck isn't there anymore. Instead, he's been replaced by what looks like a half dozen more, who are walking up and down the breadth of the entryway and beyond, guarding all the food trucks. Makes sense to me, I suppose. There's some serious kitchen gear stashed away inside a lot of the vehicles, but then again, how in the hell would someone be able to steal it?

Honestly, if someone managed to break into my food truck and somehow wrangle the entire grill out of there without blowing themselves up, I'd feel like they earned it.

It's a shame though. Here I am, driving the Ortiz food truck. Would have been hilarious to see that security guard's face watching me handle something so shiny and well taken care of. Although, all of that doesn't mean it's loved. Not like our family truck has been.

Not like my truck will be.

Ugh. This truck. It should have been my family's truck. All clean and new and spotless. I probably would have made it messy, sure. Dad too. And Mom. But whatever. It wouldn't have come looking like a hot mess. It could have become our mess.

"Lot's closed," one of the security guards says as we pull up, pointing back at the festival space. "Though I'm guessing you're here for the event?"

"We are." I fish the lanyard out of my shirt, the shiny plastic pass attached. "My truck's in there, but my, um, friend's truck is meant to park next to it." I don't even know what to call her right now. Definitely not *girlfriend*.

"Wow, this is nice," he says, peering into the truck. He takes a step back and squints at the side. "Oh, I know you. This truck. My girl loves the feta spinach wrap you make in here."

Cindy lets out a little snort, and we drive into the lot.

I park her food truck right across from mine in the spot they've got saved for her. The space between our trucks is a lot more decorated than it was earlier, with even more lights strung up and the whiskey barrel tables wrapped in them too.

"Alright, so—" I start.

Cindy hops out of the truck and closes the door.

Great.

I get out and walk around to where she is.

"Look I know neither of us really wants to do this right now, but we should make some kind of an effort," I say, crossing my arms, leaning against the steel siding of her truck. "This was your idea, to shoot a video together and all that."

"Sorry, I'm just…" She looks at her phone and back up at me. "Trying to wrangle all of this and keep everyone off our tail."

"What are you even doing?" I ask, and she nudges up close to me. Oh my God, her hair smells like that cherry vanilla shampoo she uses sometimes, and it just short-circuits my senses.

"Look." She holds her phone up, tapping a few buttons to move between the different platforms she's focused on. "I'm texting with Bethany and Drew, and posting pictures from the kitchen at home, like I'm in there, working on ingredients." She smiles. "There are even a few scheduled insults on Instagram aimed at your truck."

"Nice one, Ortiz." I smile back. There's a lingering pause between us, when another alert blips up on her Instagram.

I barely make out the username Jared Loves TV before she slides the phone back in her pocket.

"Wow, it really is serious," I huff, breaking the afterglow of that moment we just had.

"It's not like that, he just comments on a lot of stuff," Cindy says, sheepishly.

"Right."

"Let's go figure out how to fix your sandwich," she snaps.

"Fine." I nod and look around the parking lot. I'm not seeing any sign of the camera crew yet, thankfully. But really, they're going to be here any moment. The competition kicks off in three hours. They've gotta set up *something*.

I unlock my parents' truck and Cindy steps inside, standing over the grill. She glares at it like it just insulted someone in her family. I roll my eyes and start getting things going. I pull out the different ingredients I've been using for the cheese-breaks and set them out on the small prep table.

"So, this is really it." I point at the supplies. "We've got the bread, meat, cheese, eggs, salt and pepper...that's it."

"Right, so...we need to figure out how to make this sandwich better, together. Tell our own story here," Cindy says, staring at the Amaroso roll.

"I mean, that's what you and your friends said. Working together and all."

She grabs the roll, looks at it for a beat, and tosses it back on the table.

"What the hell are we doing, Jordan?" she asks, looking right at me. "What is this going to accomplish? They caught us, the show is going to blow it all up, we're going to let our families down, we can forget about that potential prize money, my parents are still going to be in debt..."

"It's about telling our story on our terms, isn't it?" I ask. "And, um, not for anything, that prize money isn't out of the question just yet."

"And what's *our* story now?" She slides down against a cabinet in the truck to sit on the floor, putting her face in her hands before looking up at me.

"I mean...haven't you made your choice when it comes to our story?" I ask, leaning against the countertop. "What is there to talk about?"

"Jordan, look... Jared—"

"I don't really care what his name is," I mutter, even though I absolutely know what his name is.

"Jordan," Cindy presses. "I'm sorry. I should have told you the second it happened. Or even...while it was happening. I couldn't tell him about us or the truth about our families, so he didn't know you and me were a thing…it's actually not his fault."

"Oh, so it's mine?"

"No," Cindy says sharply, a glimmer of irritation in her voice. "You know that. You're just upset and lashing out and I get it but…it was just…for a while it felt like I didn't have to pretend anymore. Like, we were out and about in public. Talking. It was like a glimmer of the kind of relationship I actually want. Not all this hiding."

Her eyes are a little glassy and it wrenches at something in my chest.

"I'm sorry about the kiss. I was going to tell you but then everything got messed up with the trucks' spots and the reality show and… I just got lost in it all. But I don't want to lose you."

"So…it doesn't have to end this way?" I ask, joining her on the floor. "And are you sure you want to sit down here?"

"What? Why?" she asks, gazing around nervously.

"It's just, you know, a lot of grease," I say.

She scoots up and wipes her leg, groaning as she sits back down.

"So gross, Jordan." She meets my eyes, and there's at least the hint of a smile on her face.

"Look, all of the hiding and sneaking and pretending can't have been for nothing. Can we at least, I don't know…take the time we have here and talk about it?" I ask.

"What's there to talk about though?" Cindy asks, pushing her back against the food truck wall. "I'm leaving for Northeastern in August, and I know you've never wanted to do college. You're hitting the road at the end of the summer shortly after, which I never really wanted to do—"

"Well, why not start with that, then? If you never wanted to go, why let me think you wanted to?"

"I didn't want to lose you!" Cindy shouts, slapping her hands against her knees.

"Yeah but maybe I could have planned out something different?" I suggest. "Maybe instead of us taking a gap year together I could have just gone, or you could have done virtual classes on the road with me, or I could have gone on a shorter trip and come back—"

"Jordan, you don't see it. When you have your heart set on something, it's all…starry eyes and big exclamations. Your parents are the same way. I can't be the person who shuts that down. I can't dim your shine. I just can't."

"What if I go on a shorter trip though?" I ask. "What if I come back. For you. That was always the plan. Coming back after seeing the country together."

"Is that really what you want though?" she replies, and I take her hands in mine. She squeezes them and I'm filled with warmth.

"You're what I want," I press. "Just…can we not give up on us just yet?"

"I don't know, Jordan. It feels like we're just delaying what's inevitable." She sighs.

"Listen…what Laura said back at the house. About you wanting to be in control of things," I start.

"Yeah?" Cindy says through gritted teeth.

"Just, bear with me there," I continue, squeezing her hands. "Look, I might go all-in on pipe dreams with the…stars in my eyes or whatever like you said. And I know I do. But in all of this, I've learned a little focus isn't a bad thing. Paying attention, being grounded, it keeps things close. And I want to keep you closer. And if you can let go just a bit, try to be more…spur-of-the-moment, and worry less about the outcome, maybe we can find a way to meet in the middle."

Cindy grips my hands a little bit harder.

"Alright," she says. "Let's just…can we agree to be honest with each other about everything for the rest of the summer, and see where that takes us? I'll let go a little bit more, and you can be a bit more grounded."

"Yes!" I exclaim, shaking her hands in mine. "I'll absolutely take that."

She smiles softly at me, and as we lock eyes, the air feels suddenly charged. I lean forward, and just like that, her hand reaches out, grabbing my shoulder, and pulls me in for a kiss. And before I can even tell it's happening, our arms are wrapped around one another, sliding on the metal floor, kissing and laughing. We bump against a cabinet, some pans and spatulas tumbling out and clattering on us like hard rain, and for a moment, it feels like we're actually back and us again.

This whole week has been absolute hell. The fake hating. The family secrets. The crumbling of my plans. This intern. Just thing after thing after thing when all I wanted was to find a way back to making the most important person in my life happy.

When the reality was, making her happy meant pushing all of that nonsense aside, and really talking about the things that we wanted.

It's not enough to just want and love a person.

You have to want and love things for them.

I was being selfish, and I'll never be that way again.

And then, as quickly as it happened, she pulls away from me, smacking her lips together.

"What?" I ask. "What's the matter—"

"Just...hold on..." she says, pursing her lips, her expression deep in thought. Suddenly her eyes go wide and she scrambles to her feet.

"Oh my God," she says. "That's it."

"What?" I ask. "What is it?!"

"What did you have for breakfast this morning?" she asks.

"Nothing special, just some hash browns with a little leftover truffle oil I found in a cabinet—"

"I know what we need." She grabs her jacket and empties out the pockets. "Dammit, how much money do you have in the truck?"

"What?" I laugh.

"Where's that tip jar?" She looks around. "Ah!"

She lunges across the truck and grabs the mason jar full of tips, which I still haven't emptied out from this week. She dumps it onto the countertop.

"Hey!" I shout.

"Shush," she says, flipping through the change and bills. She crams all the paper money back into the jar and turns to me, her eyes wide, the jar in her hand. "Do you trust me?"

A few days ago, under the bright lights of the cameras and the boom microphone guys chasing around, I might have said no. She barged into Laura's concert and tossed my sandwich on the ground. I saw her being kissed by that other guy...

But now, here, covered in cooking grease and the ash from

burnt bread, our skin shining with sweat and canola oil… I do. I really do trust her.

"Yes," I say, scrambling to my feet. "What are we doing?"

"Well," Cindy says, grinning. "You're gonna have to drive."

Pilot: Confessional Shot Transcript (Bethany, Producer)

Bethany: Hello? Is this on? Great. Hi. We've hit a small production snag today, as we were supposed to meet up with Cindy and Jordan at their homes, and follow them to the competition, only to discover they'd taken off hours ago.

We're going to meet up with them at Truck Off with the crew. Hopefully they are there, as we've been building up to this all week...

I don't understand what's happening here.

chapter thirty-one: cindy

Sunday Morning, Two Hours until Truck Off

"We have to find a parking spot *where*?!" Jordan asks as my family's truck roars across the Ben Franklin Parkway. I swear, we even catch a little bit of air when the truck crests the highest part of the incline, but that might just be my imagination.

"It'll be fine," I insist. "If anything, I'll just jump out and run in."

He laughs as we slow down, traffic an inevitability on a Sunday coming out of Camden into Philadelphia. I'm a little worried about the trip back, considering the amount of people who will be heading to attend the Truck Off, but that's a problem for future Cindy and Jordan.

Two people I'm thinking about a lot right now.

"Maybe, um, we can spend the rest of the summer teaching you how to do this?" Jordan shrugs, gesturing at the steering wheel and the windshield. "You might need it in Boston."

"Yeah, maybe." I smile.

I probably won't though.

"Actually, wait." I shake off that smile. "We're being honest with each other, so…no, let's do something else in these last months. I don't think I ever want to learn how to drive. I think I'm gonna get a bicycle in Boston."

Jordan glances over at me, puzzlement on his face.

"Cindy, I have never heard you so much as say the word *bicycle*, let alone ride one," he says.

"I had one when I was little! Isn't there a whole saying about how easy and familiar it is?" I ask.

"Yeah, I don't think that's meant for people riding bikes in city traffic after not touching one for a decade." He grins. "But I like this honesty."

"Good," I say, keeping an eye on both the time and the Google Maps route on my phone. "That's good. I like this."

"How much time do we have left?" Jordan asks, as we wheel into Center City. City hall quickly comes into view as we make our way into the city, the Convention Center on the right, Reading Terminal hidden a block inside.

I check my phone, which is absolutely lighting up with messages from the production team, Eesha and Ariana, and our families. I don't think I've ever seen so many missed calls and notifications.

I tap on one from Bethany and the production team, and it is…just as messy as I thought it might be.

Bethany: Hey where are you?

Bethany: We tried Jordan's house too, but they said he's at the festival.

Bethany: But you aren't here either? Neither is your truck?

Bethany: What. Is. Going. On.

Bethany: We need to get filming, this is the final piece of the story. It's the day of the competition!

Bethany: What are you DOING.

I wince at the messages, not because they're clearly getting upset that we aren't around, but because...well, she's still lying and trying to manipulate us, right? She could easily come clean that she knows about me and Jordan, but instead, she's still dancing around it and pushing ahead with the show. What's the end game there?

I don't know... I don't know if this is the life I want. I don't think I could manipulate people that way. I don't think that's part of who I am, even though maybe I've been accidentally doing it these last few days. With Jared. By not telling him the truth, not pushing him away. I wonder if saying nothing is just as bad.

There's a message from him in my Instagram notifications, and I swipe it away. But I'm going to have to talk to him eventually.

"Cindy?" Jordan asks. "You okay over there? Time?"

"Oh yeah." I glance back up at the window, and we're near Reading Terminal, driving under a skyway between two office buildings. "There's still a good hour and a half until things kick off. We can make it."

"Yeah but, are you okay?" Jordan presses. "You were staring at that phone like it was about to eat you."

"It's just…the production team is trying to find us, Bethany sounds furious, Jared is…trying to talk to me…" I swallow. "It's all going to be okay, right?"

"Of course it is," he says. "We're taking back our story. We're gonna tell it how we want. Or at least give ourselves the ending we deserve."

He reaches a hand out over the truck's console, and I grab it.

"Let's get that secret ingredient."

We circle the block once, twice, and eventually, Jordan double parks and idles the truck in front of one of the many entrances into Reading Terminal. I pivot to leap out, but stop, leaning back in to give him a kiss before taking off.

I weave through the market quickly. It's Sunday, and while we got lucky with a lack of traffic on the way over here, the crowd inside this place is a disaster. Tourists and kids are running about all over the place, and I'm dodging people with massive tote bags full of produce. I hurry by my favorite seafood stand, the spice shop where Jordan and I had our last spat, and eventually, I see it.

Sparowanya Farms' stand, and Christine is working today.

I bound over, and she catches sight of me, her expression immediately looking concerned.

"Hey, what are you doing here?" she asks. "Don't you have the big food truck thing?"

"Yes! Yeah, totally, I just…" I exhale and cough, feeling a

little winded. "I just needed another ingredient and…" My eyes search the space and settle on it. "Ah!"

I hurry around Christine and a few people who are examining some lettuce, and reach up to grab it.

Black truffles.

I grab the entire little box, and the heft of it makes my heart sink a little. I swear, it can't weigh more than a small, cup of coffee, but even that… I know it's going to be expensive. I walk over to Christine and put the little box on the counter and her eyes flit up to me, confused.

"Uh… Cindy you know those are, like, $150 an ounce. Chefs come in here to buy like, one, to last them a few days or to put in infusions or—"

"I know, I need the box."

"Yeah, but—"

"Just…how much, Christine?!" I plead and dig out all the cash from Jordan's massive tip jar. The bills flutter all over onto the countertop, and we both scramble to collect them. I think about the last time I saw these truffles, how I felt a little longing but was sure my family was okay. When in reality, we weren't. "Sorry, sorry, I'm in a hurry."

"Are you…going to use these in the food trucks?!" Christine asks, her eyes lighting up with realization. She laughs a little. "Well, I hope you win. That'll be…" She puts the little box on a scale, and coughs. "Oh, oh God, okay, it'll be $1,232."

I glance at the bills and start thumbing through them when she puts her hand on mine.

"Look just… I'll count it, you get to your competition, and you can owe me later. It looks like it's close enough."

My heart soars, I grab the little box, and… I stop.

"No, no." I shake my head, looking back down at the money. "I don't want to owe you anything." Thoughts of my dad and his mistakes roar through my mind, even though I'm wildly aware this isn't the same thing, not by a long shot. "Can we just…" I rush through counting the bills, and she reaches out across the countertop, grabbing my hand again.

"It's fine," Christine insists. "If anything, you might have too much here. Get going and I'll hold on to the rest."

I exhale.

"Thank you." And I hurry back toward the truck.

I find Jordan still idling outside and arguing with a Philadelphia Parking Authority person, which shouldn't surprise me. I've been gone less than ten minutes, so of course they're already on him like a vulture.

"Excuse me!" I swerve around the PPA guy and open the door to the truck.

"Hey!" he hollers.

"Bye!" I yell and turn to Jordan. "Go, go, go!"

He starts up the truck and takes off away from the PPA, rounding Arch Street and zooming down Vine back toward the bridge and Camden. His eyes keep shifting from the road to my lap, and eventually he smirks, staring straight ahead.

"So… I'm guessing there's a significant lack of change waiting for me in your pockets."

"Sorry." I wince, jostling the truffles around. "These bad boys are expensive. Christine is going to hold on to the rest, I'll grab it later."

"You're um…gonna have to show me how to prepare those when we make the sandwiches."

"Please," I scoff. "I'm not teaching you a thing. I'll be handling this part of the sandwich." I glance back up at him, and his eyes meet mine for a second. "We're doing this together."

The bridge slowly comes into view as we drive across Columbus. I can see the Camden waterfront right across the river, waiting for us, and whatever else might be—

There's a horrible grinding sound, and Jordan looks down at the console. The truck bucks back and forth a bit before grinding to an absolute halt not too far away from the entryway to the bridge.

"What's going on?" I ask.

"I'm not sure," Jordan says. He checks for traffic before hopping out of the truck and hurrying toward the front. He tosses the hood open, and smoke just billows out like the thing is on fire.

Oh no.

Oh no, oh no, oh no.

Jordan waves his arms around, trying to clear some of the smoke, coughing. Eventually it subsides a bit, and then his eyes flit up to me. He doesn't even need to say anything—his expression tells me everything.

It's over.

There's no way we're going to make it to—

He opens the passenger door and holds his hand out.

"You ready?" he asks.

"For what?" I say miserably. "The truck is dead."

"Sure seems like it. But we're parked here on the sidewalk, we can leave a note so no one tows it, and then…" He grins and looks up at the bridge. "We run."

"We run?" I laugh.

"We run," he says.

There are a lot of kids in school who make running their entire personality, and that's fine. Whatever makes you happy. But I am not one of these people. I am ill-prepared for a run at any time, so as we hustle over the Ben Franklin Parkway along the small pedestrian walkway, the glittering waters of the Delaware River underneath us, cars roaring past, I feel like my heart is about to explode.

This is…not how I saw this day going. Or any day going. Ever.

Jordan runs ahead of me—though really, we're briskly jogging at best—and keeps turning to look at me, a beaming smile on his face as he checks to make sure I'm still there.

And I am. I'm still here. At least until the summer ends, I guess.

I try to shake that, and all the sweat, off.

The city skyline is a burst of shimmering silver behind us. I make out a few boats and a crew team in the river below, and my hair tickles my face in the wind. It's like we're running in a postcard.

As we round the end of the bridge and into Camden, I can make out the stadium where the Truck Off is taking place in the parking lot. It's not too far away. A lot of Camden's main attractions are like that, really—near the waterfront and shore, like it's eager to hug Philadelphia.

Even if the truck did make it across the bridge, we would have never made it back inside to the festival. Cars are lined up in a standstill, blocking off seemingly all traffic. Hundreds upon hundreds of people are milling about in the streets and sidewalks, making their way up to the giant parking lot hosting the event.

It is absolutely wild.

"Come on," Jordan says, nodding his head toward the crowd. "I bet we can just blend right in and work our way to the trucks. Well, er, truck." He winces and I give him a playful scowl before grabbing his hand so we don't get separated.

It takes longer than expected to reach where Jordan's truck is set up, and where mine was supposed to be, because it's stuck in the far corner of the lot. We weave through the crowd, and when we finally approach the spot, we peek out behind one of the nearby trucks. Just about everyone who is involved in the show is waiting for us. Our families, which is fine, but there are multiple people holding boom mics, some new cameramen I don't recognize as well as Drew, and the producers. Bethany, Frank, they're all here... They all look wildly worried. And pissed off.

I'm guessing about us.

From where we're hiding, we can make out a wide gap of space between our little TV crowd and Jordan's truck, so we make a mad dash toward it around the back. No one is hanging out behind his food truck...

With the exception of Jared.

My heart sinks in my chest and my immediate gut reaction is to flee the festival, and maybe even the city, but he's standing right there. In front of the truck we need to get into. There's no other way than through. He's leaning against it, staring down at his phone and looking...despondent.

This is going to be hard.

He must catch our movement from the corner of his eye,

because his gaze flits up from his phone and settles on the two of us.

"Cindy," he says, taking a step toward me. I watch as he looks down to where my hand is still clasped in Jordan's, confusion clouding his expression.

"What's...what's all this?" Jared asks, eyes shifting from me to Jordan. "Wait...it's true?"

"I'm sorry," I say simply but genuinely. No point in hiding it now.

Jared shakes his head like he's trying to recalibrate. "Bethany has been like a tornado all morning trying to find the two of you. Says you're actually a couple and have been the whole time."

Even though he's taller than me, it seems like he's shrunk a few inches. Like...he's deflating a little. Wilting.

"I'm sorry," I say again. "I just... I thought if I told you, it might ruin the show, and...if I'm honest, there were some moments when... I didn't want to tell you."

Jordan bristles and I squeeze his hand. "Honesty, remember? He made me feel heard, but I've made my choice."

Jared sighs and hangs his head but just for a moment. "It's okay. It kind of explains a few things."

"Oh?" I ask.

"Drew." Jared shrugs. "He was...pretty firm in pushing me away. I think he's known for a while."

"Yeah, I do too." I nod.

"In fact..." Jared takes a few steps away from us, peering around the truck. "I'll be right back. He'll want to help."

There's a pause as Jared disappears around the truck, a

beat of wondering what's going to happen next, when Jordan clears his throat.

"So...*him?*" Jordan asks.

"Don't start," I laugh, nudging his shoulder. He gives me a weak smile. "Hey. It's been you since we first yelled at each other over that ketchup. You know that."

"I do."

"What are youse kids doing?" I hear Drew's voice before I see him, and he hustles around the truck with his ever-present camera. "They're all going nuts over here." Jared follows closely behind.

"We know that they know. What's really going on," I say. "We wanted to go out on our own terms."

"*Go out...*" Drew slaps his forehead. "Kids, this isn't like a heist or something, it's just a pilot for a reality television show. A proof of concept, really." He grins. "Do you honestly think they didn't have some suspicions? Hell, I figured youse both out on day one. I mean, I thought you were just friends with a secret, but I see the way your 'rival' looks at you."

He turns to Jared. "Saw the way this one was looking too."

Jared groans and Jordan chuckles.

Drew sighs, shaking his head. "It's gonna be fine. Just..." He huffs and adjusts his camera on his shoulder. "Tell me what the story is you want to tell, okay? And then maybe we can stop worrying everybody."

Pilot: Confessional Shot Transcript (Jordan & Cindy)

Jordan: I'm... I am not sure where to begin here.

Cindy: So no more lies?

Jordan: No more lies.

Cindy: The rivalry between our families, it's not exactly...real.

sound of something crashing, shouting in the distance

Cindy: Okay, well, part of it is. Tensions are running high right now and truths are bubbling up.

Jordan: There's definitely always been a hint of something there, with the amount the permits cost, with who was able to buy which truck, some petty opinions about ingredients and stuff.

Cindy: But really, our families are kind of close. Some of us closer than others.

Jordan: And now Truck Off is here, everyone is freaking out and angry and trying to find us, and well... I think it's time we found ourselves in all of this. And maybe that's how we find a way back to each other.

Cindy: Yeah, maybe.

Jordan: I'll take a maybe.

chapter thirty-two: jordan

_____

Sunday Afternoon, Thirty Minutes until Truck Off

The reaction from everyone outside of the food truck, from the second me and Cindy manage to sneak inside of it thanks to Drew and...ugh, *Jared*, boosting us up through the back window, is almost instantaneous. There's a beat of quiet when the two of us start moving around inside, and then an uproar.

Someone bangs on the shutter of the truck.

"Jordan?" I hear Bethany ask, tapping on the steel. "Come on, are you in there?"

The side door to the truck rattles. "Come on, kiddo," Bethany says.

"The window!" Cindy shouts and hurries over, closing it and wedging a baking pan across it.

"Good call." I exhale and look around the space. "Okay, so...time to get to work, I suppose?"

"Yeah, but first..." Cindy says, stepping forward. She puts

her hands on my shoulders, and slides them down my arms, pulling me in for a kiss. I stumble a little, bumping against one of the prep shelves, and I wrap my arms around her.

I lose track of time, but eventually, I feel her move away, and it takes me a moment to open my eyes.

I sigh.

"How is anyone supposed to focus on sandwiches after that?" I ask, smiling down at her.

"You'll do your best," she says, brushing a strand of hair out of my eyes. "You always do."

Cindy takes her phone and props it up on the countertop, checking the angles on the screen before hitting Record, and the two of us get cooking. I turn the grill up high and start cutting as many onions and...ugh, *mushrooms* as possible. I glance over at where the shame bell normally sits...

And it's not there.

"Huh," I say, looking around the truck a bit.

"What is it?" Cindy asks.

"Nothing, it's just...the shame bell is missing. I don't re-member taking it out." A little swirl of worry spins in my chest. That bell was from The Stateside. I'd hate to lose it.

"Maybe Steve grabbed it?" Cindy shrugs. "He's usually the one ringing the thing. Maybe he brought it home by accident."

"Hmm, yeah maybe."

"Besides, probably best you don't shame people today. I don't think anyone is going to ask for mushrooms on a break-fast sandwich anyhow."

"Yeah," I chuckle. "You're probably right."

When the grill is hot enough, I start tossing some onions on it, while Cindy holds the phone, narrating.

"We're behind the scenes inside Jordan Plazas's family cheesesteak truck, where he is prepping the handful of toppings he actually allows on his sandwiches."

I smirk at her, and she gives me a little shove.

"Don't look in the camera."

I smile and keep working on the prep.

"Jordan's family has operated this truck for years, around the same time my family opened theirs. What started with some real tension surrounding parking permits and truck purchases, morphed into friendship and eventually a faux rivalry that has delighted most of Philadelphia's residents and tourists. But that's the key word. *Faux.* It's all an act. And it's been fun, but now that high school is over and we're leaving..."

I steal a glance at her, a twinge in my chest, and she pushes my face away from the camera again. I can't help but laugh.

"We're going to be telling this story on our own terms. I don't know if this footage will be used for anything, but who knows. I think it's worth explaining ourselves."

She stops talking and then she's right there, in my space, wrapping her arms around my waist from behind.

"Careful," I say, shifting away from the piping hot grill in front of us.

"It's okay," she whispers, pressing herself against my back. She nuzzles her chin into my neck, and the smell of her shampoo blends in with the onions.

"It could be like this, every day, you know," I say, settling into her touch.

"I know," she says.

And she lets go.

Pilot: Confessional Shot Transcript (Steve)

Steve: I don't know why you're talking to me. I don't know anything.

chapter thirty-three: cindy

Sunday Afternoon, Truck Off

"One," I say, standing over the countertop, my hands under the shutter of Jordan's truck.

"Two," Jordan says, standing right next to me, a smirk on his face.

"Three!"

We both hurl the shutter up, and it rattles into the top of the truck. It's loud enough to catch the attention of every single person milling about the front of the truck, because all of them immediately turn and look at us, faces shocked and surprised.

Everyone from this past week is right there.

All the camera crew. The producers from the show. My family and Jordan's. His besties, Steve and Laura. There are even a few restaurant people that I vaguely recognize from his family's circle of friends, faces I've seen at picnics and the like. And there is an absolutely massive, sprawling line that leads from our truck all the way down to what looks like the parking lot entrance.

A few nearby trucks have people leaning out of windows on tired elbows with no one in line for their food. For a moment, I feel a little bad for them.

But then I remember we have a competition to win.

"Cindy?!" Mom gasps, looking shocked to see me as she takes a step toward the truck.

"WHERE IS OUR TRUCK?!" Dad roars, pointing at the very empty space where we were supposed to park.

"I tried to hold them off as long as I could!" Steve exclaims.

The anger and frustration just seems to build and build, our families bickering with our friends while the producers of the show complain to the cameramen. But in the sea of the chaos, is Bethany.

She's standing over where my truck was meant to be, leaning against a trash can.

And she is *smiling*.

She catches me watching and tilts her head, eyebrows lifting, and peers down at her phone. Like none of this is bothering her in the least.

So I decide to let myself feel the same way.

"Who's hungry?!" I bellow, my arms open wide. Cheers erupt from the line, and as people start moving forward, the sound of clinking kitchen utensils fills the truck. Jordan is already at the grill, onions sizzling and metal spatula scraping away. The side door to the truck swings open, and I'm fully prepared to... I don't even know, go to battle? What am

I supposed to do when one of our parents or the producers inevitably demand answers, and—

"What can I do?" Steve asks, hanging in the doorframe.

There absolutely isn't any room for that giant in here.

"Just...keep an eye on the door and the line," Jordan says, glancing at his best friend briefly before turning back to his food. "I don't want us getting interrupted."

"I got you."

"Thanks, man."

He leaves the side door open just a crack on his way out, which I am immediately thankful for. With the grill roaring and the summer sun beating down on the truck, it is already sweltering in here. I find the switch that turns on the tiny fans inside the truck, and they hum to life, but...wow. It is not great in this thing.

I don't know how Jordan does it.

"You're doing those breakfast cheesesteaks still, right?" a woman asks, our first customer of the day. She's wearing a press badge. I can't quite make out her name, but the publication *Billy Penn* is printed across the bottom. "I'm trying to sample all the hits."

I smile. "You know it, and we're doing something a little extra for the competition today—"

A sandwich practically teleports in front of me, and I whirl around to see Jordan getting to work on yet another one, his movements like a practiced, well-oiled machine. The grill hisses and his spatula clatters in a song. I reach for the box of black truffles, handling them like they're something precious, because they are, and grab the truffle grater Christine tucked inside the bag when I bought them.

I slice off thin bits from one truffle onto the cheesesteak, crumbling up the pieces so just enough sprinkles across the cheese-layered surface. They dot the sharp cheddar cheese like…cigarette ash? I don't know. It doesn't look pretty *at all*, but that doesn't change the way the journalist looks at it.

"Black truffles?!" she gasps, as I hand the breakfast cheesesteak to her.

"One day only. That's our special addition for the festival."

"But…" She looks at the sandwich, at the little truffle shredder in my hand, and back at me. "I'm sorry, but how much is this?"

"Oh." I glance at Jordan, who looks over his shoulder and shrugs at me. "Uh…seven dollars?"

I mean, that's how much he's been charging for these things during the breakfast rushes all week.

The journalist almost drops the cheesesteak.

"Sweetheart are you…quite sure?" she asks. "Those truffles are… I mean, that's gotta be wildly expensive."

"I think it'll be okay for one day." I smile.

The reporter walks away, and the people, they just keep coming. The line grows and grows, showing no sign of slowing down, but then again, neither does Jordan. He just keeps at it, chopping and scrapping. Our parents are still bickering outside the truck, and at one point, my dad takes a phone call and just bolts away from the festival.

My mom walks over and leans against the steel countertop space outside the window.

"They found our truck," she says.

"I'm sorry," I say, shaving some more truffle onto a sandwich for a hungry-looking woman with a baby strapped to her chest. "It was this whole thing and I promise we'll explain—"

"I'm sure it'll be fine." Mom gazes between Jordan and me. "So...you two bury the hatchet and all that?

"I suppose so? Maybe?" I look back and catch him peering at us over his shoulder. He returns to his work quickly. "I'm sorry, about the show. I think we ruined it."

Jordan passes me another cheesesteak, and I get to shredding for the two teenagers waiting outside the truck.

"Yeah, I don't know about all that." Mom snorts. "Bethany seemed awfully happy about how things have spiraled like this. I swear I heard her cackling when your dad and Mr. Plazas were going at it."

I hand the teens their sandwich, which they promptly rip in half and start devouring as they walk away. Bethany is still sitting where my family truck was supposed to be, watching us. Though this time, she's talking to one of the cameramen next to her. She nods at me.

"And besides, they sure did get a lot of footage of that." Mom looks over at Jordan's family, who are standing pretty far away from us, arms crossed, looking grumpy.

"Yeah, are you guys gonna be okay?"

"Honey, we're adults," she scoffs. "Your dad and Mr. Plazas will likely be laughing about this tonight in the yard. And..." she leans over, whispering "... I've been texting Mrs. Plazas all afternoon. It's fine."

I smile.

"How's...you know, Jordan holding up?"

"I'm fine, thank you," Jordan says, laughing. "This truck is like six feet wide, and you two are loud."

I lean over and give him a quick kiss on his cheek.

"You've got a lot of customers," Mom says, reaching out and grabbing my hands for a second. "I'll leave you to it."

She glances at Jordan's family and then leans toward me. "And do me a favor...keep him in there as much as you can until the end of the festival."

"What? Why—"

"Trust me." Mom smiles.

And I'm left handing out cheesesteaks while wondering what she's planning.

Pilot: Confessional Shot Transcript (Jordan & Cindy)

Jordan: Look, if there's one thing I've learned from this whole reality television experience, it's to listen more and talk less.

Cindy: And maybe...also talk more? For me, that is.

Jordan: I could have, I don't know, offered more space in the conversation about my plans, where I really asked how you were feeling about all of it. I think if I had really paid more attention, I would have figured it out sooner.

Cindy: Or I would have told you.

Jordan: You probably tried to and I just talked over you. I'm sorry.

Cindy: It's okay. I'm sorry too. For getting caught up in everything.

Jordan: I think they're picking the winners soon. Everyone is moving toward the center of the—

Cindy: I do love you, you know.

Jordan: I—

Cindy: I need to talk more. Say what I mean. And I mean that. And I know you're still leaving on your trip and I'm going to Boston and it might not last but... I'm gonna feel that, with or without you.

Jordan: I don't know what to say right now.

Cindy: Just...say it back. For as long as we have.

Jordan: I love you. And I will.

chapter thirty-four: jordan

Sunday Afternoon, Truck Off

The crowd milling around what looks to be a hastily built stage in the middle of the huge stadium parking lot is just… charged with something. Energy from too much good food, maybe? But I feel like I'm going to burst from anticipation, waiting to see if we did enough. If the breakfast cheesesteaks were good enough to win.

A hand slips into mine, and I glance down at our entwined fingers.

"You nervous?"

I look up, locking eyes with Cindy. She's wearing a small smile, and I have to resist looking into the camera that's aimed at me over her shoulder. She leans forward, pressing her forehead to mine.

"Whatever happens, I feel like we already won today," she

says, nudging my head with hers before shifting away. "I'm glad we fixed things."

"Yeah, as much as we can, right?" I say, trying to smile back. She sighs.

"I'm still going to Boston," she says.

"I'm still hitting the road." I shrug.

"Yeah."

She squeezes my hand tighter and leans against me. And I don't want to let go. I feel like the second I do, she's going to float away. But at the end of the summer, that's exactly what I'm going to have to do, because that's exactly what's going to happen.

The cameras are positioned all around, and our parents are standing in front of us, chatting with one another amicably. All that bickering and fighting that's been going on for the last day or two—and who knows, maybe it's been happening for a lot longer than this—has faded away. My dad says something, and Cindy's father slaps him on the shoulder, the two of them laughing.

A squeak of feedback echoes throughout the parking lot and the attention in the large crowd focuses on the stage. A few chefs from around town take their seats, holding large clipboards with fluttering pages. I was so focused on the grill all day that I didn't even notice when any of them came to the truck. I immediately recognize Ryan Thomas, who runs a Canadian poutine and smoked sandwich shop in Old City, and Britt Morris, one of the most celebrated seafood chefs on the East Coast. She has two locations in Philadelphia, one in Center City, another up in West Philly near the colleges. Tony

Malerba, one half of Malerba + Huss, a beloved gastropub in Fishtown, sits patiently tapping on his clipboard.

I don't recognize the woman at the microphone, but she adjusts it accordingly, and laughs awkwardly when it screeches uncomfortably.

"Hi, everyone! Thank you for coming to the first, what we hope will be, annual Truck Off competition, sponsored by some of Philadelphia's boldest and beloved restauranteurs. We hope that you enjoyed the day and that you discovered some of the incredible talent lurking in the food trucks that line our beautiful streets."

Cindy squeezes my hand, and I release a shuddering breath. This is it, everything I've been working toward.

"For those of you who don't know me, I'm Jules Leandra, probably best known for my boutiques and eateries through-out town." Oh. I'm surprised by this. I recognize her name, but why wasn't it slapped all over absolutely everything having to do with the Truck Off? She's a huge deal. "And who knows, maybe one of the chefs you met in the trucks today will end up working at one of my places in the coming year. I'm certainly going to try to lure them away."

There's some polite laughter in the crowd, including from me.

Cindy gives me an inquiring look and I shrug.

I'm with my brethren here. Nothing could take me away from this. I know where I belong.

"Now, enough talking. We'll thank our sponsors at the end, but for now, let's get to those winners."

Some cheers erupt in the crowd, and Cindy's parents and

my parents all turn to look at us. The cameras move in a little closer.

"In third place, with a prize of twenty-five hundred dollars and a free visit to Cassidy's Auto Repair for a full tune-up and servicing of their truck—Cassidy's is a sponsor, by the way...we're thrilled to award this to Whole Latke Love, who hail from right here in Camden."

Loud cheering erupts to the right of us as the crowd shifts to allow two older women to ascend the stage. They kiss and hug and everyone screams with joy, particularly at the large, fake check that the judges seem to pull from thin air. One of the women holds it up victoriously, and eventually the two make their way off the stage.

"And in second place, our runner-up, with a prize of ten thousand dollars, a free visit to Cassidy's, and a shopping spree at the local Williams Sonoma, where you'll be able to stock your truck with all matter of new gadgets and kitchen utensils..." She looks down at the envelope, squinting. "We have a rare tie here, as it seems two trucks have come together to work on a special project."

My heart hammers in my chest, and Cindy practically collides against me, holding me tight from the side.

"The Ortiz and Plazas cheesesteak trucks!" she exclaims.

Our parents jump and holler, and Cindy turns me by the shoulders and kisses me. I can feel the cameras on us, and all the eyes from the crowd.

Second place.

Split between the two of us...

I should be thrilled but...that's not enough for the dream truck. To help my parents relaunch their restaurant. For her family to explore options for a new urban farm or pay off the debt they're wrestling with.

For anything, really.

I had this image in my head for so long. Of getting a beautiful truck of my own, of traveling the country with Cindy. I know some prize money is better than nothing, and it'll go toward the truck fund I've been saving up, but... I don't know. I can't help but feel like reality is crashing down over me, and I'll be in a junker of a truck, on the road, without her.

But I push it all away.

And I hold the girl I love close.

Pilot: Confessional Shot Transcript (Jordan & Cindy)

Cindy: I mean, I'm excited. Second place? Not so bad!

loud whooshing noises from giant check being waved in the air, feedback from mic being knocked off

Cindy: *inaudible*

Cindy: Oops, sorry about that.

Jordan: Yeah, I just wish...

Cindy: What?

Jordan: I mean, it's not really going to do what we need it to, is it?

Cindy: Yeah, but that's okay. We'll keep working hard.

Your parents will, mine will. This will give us some breathing room. Besides...we don't have to worry about this whole show we were putting on anymore. We can all just be ourselves again.

Jordan: Yeah, yeah, I suppose that's a good thing... Wait...

Cindy: Hmm?

Jordan: What...what is that?

Cindy: What is...whoa. No way.

Jordan: Cindy...they didn't...

chapter thirty-five: cindy

Sunday Afternoon

I watch as Jordan takes tentative, almost delicate steps away from the wall we're standing against for our latest—and maybe last—confessional video for *Cheesesteak Wars.*

Or...whatever they're going to call the show now.

The parking lot is slowly emptying out from the festival, but a handful of trucks remain, their staff sampling food from other spots. The Truck Off winner, War & Peas, is handing out endless containers of leftover falafels. I watched one guy walk away with what had to be a dozen Styrofoam take-out boxes, clearly stocked up for the whole week.

Smart.

But right now, Jordan is standing a few feet ahead of me, my parents to the right and left, the producers and cameras watching...

As a new truck rolls into the lot.

It's fire engine red, the name "Jalapeño Your Business" written along the side in a horrible, bright yellow font, little flames licking the logo. It rolls up across the pavement and stops in front of us.

And Jordan's father gets out of the driver's seat.

"Nice, huh?" he asks, smacking the side of the truck as he closes the door, looking right at Jordan.

I think Jordan might be in shock—he's rooted in place, staring wordlessly. But then he turns to me, and that's when I see there are tears welled up in his eyes.

I can't believe it. I can't believe they did this for him.

"Go ahead." I push him forward gently, unable to suppress the huge grin on my face.

Jordan walks toward his dad like he's caught in some kind of a spell. "What is going on?" Jordan asks, sounding a little breathless.

"Look," Mr. Plazas says, clearing his throat. "I know college isn't for you. You've said it endless times. Pushing what we wanted for ourselves, onto you...that was our mistake. We should have been thinking about what *you* wanted."

He turns and gazes at the truck, and then back at Jordan.

"So...well..." his dad sighs and rubs the back of his head. "I can't believe I'm saying this, but, we dipped into your college fund to buy..." Mr. Plazas looks back to the truck and shouts, "Steve! What did he call it?"

The food truck's window shutter rattles open and Steve sticks his head out, Laura right behind him.

"Big Red!" Steve shouts, and both of them are smiling in a way I've never seen before. Not even the biggest fake fights in the park lit them up this way.

Maybe because this is real. This is all really happening.

"But…" Jordan turns away and walks toward me. "You know what this means. With a new truck, any truck, I'm… I'm gonna leave."

I reach out and grab his trembling hands.

"So am I," I say, and now I'm fully sobbing. I can see the cameras from the show, reeling right near me. "Let's just spend the rest of this summer making the best of it, okay?"

"The summer belongs to us, right?"

"The summer belongs to us."

I hug him close. It's the end of June. There's so much out there waiting for us in these next few months. Goodness, Fourth of July weekend in Philadelphia is always absolutely wild for food trucks—that'll be a couple days to remember. Maybe we can collaborate on some things at the trucks, now that the truth is out there. Maybe we can—

"Alright, that's a wrap!" a familiar voice shouts.

Bethany walks over, talking to the cameramen, shooing them away. I spot Drew in the mix, who looks at me for a second, giving me a little wry smile and a nod, before turning away and heading toward…wherever they're all going. I'm guessing there's a truck or something for the production crew here. There's gotta be, with all this equipment.

"Nice work," Bethany says, looking at the two of us, and then our parents, smirking.

"I'm… I'm sorry if we messed up the show," I say. I had been dreading talking to Bethany after everything that we did, but now that it's here, I feel strangely numb. All that anger from being manipulated, it's gone. Well, maybe not completely gone. "You shouldn't have tried to use Laura like that."

Bethany crosses her arms. "You certainly flipped things around on us," she says. "It's exactly what I was hoping for."

"Hoping?" Jordan asks, sounding shocked.

"What do you mean?"

"Look, part of reality television is knowing how to...nudge things in the right direction," Bethany says.

"You...knew that Laura would tell us what you did? That we'd do something in response?" I ask.

"I thought you might." She shrugs. "There was no guarantee, but I figured you would once you realized the story wasn't really yours anymore. You're someone who likes to be in control."

"No." I shake my head. "Not like that."

"But that's part of reality television, kid," she presses, looking at her nails for a moment. "You nudge people this way, nudge them that way, get the reactions you want. I think you'll be really good at it."

"I'm not sure I want to be."

"Ah, don't say that." Bethany looks genuinely wounded. "You learned a lesson that people on television all learn. Once you're on the screen, it isn't your story anymore."

"But it's my life!" I protest. It all seems so...absurd.

"That's the business for you," she sighs. "But I think this will make for something really special."

"You still want it?" I ask.

"Send me the videos you've been shooting during all of this," Bethany says. "Drew told me you were doing something on your phone in the food truck. All of this? A fake family rivalry that's unearthed during the filming of a TV show, two kids who are in love but can't be together in public? That's far more dramatic than the fake version you and your families were working on."

"You're…kind of a monster," Jordan says.

Bethany laughs. "I know."

With that, she turns on her heel and follows the camera crew on their way out of the lot. I look around at the remaining crowd, of both people still getting food and the folks working on the show, but I don't see Jared anywhere. Which…is fair. I wouldn't want to stick around either.

Jordan steps toward his new truck, his parents on either side of him, arms around each other they stroll over to it. As they get to the truck's shutter, to the large window peering inside, where Steve and Laura are leaning out, his dad reaches over the edge and pulls out the shame bell.

"That's where it went?" Jordan chuckles. "I was worried we lost it."

"I had Steve snag it for me." Mr. Plazas holds it like he's testing its weight, emotion all over his face. "I want you to take it in your truck. So you have a little piece of the restaurant to carry with you."

"Dad…" Jordan starts, getting choked up.

"But it's not the shame bell anymore. It's the 'I'm proud of you' bell. I'm so proud of you, son, and I don't say it enough."

His dad hoists that heavy diner bell up in the air.

And rings it like a madman.

epilogue: cindy

September

"Come on, let's go!" Eesha grabs my wrist, trying to pull me from my dorm room toward her and Ariana.

"Just a second!" I laugh, freeing myself from her grasp so I can finish hanging up a poster of The Wonder Years. Ariana hops into my room, right onto my bed, and slaps the final corner down against the white splotchy wall.

"Nope! You're done!" Ariana says, wrestling me off the small twin bed. "Let's go."

We tumble from my room and the suite we're sharing, into the hallway. A bundle of students are still moving in, their parents milling about. We pass a number of tear-streaked cheeks and embarrassed kids our age, and practically fly down the stairs and out into the Boston air.

I inhale. It's cold and crisp, even in the fading summer and early fall, and it feels like home.

The quad outside the dorm is just as bustling as the hall-ways, huge bins full of belongings being pushed up and down the cobblestone walkways, rumbling loudly. Eesha and Ariana stroll a little ahead of me, and as I walk along the old stones on the ground, I can't help but feel a twinge of something.

It reminds me of Philadelphia.

I sigh, my breath coming out in a puff of smoke, and hurry to catch up with the girls. It's close to lunchtime, and we were up way too late last night talking about…well, everything. All our hopes and dreams and plans now that we're together, assembled like the Avengers. Not like we haven't been in constant communication these last few years, but nothing compares to being together in person.

I missed this so much.

We make our way down to the student center, where a wildly late breakfast or a super early lunch—neither of which can be called brunch when you're eating cafeteria food—awaits. There's a tour of the production studios later, and I'm excited to find out where me and the girls can record our podcast…

But I'm even more excited to figure out what I want to study, based on what we find there.

Reality television… I don't know. I still love it, I still love working on *Beacon Street* with the girls, and now that we're all here together maybe we can take it to another level but… telling real stories appeals to me more.

Maybe something with podcasting? Sound engineering? Documentaries?

I have two years to be undeclared. I'll figure it out. Feel-ing like I had to lock myself into things, control every little thing around me, caused a lot of trouble earlier in the summer. I'm gonna let go a little. I'm gonna breathe.

"Hold on," Eesha says. She stops and checks her phone, her nose wrinkling as she examines the screen. She glances over my shoulder and then points to a pathway leading away from campus. "Okay, it's this way."

"What?" I ask, looking back at the student center. "Aren't we going here?"

"No, no." Eesha shakes her head. "Over here."

I follow, ducking around some small city trees and weaving through passing students and parents. Move-in weekend has been hectic. I've seen it on television and in movies and read about it in books, but in person, it's something altogether different. You can feel the anxious energy hovering and crackling in the air like the atmosphere before a storm.

The walkway leads out to the street through an opening in a small brick wall that separates the campus from the city, even though it's short enough to easily hop over. We pass several cute shops, mostly clothing boutiques, cafés, pizza places… all the things you want right next to a college campus. We turn a corner and come across a bunch of people, students maybe, up along the sidewalk waiting for something, their expressions impatient.

"Where are we—" I start.

And then I see it.

A shiny, dark red food truck with Nice to Meat You in thick black lettering along the side, sits parked near the sidewalk, a few other trucks lined up after it. But those trucks, their lines are small, a handful of people at best waiting to get what looks like ramen and some kind of fried chicken.

I don't give those trucks a second glance.

I'm too busy watching Jordan, who's leaning out of his truck, talking to someone. Taking an order, maybe?

It's like the whole world has stopped and he's all I can see.

"Thought you might want to order something," Ariana says, nudging me forward.

"How...what...how did you know he was going to—" I start, looking back and forth between Eesha and Ariana.

"Order thirty-seven for a Cindy Ortiz!"

I whirl around and Jordan is gazing right at me. The people who are anxiously waiting for their orders turn toward me, like I'm holding up their lunch.

Jordan smiles, and I walk over to the truck like I'm in a dream.

"What are you *doing* here?" I ask, the words heavy in my mouth. His truck looks absolutely gorgeous. It's the red of a fire engine and shining like one too, even though you know those trucks are several years old and have seen some things.

I glance at the menu and can't stop the groan that escapes my mouth.

"Meat. Cheese. Onions." It's the exact same stuff he served back home. I attempt a scoff but my smile gets in the way. "Some things never change."

"Yeah." He grins back at me. "But some things do."

I feel a blush heating my cheeks and creeping along my neck, and it doesn't help that Eesha and Ariana are giggling behind me.

"What happened to the road trip?" I ask, peering inside the truck. It's so...clean. There's a duffel bag in a lump in the corner, some clothes strewn around it.

"I was heading south, to that first stop we talked about. New Orleans? Got a little lost."

"Well, considering you drove north and all…" I smile.

"Got a little turned around. We should talk," Jordan says. "Maybe, after the lunch rush?"

"I'd like that." I swallow and then peer back into the truck. "Is…no one else in there with you?"

"Yeah, no, it's just me. It's kinda hard to find someone willing to, you know, go on a road trip in a food truck."

"No kidding," I smirk. "I have orientation at two. If we're gonna find time to talk, you're going to need some help."

Jordan disappears from his window, and the back door of the truck swings open.

He holds out his arm for me.

I nudge my way through the line of hungry people.

And take his hand.

★ ★ ★ ★ ★

acknowledgments

So much goes into making a book. It's not as simple as meat, cheese, bread, salt-pepper-ketchup. I was going to attempt an analogy saying these people were the ingredients, but then it kinda feels like I'm saying they all go in a sandwich. Acknowledgments are hard.

Let's go with how I'm endlessly thankful for all these cooks in my author's kitchen. Yeah, that works a lot better.

First, to Jennifer Azantian, literary agent extraordinaire. Thank you for once again championing me and my work. You're simply incredible.

To the team at Inkyard, thank you for continuing to encourage me and my Philadelphia novels. My editor Claire Stetzer for your wildly in-depth and fantastic feedback, your careful and gentle handprints are all over this story. To the rest of the crew, Bess Braswell, Randy Chan, Pamela Osti, Brittany Mitchell, Gina Macedo, Laura Gianino, and Ricardo Bessa, Kathleen Oudit, and Gigi Lau for the stunning cover.

Dear writer buddies Jennifer Dugan, Rachel Lippencott,

Gloria Chao, Christina Lauren, Tom Torre, George Jreije, Ronnie Riley, Farah Naz Rishi, Aashna Avachat, Samantha Zaboski, Chris Urie, Dahlia Adler, Jeff Zentner, Laura Taylor Namey, Brittney Morris, and Neil Bardhan (who thought of the title!) for feedback and wholesome encouragement. To Miranda Kenneally, Sarvenaz Tash, Tiffany Schmidt, Lauren Magaziner, and Jessica Spotswood for taking me to Highlights, where I was able to finish this draft.

Good pals Alex Hillman and Adam Teterus for a place to create (and for naming the bagel truck), Preeti Chhibber, Swapna Krishna, Darlene Meier, Miguel Bolivar, Andres Jimenez, Lauren Gibaldi, Helen Connor, Dana Murphy, Chris and Shannon Wink, and Dario Plazas, thank you for always showing up.

And as always, to my dear wife, Nena, and darling son, Langston. It's all for you.